The Viking Process

by Norman Hartley

Simon and Schuster
New York

Designed by Irving Perkins
Manufactured in the United States of America

1 2 3 4 5 6 7 8 9 10

Library of Congress Cataloging in Publication Data

Hartley, Norman.
  The Viking process.
  I. Title.
PZ4.H3297Vi [PS3558.A697]   813'.5'4   75-33859
ISBN 0-671-22198-1

I should like to express my particular thanks to Michael Korda and Joan Sanger, who gave me more editorial advice and help than any author has the right to expect.

For Jane and Joanna

PART I

CHAPTER 1 I awoke that first morning in my favorite sleeping position, the one my wife, Julia, calls a sexy version of the fireman's carry because I curl myself around her back, putting one arm over her breasts and the other between her thighs.

But this time I knew something was wrong. I wasn't awake enough to be sure what it was, but I knew it had something to do with the cold, smooth surface I could feel against the sole of my foot.

I lay there, drowsily, trying to guess what it was. Metal? Plastic? Leather?

Then I remembered. It was the folio case. The red leather artist's folio case. It was there, leaning against the bottom of the bed, and it was not Julia beside me. It had finally happened: for the first time in fifteen years of marriage, I had slept with another woman, a stranger I had met only the evening before.

I opened my eyes and saw a blue light flashing on the bedside table and I realized that it was the telephone that had disturbed me. It was a Futurfone. There was no bell, only the light and a "subliminal awakening tone, able to penetrate normal sleep," as the leaflet beside it said. The phone brought back the awful unreality of the room and I remembered I was in Montreal, on the fiftieth floor of the Royal Mountain Hotel, "the most modern hotel in the world, where guests are introduced, in a setting of incomparable luxury, to the wonders of the technological age."

I gently pulled my body away from the girl's to see if I could get up without waking her. She seemed to be sleeping deeply and comfortably and she barely stirred as I moved, so I got up and took the phone into the far corner of the room.

There was no cord; the whole room was bounded by an electromagnetic field, and the Futurfone could be operated anywhere within it.

I sat down on a small black sofa, one of four making a square around a brilliant white Plastiflex coffee table, depressed a switch on the Futurfone and said, "Hello," as quietly as I could.

It was Karl Harvey, the head of television news for NBC in New York, the man who was paying me $20,000 to act as "expert consultant" on his series of five one-hour specials on terrorism and urban guerrilla violence around the world. He was my reason for being in Montreal and he should have been in the next room, but he had flown back to New York for a weekend in his office because he was, as he had put it, a work junkie, wired to the seven-day week.

As usual, there were no introductory greetings.

"Philip, I know what's wrong with the series," he said. "It's too old-fashioned."

I said nothing. I already knew better than to interrupt Harvey's early morning thoughts.

"People don't care about little nationalist groups anymore. They don't care whether Quebec separates from Canada. They want something bigger."

I was too sleepy to argue and, anyway, I agreed. The Quebec hour had been Harvey's idea.

"All right, Karl," I said. "I'll see you on Monday, around noon." Then I switched off the phone and just sat, staring across the room.

The girl was still sleeping, so I sat beside the bed, looking down at her as she lay silhouetted against the milky-white glow of the huge picture window. There were no drapes at the Royal Mountain; the window glass was coated with crystals that were sensitive to light and heat. To shut out the outside world, you sent a current through the glass, and the crystals went cloudy.

I saw that the control mechanism was set to "automatic," which meant that the cloudiness would clear gradually as daylight acted on the surface. It was one of the effects the hotel mentioned proudly in its brochures: "The skyline of Montreal will appear automatically on your windowpane, as if painted there by an invisible hand." The whole room was full of such technological gadgets.

I had read somewhere that they had wanted to call the place a Komputel—for computerized hotel—but the public relations and marketing men had insisted on a reassuring, traditional name; they were soft-selling technology, "taking the shock out of future shock."

The girl stirred, pushed the sheet still farther below her waist, smiled in her sleep, then lay quietly again, breathing rhythmically.

Looking at her body, I thought how complete my betrayal had been. I had not just been unfaithful to Julia; if I had deliberately gone out and looked for a woman who would hurt her pride and stir all her deepest insecurities, I could not have chosen better than this girl I knew only as Michelle.

Asleep, she looked younger than when I had first seen her in the elegant underground shopping arcade beneath the Place Ville-Marie, twenty-five, perhaps twenty-six; but it was not just her youth that would hurt Julia, it was the naturalness of her looks. At thirty-six, Julia was, in a different way, just as beautiful, but she never quite believed her beauty because her body needed the constant discipline of diet and exercise, and her fair hair always needed attention after sleeping or walking in the wind to keep its attractive shape. Michelle's black hair was waist length. It lay tangled around her shoulders, partly trapped under one arm, but she would,

when she awoke, simply step out of bed and it would all fall
into place, a silky dark waterfall down her back. . . .

I had spent the previous day trying to write the introduction to the Quebec program, and as Harvey had flown off to
New York he had said, as if to ensure maximum tension,
that he wanted me to throw away all my previous drafts. I
had tried but it wouldn't come, and finally I had given up
and decided to go down into Montreal in search of escape.

First I had two large gins in the room, drawn from the
ComputoBar—"instant room service: mix any drink at a
touch of the selektramatic controls"—then I went down into
the glittering shopping complex under the Place Ville-Marie
to find the cinema Mont-Royal.

My excuse for choosing it was that it was snowing hard
and I could get under the Place Ville-Marie direct from the
hotel without needing heavy top clothes. The weather provided a little extra justification for choosing *Drive-In Girl*,
which had been a sellout in New York and was billed as the
sexiest film ever made.

I joined the enormous line just before it was closed off for
the final performance of the evening, and I was standing,
smoking and watching the fashionable evening paseo
through the shopping arcade, when a girl suddenly appeared
at my side.

She was carrying two ice-cream cones and she said, "I'm
sorry I've been so long. Eat it before it melts." No one in the
lineup protested and I smiled at the neatness of the maneuver. She waited for a moment until her presence had become
completely natural, then she said quietly, "I hope you don't
mind. They'd closed off the line and I did want to see it. You
looked the most attractive man to join."

What could I have done? Only a ridiculous scene would
have dislodged her, and anyway she was a very striking
woman and I felt flattered and interested. She was carrying
a red artist's folio case and she was dressed elegantly in a

fur-trimmed black maxi-coat. It hung open over a black dress, unbuttoned up the front to mid-thigh, drawing the eye inexorably up the line of small silver buttons which held it tenuously together.

She wore no bra and her hair fell casually loose into the hood of the maxi-coat; high boots and sheer black tights completed the picture.

She could have been the art director of an advertising agency or she could have been a student; it is always hard to tell in Montreal, where students wear even jeans with a chic that sets them off from every other campus in North America. Her accent told me she wasn't French Canadian; it was light and pleasant and might have come from anywhere on the eastern seaboard of the United States or Canada.

At first, all she said was, "My name's Michelle. What's yours?" I told her, then after a while she said, casually, "Where did you get those thighs? They're like a gladiator's."

I replied, without thinking, "I was a mountaineer," then, to try to restore my anonymity a bit, I added, "But should you be inspecting my thighs that closely?"

She laughed and squeezed my arm. "It's not just men that are leg-watchers, you know. That's one of those pre-Liberation myths."

She made a point of looking at me critically all over. "You've got a lot of muscle. Is that from mountaineering too?"

I said lightly, "When I was a boy, I thought I was going to be small so I started body-building to make myself wider, then I grew, so now I'm both. Six feet is about right for a climber. I'm lucky."

She nodded and I thought that would be the end of my privacy but she didn't ask any of the obvious questions, like what kind of a mountaineer I was, or what I was doing in Montreal, and she didn't notice my accent and ask if I was from Britain.

Then, as we started to move into the theater, I said, "Do

you live in Montreal?" and she replied, "Tonight I don't live anywhere. I'm taking a night off from my private life. I have no address and I don't want to know anything about you, except how you got that body."

She didn't say much else until we found seats near the back, then as the lights went down, she snuggled up to me as naturally as if we had been lovers for years and whispered, "I love sex films but they make me feel so goddam raunchy." I was too aroused and intrigued to push her away and I could feel the warmth flowing from her thigh to mine, through the double layer of cloth.

The film came on the screen and it began with a fifteen-minute sequence which had neither sound nor music. The drive-in girl of the title turned out to be a sexually neglected North American teenager who worked as an usherette and fantasized her sex life by imagining herself in each of the cars in the drive-in theater. In the opening sequence the camera tracked from car to car, spying on the frenzies and contortions of teenage sexuality, and each time the girl's fantasies added the style and grace that were lacking in the scrambling and groping of the cramped interiors.

By the time the credit titles started to roll, the whole audience was collectively holding its breath in a state of unbearable erotic suspense, and Michelle whispered, "Now that's what I really call a sex life."

After the credits, the drive-in girl's fantasies escalated spectacularly. Half an hour into the film, she was hanging upside down from a balance beam in the local high school, about to be fallen on by the entire school gymnastic team, and Michelle whispered, "This chick is getting too much action. I can't stand any more; let's go somewhere."

I was too aroused and too excited to think of the implications. We went outside and she said, "Do you have somewhere private?" and when she saw me hesitate, she said in a very matter-of-fact way, "Look, I won't cause you any grief. I'm a very independent girl in a good state of medical repair. If you want me, I'm yours till breakfast time, but you must promise that after that, you won't try to stay in my life and I won't interfere in yours. Is it a deal?"

It seemed like an offer drifting out of one of my darkest private fancies and I felt flushed and excited. It was something I had thought of doing before but never done. This time, it was as though the decision had already been taken, and without saying anything, I took her arm and led her back through the underground passageways to the hotel. I remember wondering if men who were unfaithful to their wives always felt as conspicuous as I did.

I remembered how Michelle had looked at the room, examining the Futurfone and the crystal window, and the "auto people washer" and the refrigerator full of seal-packed meals for all hours of the day and the microwave oven that would flash-heat them in fourteen seconds and how she had said, "God, how I love all this stuff," and started to take off her dress in almost the same gesture as she took off her coat.

As I sat there, looking at her asleep, the remembered images of lust were so powerful that I felt myself becoming aroused again. She had used her body as a sexual weapon and she seemed to have all the keys to unlock my deepest dreams. I thought of an image in a medieval poem that had always haunted me: of a black river of lust and violence, held stagnant by self-discipline, which, once loosed, becomes a flood that cannot be turned back and engulfs everything.

As I thought about it, I started to dress, and I felt the kind of shame you feel only when the body has gone cold again.

I became very calm suddenly and started to calculate how I could reduce the risk of Julia finding out. I went over the whole night, remembering Michelle's promise that after breakfast she would vanish from my life, and I felt a bit more comfortable and started to behave rationally.

Michelle still seemed sound asleep so I finished dressing. Then I took my wallet and credit cards and all the possessions I could find that might betray my identity and put them all in a small drawer in the desk. I collected my papers, put them in a folder, and spread some blank sheets over the typewriter to simulate the disorder of the night before.

Her departure would be easy, I thought. The big risk would be that she would come back or telephone or try to meet me again. I decided that I would take no chances at all. I would check out immediately. Instead of waiting for the flight to New York on Monday, I would go to Quebec City and check into some civilized old-world hotel and go skiing and eat *soupe aux pois* and garlic bread and be comfortable and get twentieth-century technology out of my system. If worse came to worst and I caught some kind of infection, I still had time to have it treated before I was due back in London to go home to Julia.

I remember thinking that at least in a computerized hotel, there are no eyes to check on adultery. When you flash-cook two breakfasts, the computer in the basement doesn't know a hungry man from an unfaithful one.

I was just locking, as an afterthought, the drawer where my identity was hidden, when I heard Michelle stir behind me and her voice say, "Philip Russell, for Christ's sake, don't be so naive."

CHAPTER 2 I spun round and Michelle was sitting, propped up against the pillows, wide awake.

"I was watching your little performance," she said. "Christ, how marital guilt humbles a man." Then she added, more gently, "Don't worry. It will wear off once you've got over the shock."

She got off the bed and pointed to a glass cube in the annex which made coffee by exploding the beans under the pressure of an ultrahigh-speed water jet.

"Make us some, will you, while I get dressed. I have something to show you."

I could either make coffee or start a scene and I sensed that a scene was pointless. As I made coffee I watched her pull on her clothes, standing by the window.

She dressed with the kind of arrogant indifference I always associate with Parisian women; at that particular moment she was not choosing to be looked at sexually and so seemed quite private, despite her nakedness. When she had put on her dress, she took a beaker of coffee, sat down on the bed and pointed to the red leather folio case.

"Open it," she said. "I brought it especially for you."

I took the case and examined the fastening. There was no lock, only a flap held by a single leather tongue. I pulled it back, and inside I could see the top edges of what looked like black and white photographic enlargements, huge ones, almost as big as the case itself.

I hesitated and she motioned me to take them out, so I pulled the first one upward, and before it was fully exposed, my hand started to involuntarily tremble and my heart started to flutter, disturbing a rhythm I wasn't even aware of.

It was a giant photograph of Julia and I recognized the setting immediately. She was sitting up in bed, her shoulders covered by her favorite pale blue dressing gown, in the main bedroom of the little townhouse we owned in Blackheath, just outside London.

Every detail was clear and I could even see where some of the threads had been pulled loose on the familiar olive bedcover. The lines of the pen-and-wash Modigliani sketch by the window were even more elongated than usual; so was the mirror above the brightly painted Habitat dressing table. Around Julia, spread over the bedcover, were several small objects: a plate of sandwiches and an orange, cigarettes and her silver Swiss lighter, a book of poems by W. H. Auden, and her handbag was open beside her, spilling other bits and pieces around her half-raised knees.

I recognized the scene because we had so often joked about it. I called it her bear's lair ritual. After a sad day or a lonely one she would withdraw into the bedroom, surrounding herself with little comforts, and "hibernate" until the wintry mood passed. Looking at the picture, I felt a great rush of tenderness and longing to be with her.

"Now the second picture," Michelle said. I pulled it up and it was another blow-up, a huge photograph of the biggest room of the townhouse, situated on the first floor. The townhouse was what the real estate men called a vertical apartment, with barely more space than a big flat; there was a garage on the ground floor and a narrow entrance lobby and we lived on the first and second floors.

The photograph had been taken by day, and through the big window I could see the top of the house opposite and the branches of trees in full summer foliage. Inside the room, each piece of furniture and each object were marked with a little circle and a number, stuck onto the glossy surface of the photograph.

"Turn the picture over," Michelle said matter-of-factly. She had finished her coffee and was taking a second cup.

On the reverse side, there was a column of numbers on the left-hand side and a notation against each one, in neat typescript.

"No. 1. Blue Italian pottery vase, purchased Positano, 1968. Sentimental value. Memory of a good holiday. Worth about 10 dollars.

"No. 2. Television set. Black and White. Decca. Rented from Rediffusion Ltd. 12 dollars a month. 11 months to run on a 2-year contract . . ."

I skipped unbelievingly down the list. The last line read: "Brazilian silver ladle; unusually expensive gift to Julia, marking first time she accompanied him on professional trip to South America; joint expenses paid by Defence Institute. Value 200 dollars."

I looked up from the page, but before I could say anything, Michelle held up her hand.

"One thing I forgot to mention," she said. "For Christ's sake don't say, 'What in God's name is all this about?' You're on tape and film at this moment and the man in charge of the surveillance is allergic to clichés and he hates any phrases out of old blackmail movies. He's a techno-freak; he likes all his video work to sound very hip and modern. If he had his way, we'd all talk like computerized answering devices."

She grinned as though I would enjoy the joke. "There's no point in saying anything really. This whole trip has been designed to make you feel really weird and creepy and there's no point in pretending that it doesn't. You can't understand it yet. That'll come later.

"All you have to grasp right now is that these two pictures are part of an investigation into your life. I chose them
from an enormous dossier to show you how deeply your
inner sanctuaries have been penetrated.

"Persuading you to ball me last night was the end point
of a long, long period of preparation. If you hadn't fallen I
would have given you other opportunities until you did.

"Now. There are some smaller pictures inside the case.
Take them out please."

Mechanically, I did as I was told and I found six more
photographs, smaller twelve-by-eight-inch enlargements, and
spread them out over the foot of the bed. I recognized them
all immediately. Two were views of the outside of the
Blackheath house taken from different angles, one by day,
the other by night. The night shot had the kind of contrived
artificiality that wins prizes at local camera clubs. The fore-
ground was filled with the back of a man's head and shoulders, taken as he stood watching the house, and silhouetted
at the lighted kitchen window was Julia, standing at the
sink, looking down into the tiny walled garden, clearly ob-
livious of the watcher. The daylight photograph showed the
same watcher, concealed this time at the foot of the garden,
with Julia, unaware of his presence, hanging washing on
the Spiro-dryer thirty feet away.

The other four pictures were crowd scenes, taken in the
main shopping streets of Blackheath and Greenwich, nearby.
Julia was in every picture, not as the centerpiece but as a
figure in the crowd, and the shots had been taken on different days. In one the weather was bright and clear and Julia
was wearing jeans and a sweater and open sandals and she
looked sunburned and happy. Spring possibly, but more
likely a cooler day in high summer, August, perhaps Sep-
tember. It was now March, which meant they had been
watching her for at least seven months. In another photograph it was raining but it rained so often in London that

it was impossible to assign any date. The others didn't add much either, but in each one the watcher was there, a few feet away from Julia.

"Now," Michelle said, "there's a special reason for showing you these photographs. You've spent ten years of your life studying terrorism. You know about fear and threats and coercion. This dossier is to let you know our level of professionalism, to establish our credibility. Have we succeeded?"

"Yes," I said grimly, "you've succeeded."

"Good," she said. "Because if you do have any doubts, I have a lot more material. Take your choice. Shall I show you a copy of your contract with the Defence Institute or perhaps some of those private little confidential memoranda you pass to the director, Admiral Toman."

She smiled. "We have a lot more. Bank statements, correspondence with your literary agent. I can even tell you in which drawer Julia keeps her birth control pills."

"There's no need. I've got the message."

"Well, just to make sure, I'll spell things out a bit further," she said. "In a minute, we're going to begin what the people I work with call a scenario. You're going to be hearing a lot of that word so remember that it's a planned sequence of events that we are going to go through together, with a prepared script, just as if we were acting a play, but it's happening in real life, not on a stage. Now . . ." She pointed to the photographs.

"If you disobey me on any point, or in any detail of the scenario, there are graded sanctions that will be put into effect against Julia.

"If anything goes wrong here in Montreal, surveillance will detect it. A phone call will be made to London.

"If you do something very foolish, Julia will be badly hurt. If you step a little way out of line, she may just have a minor accident. She won't even know it isn't her fault. There'll be a little fall, perhaps, a sprained ankle.

"All you need to remember is that from this moment onward, there's a terribly direct link between your obedience and Julia's well-being.

"Do you really understand that?"

I nodded.

"Good. In due time, everything will be explained to you in the greatest possible detail. There'll be no mysteries. But right now, we have to begin the scenario, so just sit tight and think of those photographs.

"While you're thinking, get some breakfasts out of that gadget over there. I'm starving."

When she had finished speaking, I could not think of a single thing to say. Her words, the photographs, the whole scene, seemed completely unreal. It was like the split second when you have cut yourself and you see the blood but haven't yet felt the pain, the suspended moment when the boat has tipped and you are still dry but you *are* going to hit the water.

I went to the refrigerated food rack and chose two "English country house deluxe breakfasts." The act of drawing them out of the rack stripped metal tabs off the undersurface which activated a pulse at the base of the unit; and somewhere in the hotel, or perhaps a hundred miles away, a computer recorded an expenditure of sixteen dollars in the central data bank.

Each tray was divided into two parts. The "part ones" were the hot food—bacon, eggs and sausages. I slipped them into the micro-bake oven which counted to six in a disembodied ticking sound then ejected the trays with the food sizzling and ready to be reunited with the cold "part twos"—the orange juice, milk and marmalade. Michelle motioned me to start eating as she picked up the Futurfone, keying three digits, an internal hotel number for the public relations office.

"Hello," she said. "I'm calling from the NBC penthouse, could you put me through to Mr. Colson, please."

She used a silly, simpering voice, making the switch in tone very professionally.

"Mr. Colson? I'm sorry to disturb you so early but I need your help rather urgently. This is Mr. Russell's secretary. That's right, NBC.

"He'd like to make a change of plan. He . . . We . . . would like to spend a few days at your ski resort. . . . Yes. That's right.

"We'd like seats on the Ski-Air helicopter as soon as possible and a room . . . I mean rooms . . . at the ski lodge."

She hesitated, simpering again, ". . . and Mr. Colson, could I ask you a little favor. Mr. Russell doesn't want to be disturbed while we're out there so could you relay calls and messages only in an extreme emergency? . . . Thank you. Yes. He has some work he wants to do without being interrupted." The voice was pure amateur theatricals now, the innuendo expressed with all the subtlety of a high school play.

She put down the phone and said brusquely in her normal voice, "I'm sorry about all that childishness, but I learned a long time ago that if you want to be remembered, you have to overact." Then she sat down, facing me, and started on the breakfast.

"You've never been to the Royal Mountain Ski Lodge," she said, telling, not asking. "It's in the Laurentian Hills and it takes thirty minutes to get there by helicopter. They take off from the roof of the hotel."

She gestured toward the window. "The snow is clearing, so there should be flights quite soon. Colson has promised us a private VIP compartment on the second takeoff at latest.

"Pack an overnight bag and don't worry about your skis." She smiled. "No one will be surprised if you leave them behind. That's not what you're going for."

I thought for a moment, then I said carefully, "I presume all this isn't going to end with a couple of days in the Laurentians."

"No, of course not," she said. "I'll tell you more in the helicopter. But right now, I'll tell you this much: We're going to be leaving Canada on a long trip and it's going to be the most bizarre experience of your life. You're going to learn more about what the twentieth century is really like than you ever have before."

She grinned suddenly, gesturing toward the pile of Royal Mountain brochures on the side-table.

"You know what these people say. They are taking the shock out of future shock. Well, the people I work with are going to put some of it back again."

I said as calmly as I could, "It sounds like the beginning of a descent into hell."

"Yes," she said, "for someone of your sensitivities, I suppose that's what it is. But at least you'll have me to replace your beloved Julia as companion for the trip."

CHAPTER 3 We were summoned to the roof at eight thirty. It had stopped snowing and there were signs of the sun trying to break through the layers of gray cloud cover. The wind was whipping powdered snow off to the balustrade and blowing it in fine spray.

When the helicopter was ready for takeoff, we were escorted through a glass tunnel and into a small compartment at the rear of the twenty-seat Sikorsky, divided from the main passenger cabin by a door as well as a curtain, with two comfortable bench seats facing each other across a card table.

A stewardess in a red and white trouser suit started fluttering around; she was obviously impressed by the VIP entry and offered in quick succession Ski-Air pamphlets, magazines, coffee and candies for takeoff.

I took off my sunglasses and gave her a hard stare. "We don't want anything else," I said. "We don't want to be disturbed for the rest of the flight."

She looked offended, as I had hoped, and withdrew into the outer cabin. Michelle said, "You did that very well; you could become a natural VIP with hardly any training at all."

"We can skip the jokes," I said. "I did it because I want some answers from you; I'm getting tired of the puppet routine."

Instead of replying, Michelle dipped her hand into the big leather carryall she used as a handbag and pulled out a gray gunmetal cube that looked like a very large cigarette lighter.

"Then we'd better use this," she said. "It's an electronic conversation mask. It eliminates any possibility of our conversation being overheard or recorded electronically."

I said, "Christ," and sat back stunned in the seat.

Michelle went on in the same steady tone. "Think of it as just another electronic toy like the ones in the Royal Mountain. It's like a tape recorder at an interview; once it's been there for a couple of minutes, you forget it's there."

I looked out of the window and saw that we were about to take off. The hawsers were being removed from the rotor blades, the chocks taken from under the wheels, and the ground crew backed away into the corners of the roof.

Almost immediately, we started to rise, slowly at first, then very fast. We hovered for a moment, like a pigeon looking for its flight-path home; then we swung out over the balustrade and headed north across the city.

The sun had broken through and there were bright reflections on the snowy roofs below and on the metalwork of the St. Lawrence bridges. It was the morning rush hour. Lines of cars, nose to tail, crisscrossed through the city streets. We flew through some clouds of industrial smoke pollution; then the air cleared again and we followed the St. Lawrence through the outer perimeter of suburbs. In a moment, we were beyond the last suburb and over the snow-covered plain dividing Montreal from the Laurentian foothills.

There was something about the morning light that reminded me suddenly of the Himalayas and I thought about the Anstatt Glacier and the overhang where we had camped, pinned under the ice wall, on that last glorious Everest expedition, my farewell to youth.

Other images followed, coming in unbidden sequence as they had so often been rehearsed in my mind's eye: the weather clearing, the step-cutting, then the last quick descent and the exultant march down into Thyangboche, and the sight of Julia, who was supposed to be in England, standing in the meadow, watching for our return.

Then the image of her running toward me, laughing, then crying. "I've ruined us. I've spent everything we had in the bank to come. I couldn't stay away. I couldn't bear you being a dot on a map in the *Times*, always a day out of date . . . always wondering whether you'd fallen since the last dispatch. I had to come. Forgive me, forgive me."

And finally the five days together in Thyangboche, in the little wooden house behind the lamasery, with the blue Tibetan good luck symbol on the door, making love on wooden pallets covered with furs.

As I looked across at Michelle, I felt the kind of regret I had not known since childhood, of having done something that has changed everything forever.

Brusquely Michelle interrupted my thoughts. "Are you ready to talk yet?" she said.

"This time I want some straight answers," I said angrily, turning to face her. "And one question first. What the hell do you want from me?"

"You're not ready for straight answers yet," she replied calmly. "You're not in the right frame of mind. But I'll give you some hints. It has to do with your book."

"You mean *The Art of the Coup d'Etat?*"

It sounded naive even as I said it, and just for a moment Michelle looked irritated, as if I had fallen below company expectations.

"No. Your new one. The study of urban violence.

"I haven't personally read it," she went on. "All I know is that the people I work with"—she emphasized the "with" again—"regard it as quite brilliant, so brilliant that they want to make use of you. You'll find out who they are in due time. All you need know for now is that they are not some half-assed terrorists who want you to show them how to make Molotov cocktails.

"We may need your services for several months. You're going to be doing complex things, right out in the open. To make you do that, we have to have real control over you. There's a limit to the amount of physical harm we can do to Julia . . . so we must retain the option of inflicting psychological harm on her too."

"For Christ's sake, what do you mean by that!" I exploded. The whole scene seemed suddenly childish as well as unreal.

She ignored the outburst and took a camera out of her bag and handed it to me.

"It's an Espion-Diversity with built-in transmitter. Instead of being recorded on film, the images are encoded in digital form and transmitted to a computerized unit which unscrambles them for projection or storage on video tape. It's one of the many offshoots of the space program.

"Last night, every single second of our little sexual encounter was recorded. These units give a complete series of images in full color in as good a quality as you'll get in a movie house. The second lens there is infrared; darkness is no obstacle whatever."

She put the camera back in her bag.

"Those images can be edited in a hundred different ways. We can destroy your marriage totally or we can just shake it a little. We can turn last night into a peccadillo—a physical weakness she will come to forgive—or we can destroy every private illusion she had about you."

I turned to look out the window, anything to escape from what she was saying, but she reached across and gripped my arm.

"No," she said. "No escapism—think about the strap."

I went very cold and still and sat, staring into space, thinking and at the same time trying not to think about the images she was trying to bring back.

It had happened some time in the middle of the night. We had lain, talking about the movie, and she had turned the conversation to a sequence in which the drive-in girl had imagined herself pinned across a motorcycle seat and beaten with a studded leather biker's belt.

Michelle had talked sexily and teasingly about the image, about how it was a common female fantasy. Gradually she had admitted that she was turned on by it, and then, at a point where the sexual tension was nearly unbearable, she had produced from her handbag a tiny leather strap.

"There are no studs in it," she had said, grinning. "This is just for fun." And then she had drawn me gently to the point where, quite naturally, she had lain across the bed and I had picked up the strap and started to use it on her.

Interrupting my thoughts, Michelle said, "It all feels pretty sick in the cold light of day, doesn't it? That's the trouble with sex—you do some funny things when the black river is running."

She saw me start and she said lightly, "Oh, yes. I know about the black river too. I've heard you mention it to Julia."

I said viciously, "I hope to God at least I hurt you." And she laughed, the big happy laugh she had used after the cinema.

"You remember I went to the bathroom just before we started?"

"Yes."

"I gave myself a small amount of local anesthetic. It was just as well, too. You hit very hard."

The obscenity of it all left me stunned and I had to turn away from her, and this time she let me stare out of the window for a while.

But the landscape below was little comfort. The sun had gone down and the fields of snow looked cold and desolate. Plows had been used on the single main road, but the side roads were covered in deep snow and identifiable only by the thin black line of the fences beside them. In one field, someone had been out early having fun with a snowmobile, making crazy tracks over the surface.

As we passed over St. Jerome and started to climb, skimming the tops of the low hills, Michelle said, "I'm sorry I had to be so nasty about the strap."

"What am I supposed to say?" I said. "You're welcome?"

"We'll be there soon and you'll be finding out more about all this, then you'll feel better," she replied. "For now bear with me. I have several jobs in this operation. One of them is to make you understand the implications of the technology we use. . . ."

"I'm beginning to understand more than I want to," I said.

"But not more than you need to." Her reply had a sharp edge, then she smiled again. "You can't be expected to understand what surveillance is really all about. They call it the soft sell and that's what I am. . . . I'm here to get you used to the technology of terrorism. Now why don't you just sit back and think about which parts of your book anyone might be interested in. . . ."

When the helicopter landed, my spirits lifted.

All my life, I've been around mountain resorts, and the Royal Mountain resort was my kind of environment. I can read signs around me like a woodsman who sees the significance of every broken twig on a path or configuration of mud on a river bed. I notice little details quite naturally: the prices, the attitude of the instructors, the types of equipment for rent, the layouts of the descents.

The signs at the Royal Mountain told me it was an expensive resort but a good one, where winter sports were taken seriously and there was much more to the snow scene than apres-ski dancing until 3:00 A.M. in a discotheque with wood paneling and a log fire.

The lodge was situated at the edge of a completely frozen lake, nearly four miles long and two miles across; two ranges of hills sloped down to the lakeshore and there were chair lifts and ski trails on both. There was also a skating rink with outdoor bar, a fenced-off snowmobile park where the rental machines were stored and a circuit marked out on the lake ice for horse-sled racing.

The hotel was protected from the noise of the helipad by a wall sculpted out of ice, reinforced by wood, and we walked right into the lobby, through a narrow cut, like the entrance to a snow-covered mineshaft.

As we entered, Michelle whispered, "We won't be sleeping here tonight. There'll be a message at the desk. Do exactly what it says. Pay everything by credit card and if I make a suggestion, follow it exactly."

The assistant manager was a cheerful young French Canadian with a build and tan that said he spent a lot of time on the slopes himself.

As soon as we got to the desk, he greeted us, then turned to me. "Mr. Russell, I have a message for you. It came this morning. I was told it was very urgent."

I opened the slip of red and white paper.

"Welcome to Royal Mountain," the message said. "Won't be able to get down to the hotel to see you. Can you come right away to the Cabine des Pins? Bring Michelle."

I handed the message to Michelle and she read it quickly.

"That should be fun," she said. "We can go by snowmobile." She turned to the assistant manager. "We've been invited to one of the villas on the far side of Lake Condet. Will you arrange a snowmobile for Mr. Russell?"

She smiled at me. "We can leave our luggage here." I knew it would not have escaped anyone's attention that Michelle did not have any luggage, so I smiled back and said, "Well at least leave your coat. We'll have to rent snowmobile suits if we're going across the lake."

The assistant manager nodded and gave me some forms to fill in. I signed the register as Philip Russell, and when I hesitated on the second card, Michelle took it and signed Michelle Foxton, c/o NBC, New York.

"Shall I charge the snowmobile to your room?" the assistant manager asked. Michelle nodded imperceptibly and I said, "Yes," and handed him my American Express card. He made out a credit form, ran the card through a machine, together with a blank hotel bill, then handed me back a slip with a room number in ink over a hotel stamp.

"Just give that to the rental manager in the snowmobile park," he said. "Will you be needing any skis while you are here?"

"No. We won't have time for skiing, I'm afraid." Michelle flashed a quick leer at the manager, hesitated a fraction too long, then added, "And anyway, we'll have the snowmobile."

"Eventually," I said lightly, "there won't be any skiers left in North America, only snowmobilers."

As we walked out of the hotel and down to the snowmobile park, Michelle said, "I suppose you hate snowmobiles. I expect you like backpacking and communing with the wilderness in its natural state."

It was only a casual remark but at the time it seemed a small triumph for me. They knew how much I paid for my television set in a house four thousand miles away but they apparently didn't know that snowmobiles are my secret passion.

On the face of it, she should have been right. I don't like technology in the mountains. In the climbing books I'm classified with the purists, but snowmobiles are my private sin.

It seemed all the sweeter when I sensed, in the snowmobile park, that she herself was ill at ease around the machines.

"What's the matter," I asked, "don't you like snow machines?"

"Not much." It was a grudging admission. "But I'll be all right as long as you take it easy. It's the cornering that scares me and I don't like going fast."

I nodded. "And what's the scenario, as you call it?" She pointed across the lake to a ridge, covered with pine trees.

"The Cabine des Pins is right on top, up there. It has a red roof."

"And the scenario is to go there?"

"Yes."

The rental manager, a cheerful-looking young ski pro, came up and I handed him the card the hotel manager had given me. When he asked what kind of machine we wanted, I said, "I'd like a Skidoo Vautour X-19 please."

"We do have a couple of those machines, sir, but I'm afraid we insist that guests take lessons first. They're a bit hairy for touring," the manager replied in a friendly but firm voice as he smiled apologetically.

I reached into my credit card case, flicked over the plastic windows and took out a green printed slip.

The manager read it and grinned. "That's okay, then, sir. I'll get the machine right away. Would you like to choose your suits and boots from the ones on this rack?"

As he walked away, Michelle snapped, "What the hell was that you just showed him?"

"My snowmobile racing competitor's license," I smiled. "I took part once in the Quebec Winter Carnival Races. I didn't win but I had a helluva lot of fun."

Michelle looked really angry. "Have you forgotten the folio case already?" she said. "You really can't be that dumb."

I looked at her very calmly and said, "Don't worry, I'll keep to the scenario. We'll get to the Cabine des Pins."

"How is the ice?" I asked the rental manager when he returned, zipping up my snowmobile suit.

"Good all over. We've never had a March like it. We've been exceptionally lucky."

I grinned at Michelle. "Did you hear that? We're exceptionally lucky. Hop on."

She climbed on behind me as I adjusted my goggles and I could feel her grip unnecessarily tightly around my waist. I gunned the motor hard and felt her tighten even more, as if we were on the pinnacle of a roller coaster. A glance be-

tween the rental manager and myself was a little sign between us that this was strictly for sex, not because I couldn't
control the throttle.

There was a short trail of hard-packed snow leading down
to the ice and I took it at a rush, feeling the heavy machine
skittering over the glassy surface. I could feel Michelle's
anxiety turning to real fear.

She shouted something but I made a sign against my helmet that I couldn't hear, then I opened the throttle and we
shot out over the ice.

About a mile ahead, four snowmobiles were coming
toward us, three together, with a fourth trailing behind.
They were staying close to the tracks to have a smoother
run, and I decided to find out how Michelle would enjoy
playing chicken.

I gunned the throttle to get the last surge of power from
the engine. Adjusting my stance for maximum menace I
roared straight at the oncoming machines, not caring that
their final, panicky swerve came seconds before a dangerous, metal-jarring spill.

I could feel Michelle clawing desperately at my back but
I ignored her and held the machine at 40 mph, using
strength to haul the runners off the ice into a jump that took
us directly onto the upward trail.

Though we barely left the ground, the return was jarring.
It takes practice to learn the right position to cushion the
shock and I felt Michelle thud back onto the seat with a
force I knew would send pain right up her spine.

When I was sure of the feel of the surfaces, I started to
crisscross over the ruts, swaying from side to side in a little
ravine like a bobsledder testing the outer limits of his curve.

I was doing it now for the sheer hell of it.

Each twist of the guidebars risked a spill but I didn't care,
and when I saw the yellow flash of another Skidoo, heading
down toward us through the trees, I accelerated instead of
slowing to let it pass. The other rider saw, just in time, that

he had nowhere to go and threw his machine into a snow-bank, hurling himself off and rolling sideways into a deep drift.

As we skidded by, I gave him a friendly wave, as if thanking him for letting us pass, and gunned the engine again to drown his abuse.

Then I saw we were almost at the top. I could see the red roof of the villa and I waited until we were close, then slowed the snowmobile and pulled into a little clearing in the pine trees.

Before we were fully stationary, Michelle had jumped off and was starting to vomit into the snow, bending double, the heavy mitten cupped to her face.

I watched her without speaking, and after about a minute she stood up, her face scarlet with anger.

"You bastard, you stupid bastard. You're going to find out just what control means."

Just for a moment, I wasn't sure if I had judged the situation correctly; then I relaxed and said very quietly, "I think you'll find the people you work with won't want to waste any sanctions just because you had a hairy snowmobile ride. I've followed your scenario. You have no complaints."

Then I added, in the same professional tone she had used so much, "Tell me, would *you* seriously recommend sanctions in the circumstances?"

She didn't answer and I could see she was putting all her energy into getting her fear under control.

"That ride was a message," I said. "It says I'm not a toy. You've set up a game, a vicious, nasty game and I'm playing by your rules because I don't want Julia hurt. I acknowledge your control. But that ride was to tell you what may happen if I ever get out of it."

She missed the end of the speech because she had started vomiting again, so I sat on a log and smoked a cigarette and waited for her to compose herself.

After a while, she lit a cigarette too, then she smiled. "I

guess you did owe me that," she said. "Shall we call it quits?"

I put my cigarette out on the tree stump.

"In the kind of game you're playing, debts aren't paid that easily," I said. "You keep on winning, or you don't turn your back."

CHAPTER 4 "My name is Peace, Simon Peace—and I never turn my back."

We were standing at the doorway of the cottage and the man said it as a greeting, holding out toward me in mock handshake a thin, cylindrical tube with a parabolic sound reflector at the stem. I recognized it as a long-range, high-sensitivity, directional microphone.

"Come in," he said easily. "I wasn't really spying on you. Take off your snowmobile suits."

The voice was friendly, educated, American, not unlike Michelle's.

The man was young, probably not past thirty, and he was dressed in stylish, flared brushed denim slacks and a white sweater. I noticed on a coathanger beside the door a $400 version of an Afghan sheepskin coat, the ultimate in hip-style among North American kids that year.

The most striking thing about him was that he was thin —bony thin, not slim, with too many sinews showing in his hands and neck. Even his forehead looked too naked despite a thick head of sandy-colored hair.

He waited until we had taken off our snowmobile suits and put our overboots on the rubber mat, then he said casually to me, "That was a fine dramatic little speech down there. I hope Michelle was suitably scared."

"You heard, but you were not spying," I sneered. He took my arm and led me through into the huge open living room of the cottage.

"To be absolutely truthful," he said, "I overheard the conversation by chance. I was just filling in time until you arrived and I happened to be playing with this old microphone."

He handed it to me and waited for me to inspect it.

Michelle said, "Philip's rhetoric didn't scare me," and Peace laughed.

"No. But I bet his snowmobile driving did," he said.

"You saw that too, did you?" she snapped, and Peace laughed again.

"Not all of it, but I guessed what would happen.

"I'm afraid it was a little joke of mine not telling you about Philip's love of those ghastly machines."

He reached into his pocket and handed her a folded sheet of paper. When she opened it, I saw that it was a photocopy of the snowmobile competitor's license and I noticed that it was a dry-process color copy, the latest advance in xerography which produced copies almost indistinguishable from the original.

Michelle handed it back. "That wasn't funny," she said. "He's a maniac with those machines."

"I thought it would do him good to let off a little steam," Peace replied, nodding casually in my direction. "You told me yourself it would take a while for a man like Philip to get used to all his new constraints."

He sounded completely unapologetic and he had taken it as his right to enjoy an amusing but slightly cruel joke at her expense.

I could see too that the friendly welcome had also been carefully designed. I had arrived feeling strong and aggressive, exhilarated after the snowmobile ride, adrenaline flowing, ready to confront the architect of the scenario I was being forced to act through.

But there was no confrontation, no conflict, only the awful, deflating realization that everyone felt safe in assuming that I was under control. There were no guards, no apparent security precautions.

"We've tried your patience long enough," Peace said. "Let me get you a drink, then we'll tell you what this is all about."

I asked for a scotch and inspected the cabin while he got the drink.

The cottage was typical plastic Canadiana, clearly the "nineteenth-century rural Quebec package."

"Now," Peace said brusquely, as he returned with the drinks, "how much has Michelle told you?"

"I told him that we wanted him to join us for a long period, so we could make use of his particular skills," Michelle said. She smiled. "I also told him we were not Quebec separatists." The smile seemed to be a signal to Peace that her anger had passed. Peace smiled back.

"I'm relieved at that," he said. "The Quebec separatists really are one of the truly irrelevant movements of our time."

He turned to face me. "We are a radical group, it's true," he said, "but of a very much more interesting kind." He paused. "Tell me, Philip. Do you know what the Institute for Social Change is?"

I thought for a moment, then I said carefully, "It's a new think tank, isn't it? It opened about six months ago, somewhere outside London."

"It's in Chislehurst, actually, less than ten miles from where you live," Peace said, "and it is, officially, six months old."

He smiled. "Only the institute didn't actually open six months ago. It came above ground, as it were. I created the ISC over two years ago, as an underground think tank, one that could work away from the eyes of governments and security organizations. We had a good reason for coming out into the open, but that needn't concern you yet.

"In fact, the ISC is the world's first genuinely radical think

41

tank. Its purpose is to study corporate power, in order to be able to destroy it."

He paused in a consciously theatrical way to underline the revelation, then he went on: "As you've often said in your writings, most radical groups really don't understand corporate power. Mostly because they get hung up on the idea that most of the big corporations are American-owned.

"We don't make that mistake. We recognize that corporations aren't American, or British, or German. They've become nation-states in their own right."

He smiled. "The big U.S. based multinational corporations are about as loyal to the Stars and Stripes as Chairman Mao is. Corporations move across national boundaries and between them. They understand that real power is in monopolies not patriotism—in oil, natural gas, food and transportation. We make it our business to understand our enemies properly. That's what the Institute for Social Change is all about."

"Well," I said, "if I'm to be pressed into the service of radicals, it's nice to know they are competent ones."

I made the sarcasm very heavy, hoping to provoke Peace but he smiled as he rose. "I think we could put an end to your doubts, Philip, if I introduced you to the person who provides us with the access to the resources we need for this kind of activity. As you know, a think tank needs more than money. It needs access to the right people and the right information."

He walked over to the foot of the staircase that was just visible at the entrance to the living room, "Hairy, can you come down a minute please."

As he said the word Hairy, an instant image came to mind, as I knew Peace intended. It was a *Time* magazine cover of a man so covered with hair that even fully dressed he looked like an ape.

I heard him coming down the stairs and as he walked into

the living room there was no need for the introduction Peace made.

Ever since he first made his appearance on the California hippie scene in the middle of the 1960s, no one had ever called him anything else but Hairy. I had seen pictures of him in *Rolling Stone* and in underground movies and in newsreels after one of his arrests, and it was always the same: you never remembered what he was wearing, you remembered only the hair.

Michelle went up to him and put her arms round him, hugging him warmly. "Meet the only man in the world whose pubic hair doesn't stop at his ears," she said. "Isn't he beautiful?"

Hairy grunted and sat down. I remembered reading that, the journalist put it, he was an unenthusiastic conversationalist. But I knew that he didn't need to say anything; his presence alone gave Peace all the credibility he needed.

Hairy was one of the three or four gods of the world's hip youth, the number one techno-freak who had earlier been the first and the greatest underground drug chemist.

In the basement of a suburban home in San Francisco he had built, while barely out of high school, the most notorious acid lab of any the narcotics bureau had tried to raid. He had invented time-release LSD, then developed it into the six-day multipill, in which twelve different highs were released from different drugs contained within one capsule at timed intervals like a long-acting cold cure.

Like many of the most aware kids of his generation, he had quickly tired of the drug scene and turned instead to electronics, to biofeedback, to brain-wave control circuitry and sound technology. He had built the ultimate sound and light show that had put 50,000 kids into a state of catatonic shock in a San Francisco auditorium.

For a change, he had dabbled for a while in phone-freaking, and set a record with $11,000 worth of free transoceanic phone calls in a single day, distorting the circuits with a gadget the size of a matchbox. When Ma Bell had prosecuted him, he had reacted angrily with a device which had wiped clean the storage drum in their central billing computer in Los Angeles and everyone on the West Coast had had free phone calls for a month.

Bell had dropped charges and offered Hairy a $60,000 a year research job, but he had become bored with telephones and had turned to guerrilla television. He had invented a system of spiking into local cable channels and given it away, free and for fun, to underground groups supporting everything from ecological preservation to abortion on demand. Before long, there was scarcely a TV cable company executive in the United States who didn't watch his shows in the constant fear of the strange pirate images that would suddenly surge onto the screen in the middle of the evening's viewing.

Peace let us all sit for a while, while I weighed the implications of Hairy's presence. Then he said quietly, "I want you to think of Hairy as the tip of a very large iceberg.

"All over North America and Europe there are hundreds of kids like Hairy who were part of the freak scene when that was appropriate, then went into laboratories at NASA or Bell or General Electric—kids who smoke a little dope and who like having a big lab to play in and don't mind helping put a man on the moon, but who are still freaks at heart.

"Call it an iceberg, or call it a network. When Hairy needs help, Hairy calls them up. We have the money we need from other sources. Through Hairy, we have the access we need to the places where there are things that can't be bought on the open market.

"Does that put an end to your cynicism, Philip?" I didn't say anything but he could read the answer in my face. "Good," he said. "Now we can show you why you are really here."

He led me into a tiny book-lined study next to the living room, and Hairy and Michelle followed. Peace indicated a chair in front of the television set, and I noticed that Hairy was taking out of a cupboard behind me a black box, the size of a large tool kit.

I sat down and Hairy knelt beside me. I guessed he must be in his late twenties now, but he still looked basically the same as he had always looked: his huge beard seemed to flow equally strongly in all directions; his hair made a gigantic aura around his head and his body hair protruded from every edge of his shirt, at the collar, cuffs and between the buttons which bulged open over his heavy stomach.

I remembered the *Time* magazine phrase: "The body of a 200-pound ape, with one of the greatest scientific minds of the 20th century inside it."

Hairy opened the box to reveal eight dials on a display face and a set of electrodes with wires, leading into jack-sockets.

"What the hell's that?" I said.

Michelle laughed. "Don't worry," she said, "it's a device for reading emotional reaction through the skin. We're going to show you some pictures and we want to get your reaction."

She smiled. "This way, we don't have to ask for your reaction. This tells us more precisely."

"Don't start making a fuss over nothing, Philip," Peace said offhandedly. "Look on it as a chance to begin to really learn something about technology for a change, instead of fighting it, as you do all the time. You are going to be working with scientists."

I had been trying to place Peace in some category that would help me understand what he was doing. I couldn't see him in any of the radical movements; politics and street fighting wouldn't be his style. He liked to cultivate the distant stare which implied some secret understanding. He had a peculiar kind of charisma that worked not by dominance but by remoteness, and he affected slightly flowery, over-precise language. I decided suddenly that whether he fully realized it or not, he was styling himself a prophet. He had a message, a Word.

As I thought about it, I realized too how acquiescent I had already become in this weird new environment. I was sitting in a chair, letting Hairy attach electrodes to my head and arms and chest, waiting for them to test my reactions to whatever they might put on the screen.

"He's ready," Hairy said, interrupting my thoughts.

Peace leaned over to the TV set and touched a switch on the video-cassette player, and a picture flashed onto the screen.

It was an English country house, or a close imitation of one. There was no mistaking the style, and even the ivy on the walls looked authentic. The camera was panning through the grounds on a wet blustery day and the rain was blowing in sharp gusts over the neatly trimmed lawns. As the camera turned the corner, it focused on a side of the building that was shiny black and had been reshaped from what was once a glassed-in conservatory.

"I take it that is the Institute for Social Change," I said. "I don't know many country houses that have black spheres grafted on the outside."

"The black stuff is Neroflex, that's Hairy's laboratory. When we resell the institute, as we no doubt will, we'll simply roll it up and it will be a conservatory again," Peace said. "That's the only change we've made in the structure of the building. We like to travel light through the communications age; we don't build institutions."

I glanced down at the dials and saw that no readings were showing.

"Apparently you haven't grabbed my interest," I said. "I don't seem to have any reaction."

"No. But then we haven't told you the interesting part. What you are looking at is your institute."

I didn't need to look at the dials. I could feel my own pulse racing.

"In a very short time, you are going to be appointed the director of the Institute for Social Change at a salary of forty-five thousand dollars a year, net of English tax, paid in the United States. You will have a glossy car, a top-hat pension scheme and a grossly large expense account. The title, of course, will be a little phony, but the prestige and the financial rewards will make your 'defection' from the Defence Institute seem plausible.

"You won't actually be the director; but you will be a consultant, with a great deal of power and influence over what we do."

Peace pointed down at the panel of dials. "Look at the readings, now," he said, "as I tell you that I've been telling you one big lie all through this discussion."

Two of the needles moved across their scales to a halfway point.

"Anxious, but not scared," Michelle said. "That's good."

"Tell me what the lie was and stop playing games," I said.

Peace put his finger on a dial. "Unfortunately, it's very hard to manage theatrical effects while you're hooked up to this," he said. "Your voice was trying to convey anger; the needles still say anxiety."

I looked down and guessed that the third dial was the anxiety reading and it was holding constant just below the halfway point on the scale.

"The lie had a purpose," Peace said. "I wanted to give you some point of reference so that you'd have somewhere to fit the institute. So I called it a think tank."

He smiled. "But in fact it isn't. It's an action tank. You're not being hired to do more studies and analyses. You're going to help us put some of your ideas into practice. Now, Philip, I'll explain a little more," Peace said. "For the past two years, we've been studying terrorism as a weapon to fight corporate power.

"We've watched your work closely and found it brilliant. Like you, we came to the conclusion that most radical guerrilla groups are useless. Most of the big ones—the IRA, the Arab organizations—are so committed to various ideologies that they've turned terrorism into a new kind of trench warfare. Good old attrition stuff. We'll blow you up and you blow us up, and the ones left at the end win. The small groups like the SLA are mostly low-grade crazies who somehow managed to avoid getting stuck in some twitch-bin or other. Generally speaking, what is saving society from the scourge of urban guerrilla warfare is that most urban guerrillas are idiots."

"But if you know all this," I said, fascinated despite myself, "why do you need me?"

"You have one thing we lack," Peace said. "We have financial backing, enough for the incredibly sophisticated games you've seen already. Not all the world's wealthy are right-wing fascists, you know. We have access to the technology and Hairy provides the scientific genius.

"We've put together a team of urban guerrillas. We call them the Vikings." He smiled. "That's another of our quaint, reassuring romantic names. And we're giving them all the basic skills to become supremely competent techno-guerrillas.

"But we still lack one thing . . . your artistry in terrorism." I noticed Michelle nod in agreement at the word. "You are going to help us design some truly ingenious urban guerrilla scenarios. We need your bizarre mind and your experience in the techniques of terror. We need an artist.

"We are going to launch a war against corporate power. But we're not just going to blow up buildings and kidnap executives and shout angry slogans. We're going to use terror to bring about changes—specific changes. And to open our war, we have a very special campaign in mind, which we'll tell you about when the time comes."

He stopped speaking and pointed downward. "Now look at the dials."

I looked down and there was a very complicated set of movements on all eight dials which meant nothing to me.

"If you hadn't been wired up, you'd probably have made all kinds of protests but the readings say that you're only a bit confused but interested. You'll find the work very interesting," Peace said. "You'll be traveling to some interesting places, and for some of the time you'll be living in your own home in Blackheath. You'll go to the institute in the morning and come home in the evening to find Michelle waiting lovingly to take care of all your needs—including your sexual ones, if you wish."

"For God's sake, what about Julia?" I said. "What will you do with her?"

"Don't worry," Peace said reassuringly. "I'll tell you all about Julia now. Watch the screen."

The cassette started to turn again and a mountain flashed onto the screen. There was some snow on the peak but the lower slopes were purple with heather. At the base there was a lake and along the water's edge a narrow road wound through a one-street village.

"You know where that is, don't you," Peace said quietly.

"It's Kinlochbannon," I said, "the village in Scotland where Julia's mother lives. Is that where'll she'll be?"

"Don't ask questions yet," Peace said, "just watch the screen and think of all the beautiful memories you've shared with Julia there, while you were courting her."

I looked back at the screen. On the hillside, just above the village, there was a shepherd's hut, just visible on the film. We had made love there one night, on a vacation soon after our first meeting at Cambridge, staying out all night and inventing a ridiculous story to soothe her mother the next day.

My thoughts drifted on and I heard Peace say, "Now you see the road, follow it in your mind through the village toward the mountain . . . now, you see the point where it bends? Well, there, exactly, is the place where Julia is going to die. . . ."

In the instant he pronounced the word, Hairy jerked the box up in front of me and I saw half the dials swing wildly to their maximum reading.

Then Peace said, "Or rather, I should say, appear to die," and this time the other dials swung over to their extreme outer edge.

I tried to get out of the chair but Hairy held me down leaning all his weight on my arm.

Before I could struggle, I heard Peace say, "It's all over, Philip, and that was a beautiful set of readings. Almost perfect. Total shock at the idea of Julia's death, total relief at news of her safety."

He switched off the television set, and suddenly there was no friendliness in his voice.

"That was to show you that we do really have control of you," he said. We *are* capable of causing death and suffering to Julia. You *will* go along with what we say." He dropped back again into his conversational voice.

"At this moment, Julia is on her way to Scotland, answering a message from her mother. Tomorrow, there will be a car accident, followed by a classic sequence: the finding of a burned body, a substitution, an autopsy and the issuing of a death certificate.

"The only difference is that this sequence will be contrived with all the technological perfection we can command and it *will* be convincing." He paused. "A week from now, there will be a funeral. Your friend on *The Times*, Jack Wescott, will have to take care of the arrangements because there will be some trouble locating you.

"When you are found, it will be rather sordid. You will be in the middle of a torrid affair with a sexy black-haired chick called Michelle, and you will have to be almost dragged from between the sheets to attend the funeral.

"There will be other little details planned to shock and alienate your friends. When you get back to London, we don't guarantee we can have you ostracized totally . . ." He smiled. "Just enough so you can begin your new career, planning the first really efficient terror campaign in the history of guerrilla warfare."

CHAPTER 5 Five days later I was in London. On the drive to Greenwich to attend Julia's "funeral," I saw my first real chance to break out of my invisible prison. We had been circling the Heath, killing time, before the final descent toward St. Mary of All Seamen, the beautiful Thamesside church where the ceremony was being held.

The delay was part of the scenario. "There's nothing quite so socially gruesome as a man who's late for his own wife's funeral," Peace said, as he sat beside me in the back of the limousine, briefing me on the arrangements. Like me, he was wearing a dark suit and looked a conventional mourner and I thought at first he was going to the church with me, but he said, "No. You'll be there alone." Then he smiled and put on his distant, prophetic look and added, "Psychologically speaking, you'll be very alone. We've been feeding back rumors about you and Michelle. I'm afraid some of your friends will be a bit chilly."

When he motioned the driver to pull over to the curb I realized there had been another car following.

"I'll leave you here. Our driver knows what to do." Then, as he closed the door, he added in a deliberate, menacing tone, "Remember, our people will be close to you all the time. They'll be all around you. You'll be watched more closely than you've ever been watched in your life."

Instead of scaring me, his words woke me up from the torpor I had been sliding into a little more during each day of waiting in Quebec, as I listened to them designing the scenario for my return to England.

Until that moment, I had assumed there would be the same total electronic surveillance as in Montreal and I had taken no interest in the funeral. Peace's remark changed it back into a real-life event. If I was to be watched by humans, then I might be able to match wits with them.

The weather was dark and threatening, and as we started to glide down the A-2 into the center of Greenwich, a few raindrops started to splash against the windows. I looked at my watch. The coffin was due to arrive at the church at 3:00 P.M., ten minutes to go.

I picked up the speaking tube clipped beside the chauffeur's partition and said through it, "Driver, we're late already. I think we'd better go right into the church."

Without turning round, the driver shook his head. He was a youth of about twenty with a face as nondescript as the gray chauffeur's uniform he had been provided with.

"We've got t'arrive after't coffin." Through the speaking tube, the north of England accent sounded flat and thick.

Looking ahead, I could see the gates of St. Mary of All Seamen. If I could only persuade him to go in, I could have ten minutes to talk to the mourners, more if the hearse was delayed by traffic. There would be so many people there I knew well. Whatever Peace had made them think of me, there had to be a chance for a hint that something was wrong, a signal for someone to try to contact me quickly after the funeral.

"Look, five minutes isn't going to make that much difference," I said urgently to the driver. "It's stupid just to drive around the churchyard. If anyone sees us, it'll look more suspicious than going in now."

"We're going round t'other side, so's we can watch fer't coffin," the driver answered mechanically as he made a sharp left turn in front of the Seamen's Hospital. The gates of the church were blocked from view by a red double-decker bus. It was infuriating to be so near and yet so helpless but I could think of nothing to do.

At the end of an alley, the driver made a right-hand turn, keeping us parallel with the churchyard, and we started to climb toward the lower slopes of the park under Greenwich Observatory. At the top, the driver turned right again and eased the car into a small children's playground, deserted now in the poor weather, with a view out over the church and the river beyond.

"Yer can get out if yer want to. We'll watch from 'ere." The driver made no signs of moving, so I got out. There was always the same maddening certainty that I was under control.

In the churchyard below, there were over a hundred mourners gathered in a circle around an empty gravesite, right at the water's edge. The circle was too far away for me to make out all the faces under the umbrellas but I could recognize, just from their outlines, at least seven or eight people I longed to talk to: Ivor Pearson, the apparently copy-book diplomat who cultivated an extreme Foreign Office manner as part of his cover as a member of the British Intelligence Service ("It does no harm if they think us paper lions," he always said). George Wilket, the huge raw-boned colonial police commissioner. Melton from Scotland Yard, a childhood friend of Julia's. . . . If I could only get down there in time, I was sure I could convey to someone that things were not as they seemed.

I was staring so intently at the circle of mourners that I didn't notice the hearse draw into the entrance to the cemetery and pause under the lych-gate.

"Coffin's comin'," the driver said behind me, pointing down the slope. "We'll give 'em time to get 'er into't church, then we'll go down."

I stared at the coffin, just visible through the narrow windows of the hearse, and for a moment, I felt real tears beginning to form, so I turned away and walked quickly back to the car. If I started letting my imagination play tricks, I knew I could lose all capacity for action.

"Dammit, we've got to go now," I said to the driver. "I'm already late for the funeral. Isn't that enough?"

It took three long, agonizing minutes to drive down the hill, turn into the main street and draw onto the little asphalted circle under the lych-gate. I was almost there. All I needed was to see which of the likely contacts was free of strange faces around them; relatives and friends tend to bunch up at funerals and, anyway, surely a strange watcher could not go too close to security people like Pearson or Wilket, for fear of having to make conversation.

Then, suddenly, as the driver was ready to begin our stately entrance, a huge tractorlike vehicle, with a pair of mechanical claws towering high above it, like the antennae of some giant South American insect, rumbled out of a driveway beside the gate and smashed into the front of the car. The impact crumpled the whole side of the limousine, scattering broken glass all over the gravel. It took me an instant to realize that it was a mechanical grave-digger. I had seen them before only in California, rolling back and forth under the pine glades, pausing at measured intervals to take single human-being-sized bites out of the grassy slopes of Forest Lawn. It was a grotesque object to have in an English country churchyard and I thought, "Christ, this must be some bizarre twist in the scenario devised by Peace." Perhaps it had been intended to injure me, giving an excuse for not going to the funeral at all.

I leaped out of the car and saw that I was trapped outside the church. The sheer weight of the huge tractor had pushed the limousine sideways under the narrow vaulted gateway; on either side, the stone church wall stood eight feet high. The driver had squeezed himself out of the offside front door but I couldn't get through because of the chauffeur's partition; the only way was over the top of the car.

I used the doorhandle as a first foothold to swing myself up onto the roof. The car was wet with rain and I could feel my leather soles slipping on the glassy surface. I sat on the car top and slid over the windshield and as I swung my legs over the hood, I saw Hedley, the vicar, running toward me.

"Oh, Philip," he cried, "what a way to have to arrive for the funeral of our beloved Julia."

The pomposity of the tone was too much. I seized Hedley by the collar and yelled, "You goddamn fool! Can't you keep your grave toys under control."

Then I saw the wiry, muscular figure of Jack Wescott, hurrying down the gravel drive. I had almost pushed Hedley aside and strode swiftly toward Westcott. This was my opportunity. There was no one who could overhear on the path. I couldn't tell Jack the truth, that Julia wasn't really dead. But Wescott is a journalist, a financial specialist with *The Times* and one of the sharpest-witted men I have ever known. A hint, even a tiny one could be enough.

I decided to try to break the tension of our mutual approach with humor. He had seen the arrival and I knew what he thought of Hedley. As he held out his hand, I said wryly, "I'm sorry, Jack, that was some way to arrive at my wife's funeral."

It should have brought a smile, but Wescott ignored the remark and said only, "We're ready. Julia is inside."

It was the first time in twenty years of friendship that there had ever been such a frost between us. We had had rows often enough; we had even fought physically once after a drunken party at Cambridge; but never this. He simply did not understand what had happened to me.

I said as warmly as I could, "Jack, thanks for taking care of everything. You know how I appreciate it."

His reply was cold and formal. "I understand you had problems in Canada. I heard you brought them back with you." I could only guess at what rumors Peace had circulated; I knew Wescott was extremely fond of Julia but he did not shock easily.

We turned together down the path toward the churchyard and I tried to walk slowly to give him time to soften, but then his wife, Jane, who had been hanging back strode to meet us. She had been a close friend of Julia's and she was blazing angry.

"Philip, tell me one thing," she greeted me. "Is it true that your new woman is in Blackheath even now, warming Julia's bed?"

I hesitated, afraid to answer. I wanted to say, "No, of course not," but I hadn't yet been to the Blackheath house. Michelle could well be there.

Jack saw my hesitation. "Jane, I think we'd better discuss all this later."

"Yes," I said desperately, "I'd like that. I want you to *understand*."

"Perhaps you'd better give the final instructions to the bearers," Westcott said formally. "It will give you a chance of a moment alone with Julia."

I looked desperately down the drive. The circle of mourners was re-forming. In a few moments the service would begin; then, afterward I would be whisked away. I had to speak to someone.

"Look, Jack," I said. "Would you mind doing it? I can't explain. But I don't feel I can. I'd rather leave it to you."

Jane exploded. "For Christ's sake." She turned and took Wescott's arm. "I'll come with you. I don't want to be near this man."

Wescott was caught in a classic dilemma: wife versus closest friend. Just for a second, we exchanged glances: he wanted to know what the hell had got into me; we had shared too much for him to shut me out of his life without giving me a chance to explain, but it would have to come later. He turned with Jane and walked into the church.

I pushed past them and worked my way to the very edge

of the grave through the crowd of mourners, fearing at one moment that I might actually fall in, and finally managed to take a place next to Ivor Pearson.

He was looking elegant and cool, a slick sheen of damp on his black Aquascutum topcoat. His hair was trim, but fashionably curly under the black homburg.

He put out his hand and I shook it, but as he started to express his sorrow, I started looking around like a socialite on the make at a cocktail party, as if I didn't care about his grief. I realized I was no longer being cautious enough but I had to be sure there were no strangers close by.

I counted heads, checking off familiar faces, nodding to each one as Ivor spoke. I felt suddenly elated. Within twenty yards on every side, I knew everyone; there were no unknown watchers.

Edging closer to Pearson I turned my back on the rest of the crowd. "Look, Ivor," I said. "I'm sorry. I'm a bit overwrought. Please forgive my manners."

He nodded. He wasn't convinced the apology was enough but at least I was making an attempt.

"It's a difficult time, I know," he said. "I'm truly sorry about Julia. She was a wonderful woman."

I saw the coffin appearing in the church door; the music was growing louder.

I said, "Ivor . . . before all this, we hadn't seen you for so long. We were going to have you over for dinner. . . ." I hesitated. "I'd like us to still get together. I'm sure Julia would have wanted it."

He said, nervously, "Yes, of course . . . but you must come to us."

"Soon," I said. "Let's make it very soon."

He looked at me unbelievingly. "Yes, of course, we'd love to. Mary is away. As soon as she gets back, I'll call you."

At that moment, the choir emerged from the church a few steps behind the coffin. I closed my eyes so as not to think of Julia and I started to relax.

I hadn't done much, but I had done something. Wescott would come round. It would take time because of Jane but there would be an approach. And Pearson would invite me and I might be able to invent some reason to convince Peace that I had to go.

The choir began to sing Julia's favorite hymn, then I felt a tug at my elbow and the sacristan handed me a note.

I opened the single folded sheet of paper and read:

"Wait five minutes. Then feign grief and leave. A sanction has already been put into effect against Julia. There is a car outside the gate. Bring this message with you. You have just made some very bad mistakes. . . . Do not make any more."

There was no signature.

CHAPTER 6 "Yer'll find a tape-recorded on't back seat; give me't message you were 'anded." The driver motioned me into a black limousine identical with the one that had been wrecked.

I put the paper through a slot in the partition and picked up the recorder on the back seat; it was a miniature Sony, the smallest executive note-taking model.

I pressed the play switch and settled back into the deep cushioned seat, trying to appear cool again, as we pulled away from the church.

The voice on the tape was Peace's. "The tape on this cassette erases itself as it is played. Listen carefully."

There was a pause then the voice continued in clipped, authoritarian tones.

"The driver is taking you to Greenwich Naval College. I will be waiting for you in your office. Just about now, a needle is being inserted in Julia's arm. It contains a minor tropical virus that will cause her extensive discomfort for four days. She will suffer fever, headaches, sore eyes, considerable loss of sleep and the sensation that her throat is swelling. By the third day, she will be over the worst of it. If she is not, we will intervene with medication.

"Compose yourself. There must be no outbursts or histrionics. This is your last chance to prove that you can adapt to life on our terms."

There was a click, and I knew it was the end of the message, but I let the cassette play on, listening to the faint mechanical hiss, hoping for something more, some explanation.

But there was nothing. The car sped on through lower Greenwich, slowed, and we turned into the grounds of the Greenwich Naval College.

My room was a small one, in the west wing. The navy men called them good-humoredly the "thinkers' cells"; there was a row of them, used by naval librarians and lecturers at the college.

I took out my keys but the door would not open, then I heard a bolt being drawn from inside and Peace opened it, standing back so that I could see into the room.

But for the warning on the tape, I might have cried out, but I just stood, shocked, staring at the scene, as Peace closed the door behind me.

Everything about the room had been transformed. The mountaineering pictures had been taken off the walls and the furniture thrust to the sides of the room, and the whole central portion looked like a miniature control center for a space shot at Cape Canaveral. Two young freak-looking men with long tousled hair, wearing headsets with tiny pin-sized microphones, were sitting at opposite ends of my work table. On the table, in place of the usual clutter of books and papers, there was an electronic unit with a double-faced TV screen. On the screen was a grid, etched out in green, and within each crisscross segment colored dots flitted about.

Without looking at me, Peace said, "Can we have audio please?" One man touched a small switch and immediately the room was filled with the sounds of voices. It was the funeral. I could hear Hedley's voice, intoning the funeral address.

"Track onto quadrant two," Peace said. I could hear him savoring the words.

Another switch was touched and Hedley's voice faded to

a hum. Now the main sound was George Wilket, whispering to his wife Annabelle, who was crying softly. Her grief, horribly amplified, echoed round the walls of the study.

From the table, Peace picked up a small cartridge, barely an inch long, and handed it to me.

"This is your voiceprint," he said curtly. "It is, if you like, the encapsulation of the frequency of your normal speaking tones."

He reached over and fitted the cartridge into a slot at the edge of the electronic unit.

"This device"—he gestured toward the table—"picks up every sound within the loop of the lariat surrounding the cemetery. We are online to a computer which unscrambles the sounds and re-forms them into intelligible speech patterns.

"This"—he pointed to the flickering grid—"sorts out the sounds into those we are interested in and those we are not."

He turned on me with a vicious, angry look.

"What matters right now is that you could have been stupid enough to believe that we would rely on people eavesdropping in the church to make sure you did nothing wrong. It lost you credibility in a way you cannot afford to lose it."

I said desperately, "I've understood. I've got the message now. There's no need to harm Julia."

"The needle has already entered Julia's arm," Peace said. "One of the things it is essential for you to learn is that we *always* do what we say we'll do."

He gestured toward the men at the table. "Okay. Terminate surveillance."

He turned back to me. "There's a second part to the lesson. This time you *will* learn. I told Hairy to make damn sure you do, because if you don't, then you're no use to us. . . . Come with me."

Numbly I followed Peace to the car. He told the driver, "Go to the house."

I remember crossing the Heath, then I realized we were outside my house in Blackheath and I relaxed a little, reassured by the familiar olive-painted facade and the cream garage door. Everything looked just as it had when I left for New York a month before.

Peace watched me looking around, then he said, "Outside, everything is the same. Inside, you'll find some changes. Go in and wait. We'll contact you."

I knew from his tone that this was to be the second part of the lesson.

When the car was out of sight, I took out my key and cautiously opened the front door. Inside the tiny hallway, everything was in place. I started to climb the narrow wooden staircase leading to the first floor living room, and the muffled echo of my tread under the thick stair carpet sounded familiar, reassuring. The living room door was open and the parts of the living room I could see from the top of the staircase all looked untouched, but as I entered, I saw the changes that Hairy—it could only have been Hairy—had made.

In the center of the main room, replacing the modern crystal chandelier, hung a glittering, multifaceted orb. In the corner the black and white television had been replaced by a huge forty-inch color model. It was the biggest I had ever seen outside a television studio.

Beside the set was a gadget I recognized as a video-cassette player, like the one Peace had used in the cabin in Quebec, and in the corners of the room were four new floor speakers, but I couldn't see any tape player to which they were connected.

But the strangest change was in the curtains. The whole of the single window which spanned the width of the room was normally covered with floor-length drapes, which had been hand-sewn by Julia from heavy turquoise cotton. These had been removed and the new drapes stood open, bunched up against the walls. It was their material that was odd. They seemed to be made of tiny glass beads rather than cloth.

I looked around hesitantly. At least the drapes were open. Even the pale daylight was reassuring and all the gadgets looked a little less threatening.

I stepped farther into the room, still unsure what to do. Was I supposed to turn on the television set? I took one more cautious step toward the window and suddenly I had the answer.

I felt something heavy and unusually thick under the carpet, and before I realized it was a foot control, I had stepped on it and the drapes closed with a metallic swish. Instantly the room was totally dark and I knew that the drapes were made of starbeads which sealed out all light, creating absolute, baseline blackness. An instant later, there was a piercing ear-jarring shriek which rose higher and higher in pitch, sending pain searing through my ears. It was so loud I thought I had gone deaf, then it stopped, but as I tried to speak to test my hearing, the noise started again, louder yet, and it became an eerie, unnatural wail.

Then there was silence again and I tried to move toward the window to open the curtains, but I found I had lost my sense of direction and I could no longer even guess which way I was facing.

In the silence, I stood, waiting, trying to orient myself; then I heard a loud whisper that seemed to be coming from all corners of the room at once.

"Darling, Philip . . . I love you, darling, Philip." It was Julia's voice, magnified grotesquely, and as one phrase died away, another began. "Darling, I love you. I've missed you so. . . . Philip, I love you. . . . I wish we could go on like this forever."

Without warning, Julia's face appeared in the center of the screen, emerging from a white halo of light.

I felt my fear rising again. I looked at the halo of light for reassurance. Julia was there, walking happily across a field. I recognized the white dress. I remembered how much she liked it.

I stared at the ball of light, willing the picture to fade, but when it did, it was replaced by a series of jerky flashes, like a speeded-up old movie. The images kept flickering and I looked in horror at what was coming, superimposed over the white dress.

I could make out a hospital bed. Julia was lying in it. Then the underimage of the white dress faded and the flickering stopped and the new images started coming onto the screen clearly, in quick succession. The hospital bed, a saline drip, flowers on a table, the bed again, an operating table, Julia, the hospital ward again. Julia bandaged across the chest.

Then the sequence started over again, the ward, the bed, the saline drip, the flowers, only this time Julia was screaming and I could hear nothing but her pain, her sobs, her cries. I wanted to cry out, to leap toward her to comfort her. I knew what was happening. This was the operation she feared; the removal of a breast. I could feel her sobbing, her tears. . . .

The image faded and the white circle was filled with blue sky. A bird flew across it. A small bird. No, it looked small but it was large. It was, suddenly, a huge bird, an eagle with fully spread wings, then a moment later the circle of light contained nothing but its claws.

The claws faded, and in their place came a single image: a soldering iron, a thick lump of metal, bulbous-tipped and ugly; then the eagle's claws reappeared and I knew what the message was.

I couldn't form the thought coherently but I knew what I was looking at: the eagle's claw, the most feared instrument of torture in South America . . . the soldering iron which was plunged into the orifices of the body and slowly heated to produce a burning cancer, relentlessly destroying the internal organs with unbearable pain.

I stared at the claws and started to shout, screaming at the image to go away. Then, in an instant, it was over and I was back in the living room again.

The white light was gone, the curtains were open and I was staring at a blank television screen.

The screen lit up and a voice said, "That was a nasty nightmare wasn't it . . . but we'll show you how to avoid nasty nightmares." The voice was in a singsong style of the kindergarten cartoons used to teach road safety. "Now," said the singsong voice, "to avoid nasty nightmares, stay away from mailboxes."

A mailbox appeared on the screen with a red cross superimposed on it.

"Stay away from telephones . . ." The images went on. ". . . and stay away from people."

The screen went blank. I pulled myself into a kneeling position and I realized that I was in shock. My limbs wouldn't respond properly. There were dancing lights at the back of my eyes and I was trembling uncontrollably.

Faintly, in the distance, I heard a voice and I realized it was coming from below, from the front door of the house.

"Hello, is anybody there?"

The words might have been Julia's, but the voice was Michelle's. I heard her coming up the stairs; then she knelt beside me and said quietly, "From now on, think of yourself as one of those desk ornaments, an object frozen in an acrylic cube. Whenever you try to reach out, you'll be blocked by an invisible shell."

She looked at me with a hard, staring intensity. "You'll be at the institute for two weeks and you mustn't make a move. Not one. Do you understand?"

I nodded and her voice softened suddenly.

"After that you'll meet the Vikings but you won't be alone

in the cube anymore. You're going to have a partner. Someone you like. We're bringing you one of your oldest friends."

From that point on, my life became a bizarre parody of the life I had lived at the Defence Institute. Instead of Julia, I had Michelle. Each morning I breakfasted but instead of going down to get my Mini-Cooper out of the little garage, I waited for a glossy, black Rover 3500 to pick me up at the door.

Instead of turning left, down the hill toward the Naval College, we turned right and drove to Chislehurst and through the gates of the Institute for Social Change, to a faint salute from the rent-a-cop on the gate.

My neighbors watched the transformation and I could imagine their comments but no one spoke to me. At about the time when the first neighbor might have come to the house to express grief and condolence, Michelle stripped off her dress and unpinned her hair, letting it fall to her waist. Wearing only black bikini underpants, she started to dust the main living room with the curtains drawn far back.

"Do you think your street is ready for a topless housewife?" she laughed. "Do you think they'll accept these black things as my concession to mourning?"

I watched helplessly as, one by one, the neighbors noticed: a child called her mother; a mother called another mother; Sedbon, two doors down, who worked on the BBC nightshift, woke up and brought his binoculars.

In less than twenty minutes, she transformed our supercool, arty, liberal neighborhood into an old-fashioned, gossip-over-the-wall street. Then, when she judged her audience attentive enough, she called me over and exploded in laughter, throwing her arms gaily around me and lifting her feet off the ground in a joyous embrace.

There were no calls of condolence.

At the institute, most of my work seemed to consist of devising computer simulation games to assess the impact of various types of terrorist tactics. They learned very quickly and at night I began to have dark dreams about how much I was teaching them. I was beginning to accept my helplessness.

But as the computer games went on, I became more and more curious about why they had created the institute at all. There were two IBM computers on the ground floor but they could have been placed anywhere in London—or in New York for that matter. All that was needed for our purposes was a small room and a computer terminal.

In nearly a month, I saw barely twenty people. They were all under twenty-five, male and female, and all of them too sedentery to be any use as urban guerrillas.

I came to think of the institute as pure theater, a huge hollow shell containing nothing of substance, a stage set; but for the benefit of whom? That I couldn't decide.

Nor could I understand the way they kept me in touch with Julia.

It began right after the funeral with a telephone call. We were not allowed to say much and the words came to both of us in an awkward, stilted way, but Julia's voice sounded very real, for all that, and I felt her presence very strongly.

The same night, she had come even closer, in a video tape she had been allowed to make, in which she laughed about the telephone conversation, making fun of our awkwardness and the way we had both failed to act our parts properly, even though we had seen people in similar uncomfortable situations a hundred times on television.

The video clips continued to come, usually at three-day intervals, and I waited for them as expectantly as I had for my first teenage love letters. At first they were similar to the first clip, and though I was allowed to send no message in return, I felt we were in touch because the lifelike images conjured her up so vividly. I had never seen her on film or video tape before, and I realized she had a strong electronic charisma of the kind politicians dream of possessing; she seemed to jump out of the screen and I felt her alive and warm.

Then the video clips started changing in character and each one began to come in two parts.

First there was a very workaday clip, in which Julia read aloud to the camera, headlines and random excerpts from the day's paper. In the first one, she made little jokes about the corniness of it; then she stopped that and just read, at each sequence, enough to convince me she was alive on the day the clip was prepared.

The second part could not have been more different. The video tape was silent, or rather, there was no voice; only images of her performing some action with appropriate background sounds.

She seemed to be in England, in a cottage somewhere in the country. Gradually, the images took on a more and more dreamlike air. In the early ones, the camera moved in close, once as she planted some flowers in a rock garden, once as she walked down a country lane.

Then, over the days, the camera work became less and less realistic. Twice they showed Julia horseback riding and I was glad they were letting her do something she loved, but the images were tantalizingly vague. I knew it was her— there was no doubt about that—but the camera never stayed close enough for me to look at her properly; she just seemed to drift across my consciousness.

Sometimes—and they were the worst—they showed Julia undressing, preparing for bed, and again the clips were full of ephemereal images that tantalized and aroused me.

Eventually the video clips all became unambiguously dreamlike, and my work at the institute started to seem totally surreal. And on top of it all, I was feeling restless and irritable from lack of physical exercise.

Then, one night about four weeks after the funeral, I came home from the institute and I found Michelle in the bedroom and my bags packed and laid out, open, ready for a final check before locking.

As I looked at the bags, I could feel her reading my reactions, then she laughed.

"I think I won," she said. "I really think I won."

"What do you mean?"

"There was no need for Hairy's dials to tell what you were feeling. You were relieved, then excited. You're ready to go. You don't care what the packed bags mean; you're ready whatever it is."

I nodded, and she said, "Then I did win." She smiled. "I've been playing games with your head for the past month."

Her tone shook me. I suppose it was partly the easy way she said, "*I've* been playing games with your head." I knew I was being manipulated, but I had assumed it was Peace or Hairy or some shadowy figure I hadn't met. I had been thinking of Michelle as a minor character in the scenario.

Michelle saw my look and read it correctly.

"No," she said, "I'm not some kind of sophisticated whore and I'm not the Pasionaria of the urban guerrilla world. I'm a sexual psychologist. I was hired to entrap you and devise the flexible sanctions. And I'm also supposed to prepare you for action as commander of the Vikings. That's what I've been doing for the past four weeks."

She laughed again. "I've been bringing your nasty edge a bit closer to the surface."

"What the hell do you mean?" I said.

"I've been putting you through something similar to the process the army uses, partly consciously, partly by an unconscious tradition that's been growing up for centuries. You could call it 'clearing the decks,' preparing you to leave civilian life behind."

She made a throwaway gesture with her hands. "You can see the elements yourself, if you think about it. You've been killing time at the institute. Killing it usefully as it happens, but we still had to prolong the computer games two weeks longer than was necessary. Not a bad simulation of depot life, in fact.

"You know as well as I do that after a year in depot, a soldier can be persuaded to fight his own grandmother, and I've been helping by upping your physical frustration. You're used to enormous amounts of physical activity. I've turned you into a house pekingese."

"And Julia?" I said. "What the hell have you been doing with all those changes in the video clips?"

"Oversimplifying, I've turned Julia into a pin-up," Michelle said matter-of-factly. "She's much less real to you than she was a month ago. When you feel close to her, you feel too tender, too gentle. But you do have a very violent side to your nature.

"I need a tradeoff. I need you to be conscious enough of Julia that you won't forget the sanctions, but I want her to be less real to you, so she won't inhibit you too much."

"And now you're satisfied," I said bitterly.

"More or less."

She folded the lid over one of the suitcases. "Tonight is the night your frustrations end, and I've got a really nice surprise for you for a change."

"What?" I said. "Another new toy? A new status symbol to add to my director's image?"

Michelle smiled. "No, much better than that. We're taking a plane ride in a small charter plane, which I know you like. You'll be able to rock climb, and better yet, you're going to meet an old friend, a really good friend."

"For God's sake who?" I said. "Not Wescott?"

"No."

"Then who?"

She smiled more broadly. "Who is the person you've become most friendly with in your adult life, leaving aside friends from university days like Wescott?"

I thought for a moment then I said, "Not Alan? Not Alan Gellman?"

"On the nose," she said. "Alan Gellman, the great Harvard economist and sandwich-eater himself."

I hesitated. "If you know about the sandwiches, that means you've studied him," I said. "Does that mean . . . ?"

"Yes," Michelle said. "It does. Alan Gellman is to be your partner and technical adviser. You'll be with him in less than an hour. We're flying together tonight."

She closed the other suitcase.

"Finally, you're going to meet the Vikings."

CHAPTER 7   "Does it remind you of Biafra?"

Alan Gellman looked down through the tiny rectangular window at the cluster of lights in the dark hollow between the mountains and grinned.

"Sure," he said. "Apart from the fact that it's too hilly, has no palm trees, there's no gunfire and the weather's too cold, it's just like Biafra."

The soft Texas accent was like a cat's purr, identifiable even with the noise of the engines. "The accent Harvard loves to hate" one writer had called it in a *New York Times Magazine* article titled "Alan Gellman, Why Aren't You One of Us?" which described beautifully how the eastern academic establishment had never forgiven their most brilliant economist for being a Texan.

Just hearing the voice again eased so much of the tension of the past weeks. As we had shaken hands at the little airport outside London, I had seen the unfamiliar stress lines around his eyes; then he had smiled and I knew that he wanted to stick with the motto he had lived by through all the ten years I had known him: "If you can't smile, then you aren't just close to death, you're dead already."

During the three-hour flight, there had been only one moment of real strain. Gellman's wife, Esther, had been killed in a boating accident and his two sons were at boarding school in New England.

When I asked how they were he had said, tensely, "Fine . . . for the moment," and I did not need to ask how the Vikings had snared him. Nor did I need to ask why. Gellman was one of the world's leading experts on multinational corporations.

I looked at my watch and saw that it was half-past eleven. The plane was losing height, following the track of a narrow valley between the rocky hills that stood out milkily in the moonlight.

We were in the Peak District of Derbyshire in the north of England, and this was for me another, much older nostalgia trip, to the hills where I had first learned to climb as a boy. As the plane dipped lower, I could see the outline of a circle of plain wooden huts of the kind I had slept in on so many weekends with my first climbing club.

"Time for a last sandwich," Gellman said. "Do you want one?"

I grinned. "No thanks. I'm trying to keep to a pack a day."

Since London he had eaten twelve sandwiches, the only food I had ever seen him take a serious interest in. He was a short man with a jowled face and spreading waistline, and it was only by some metabolic accident that he had reached the age of forty without going far over his 230 pounds; his private passion was doughy food and his biggest hatred was physical exercise.

He had said often that if a dish was worth eating, it was worth making into a sandwich, and on many joyous occasions I had seen him stun a headwaiter by taking a carefully arranged salad or fish delicacy and piling it between thick slices of bread.

But after the initial shock, none of them ever took offense. There was something about Gellman that defied you to get angry with him. Writers profiling him had tried time and again to find ways to describe the quality. They had tried phrases like "genuinely nice guy" and pompous lines like "a man who carried with him a special aura of humanity," but the one who had come closest had called him "one of those rare truly human human-beings."

Just being around him made me feel comfortable again.

"You're still dressed for Harvard," I said, pointing to his dark blue blazer and slacks. "Didn't you have time to change?"

He grinned. "This is one bus I didn't ask to get on," he said. It was an old joke. When he had first come to Harvard with his Texas accent and easy manners, he had bought the right kind of suits and blazers and faculty colleagues had styled him, with a delicate edge of contempt, as a farm boy with pretensions to eastern gentility.

By the time he was famous, they had discovered something else about him: that he simply didn't give a damn.

The New York Times man had understood it and written, "When Gellman arrives somewhere, he buys a couple of things that he feels appropriate, like a tourist getting off a Greyhound bus. When the bus stopped at Harvard, he bought a blazer and a crested beer mug."

During the flight, we had talked very little. I wanted to ask him a hundred questions about how they had taken him and what he had learned about the Vikings, but I could see that Michelle's presence beside the pilot was making him cautious.

He had said only that this was his second visit to the camp, as Peace had summoned him there for a briefing. I gathered that he had seen very little, but had acquired a strong distaste for the Vikings.

The small aircraft was beginning its descent now and I said quietly, "Am I not going to see the flask?"

He nodded and pulled out his familiar silver hip flask. "Does that make you feel better?" he said, putting it to his lips.

The flask was our talisman, a reminder of the times we had flown into—and then out of again—so many dangerous situations in Africa, South America and the Middle East, as he had documented the maneuverings of multinational corporations around the world.

As the plane's wheels touched the grass, Michelle pointed through the window and I saw Peace standing at the side of the landing strip. He was talking to a tall, raw-boned youth in climbing breeches and a black sweater. Peace himself looked too stylish for the setting, in a dark brown safari jacket and slim corduroy pants that showed their elegant cut even in the landing lights of the aircraft.

We climbed out and Peace greeted us with warm handshakes and introduced us to the young man with a slight flourish, setting us up as senior and important arrivals. To me he added, "This is Rory, one of our best climbers. You'll find you have a lot in common."

I shook his hand and felt his powerful, muscular grip. He was a little over six feet, slim but with powerful shoulders and a well-defined waist. The only incongruous touch was his bright red hair which fell nearly to his shoulders, limply, without curls or shape. Hippie hair on a marine body, I thought, and wondered, hearing his Irish accent, whether the hair was the symbol of his graduation to techno-guerrilla status from street-fighting in the slums of Londonderry.

Peace gestured to a small English Ford car parked on the road beside the field, on the other side of a low stone wall.

"It's only a few minutes to the camp," he said. "I'll drive you down."

"I'd rather walk," I said.

"As you wish." Peace smiled. "There'll be surveillance of course. Not total. Just random checks." He said it with an expansive gesture, as though that constituted the technological equivalent of fresh air.

"You don't have to keep saying nice things about us," he added. "You're here to work for us, not to join us."

"In that case I'll walk too," Gellman said.

Peace turned back to me. "Michelle says she promised you some climbing to get Blackheath out of your system. We won't be starting work until late tomorrow morning, so why don't you go out early and get rid of your restlessness. I'm afraid you'll have to go out alone, but some of the Vikings may join you later."

He said it casually but there was a slight undertone in his voice and I felt a crawling sensation in the neck.

Was it another scenario? If it was, at least I would be on the rocks where I felt at home. I looked across at Rory, measuring him suddenly as an adversary, rather than as another man on a rope, but he turned away and walked toward the car, carrying the bags the pilot had unloaded from the plane.

Peace walked after him and Michelle followed. Gellman and I were left alone in the center of the grass.

Gellman grinned at me. "You realize, I trust, what a compliment I'm paying your company."

"I won't tell Peace," I said. "If he knew what it takes to make you choose a walk over a car ride, he'd start believing he was the ultimate incarnation of evil, and a man should have room to grow."

We walked in silence for a while and I shortened my pace to allow Gellman to keep up without difficulty. We strolled through a gap in the stone wall and set out across a second rough meadow, picking our way carefully to avoid rabbit holes and twisted tufts of the wiry grass which covered the poor upland soil.

Gellman trudged as if he were on wet sand, plunging one foot in front of the other with no sense of the right balance for his weight on the sole of the foot. A mile of it and he would jar his knees enough to feel as tired as after a full day's exercise.

Only his friends realized that while he wasn't an eastern gentleman-scholar, he wasn't really a farm boy either. He disliked the outdoors, couldn't ride a horse and enjoyed watching cowboys only in the movies.

Asked once whether he missed ranch life, he had replied, "Not really. If I hadn't been lucky enough to be born with a few brains, I'd have been one of those dumb fat kids who hang around the general store and shout after passing cars."

When we were well away from the airstrip, I said cautiously, "This is quite a place to plot the destruction of corporate power, isn't it?"

"You know about that, do you?"

"Yes," I said, "but not so damn much more. What about you?"

"Nothing that will help." He looked thoughtful and I could see he was wondering whether he dare drop any hints despite the surveillance.

I decided to try a little gentle prompting, to see if he had any idea of who we were supposed to be working for.

"If we do smash corporate power," I said, grinning, "I wonder what kind of new order Peace will put in its place."

Gellman smiled. "That's a *good* question." He intentionally let the drawl come through clearly. "If it's to be some kind of socialism, I would say it would not have to be too heavy on austerity and self-sacrifice."

"Maybe Peace believes that line about how there's no point in being a unilateral socialist," I said. "Maybe when the new order comes, he'll give up the one-in-every-color safari jackets."

"Maybe," Gellman said, letting the drawl come back again. "Wondrous things may happen, come the revolution."

I wanted to say more but we were both uneasy and I couldn't think of any subtle way of hinting at my doubts about the institute and about Peace.

By the end of the four weeks I had felt as though I was drowning in radical rhetoric, but there were times when Peace seemed to talk like a corporate executive, rather than a radical leader. When I had commented on it once he had replied offhandedly, "You have to learn to think like the enemy; the quickest way is to be a bit like them." I wondered if Alan had sensed the same thing but he obviously felt it was too early for serious guessing so I said lightly, "Well at least there's nothing wrong in believing that multinational corporations are too powerful. Some of our best economists believe that."

"*This* one made his reputation saying so," Gellman remarked.

I nodded, "Alan, you've seen the Vikings and I haven't. What makes them so frightening?"

"They scare me because they're so spiritually empty. You always have the feeling that they lack any interior life. I can imagine them capable of completely mindless viciousness because they haven't any values, however old-fashioned, to hold them back."

He stopped suddenly. "I don't even want to think about them until tomorrow," he said. "Tell me instead what the difference is between a black and white scenario. Peace told me to ask you."

"He's been ripping off my book again and adding his own jargon. I called it white and black terrorism."

"Meaning?"

"Well in Peace's terminology, a black scenario is vicious, total violence. Throwing nailbombs into shopping centers, kidnapping people and torturing them to death, firing randomly into crowds to create panic. All the stuff you do when you want to spread fear and loathing."

"And white scenarios are presumably the opposite?"

"Yes," I said. "White scenarios are the Robin Hood stuff. You use them when you want to create sympathy for the guerrilla movement. In the white scenario you use finesse, often humor. When you kidnap someone, you don't beat them to death, you try them in a people's court and sentence them to hand out food or pay raises for the workers."

Gellman sat down on a rock and pulled out his hip flask. "That sounds more like the house style we should be aiming at," he said. "Let's drink to that."

He handed me the flask, and we each took a quick pull at it.

But the difference between black and white was to be rather finer than I had thought.

CHAPTER 8 The next morning, I was on the rockface behind the camp before it was fully daylight and I climbed myself into a state of oblivion.

I broke all the rules; I just didn't care. I climbed alone and I climbed too fast. I did a traverse free where I should never have gone unbelayed. At one point, I went needlessly into a sticky gulley, just for the hell of it, when a moment's study would have shown easier holds on the face beside it.

I did a "very difficult" to shake the bed out of my bones, then I abseiled down like a crazed commando and went up a "very severe" as if I were playing monkey-up-the-stick.

This was the rock I had learned on and the surfaces felt like an old friend. The Peak District is climber's climbing; the climbs are all too short for it ever to become a big-time mountain resort, but there are pitches as difficult as anything in Europe.

The rocks just soar up out of the grass for reasons only a geologist would know. It is fun climbing and for an hour Peace didn't exist. It was, simply, a happy return to my youth.

I wasn't as fit as when I had first come here but now, as the prostitutes say, I knew tricks to help me along. I climbed until I didn't care about shotgun microphones or random surveillance. I knew it was all programmed but I didn't mind; the right-sized boots had been waiting in the cubicle I shared with Michelle, with the kind of Vibram soles I like best for dry rock, breeches and sweater that fitted perfectly and some heavy old-style rope that I feel most at ease with.

It was a scenario, just like everything else, but it was one I wanted, and it didn't matter whether Michelle would be watching, recording my frustration levels on her private chart.

I climbed until I got them all out of my system, then I went up one last time, taking the kind of route we had called as kids a "very bloody impossible," and then I sat, high on the clifftop, finally at ease, and smoked a cigarette.

Below, the camp was just waking up. From up there, it had nothing to do with Vikings or urban guerrilla warfare; they were just huts with smoke starting to rise from the metal chimneys and people coming out into the morning air, to stretch their legs and start thinking about breakfast.

Then Rory appeared. He was a dot at first outside one of the huts, but he started to stride toward the rockface below me, and I could see the hair and I knew for sure who it was.

He had a girl with him and another man, both in climbing gear, and they seemed to have too much rope and little boxes in their hands, like workmen's lunch buckets. As they came into clearer view, I saw that Rory had around his shoulder what I thought at first was a bandolier of bullets, but I could see no weapons and it took a moment for me to make the connection between the bullets and the metal boxes. I realized with a horror worse than if it had been a weapon that the rockface and my aerie were going to be invaded techno-style.

I knew about electropiton hammers, but in the way that yachtsmen know that motorized houseboats exist but try not to think about them. Wescott had found the perfect name for them: electric drills with a Black and Decker mountaineering attachment on the end.

The climber drills into the rock with his power tool, driving in the small metal pitons, creating holds where none existed and turning every pitch into a crawl up a scrambling net made of thin, plasticized rope passed through the eyes in the end of the pitons and woven into an obscene cat's cradle of steps and loops to hang by.

I watched the three climbers, three hundred feet below, and saw in fascination that they were preparing for the ascent like steeplejacks about to haul themselves up the face of a skyscraper in a window-cleaning cradle.

I watched Rory closely and I could see he was going to lead, but he wasn't looking for a route, searching out choices of holds and crevices; he was working out how many nails he needed.

When they started up the face, I knew roughly what to expect, but the speed was a surprise. From the preparations, I had expected a very mechanical performance: straight up the middle, hand over hand, one piton after the next, but Rory was an artist with his power tool. Even though I hated that style of climbing I had to admire his technique. He came up the rock like a mechanized beetle, drilling holes with short quick bursts of the piton-hammer and sliding the metal pins out of his bandolier and into the cracks in a single smooth movement.

He didn't stop, in fact he barely even paused at the end of each burst, and by the time he had done the first hundred feet I knew that for all his gadgetry and plasticized knitting wool, he was a fine climber.

You can always tell a good rockman, especially when you're watching from above; you can see how quickly he surveys the options, how long he hesitates before he decides to push himself into the hold that is just a little bit too far away for comfort, the one you have to lean away from the rock for. Rory could have climbed impressively without the scrambling net he was shaping around him, not by the direct route he was taking perhaps, but by one close enough to it to make little difference.

He used his toys as extensions of himself to ease his way

through the impossible bits of the climb and then he went a little beyond, with a style that told me he was in real control of himself on the rock.

The other kids were competent too in a more mundane way; they came up behind, going through the boring process of raveling the strands and threads of the rope ladder up behind them. By the time they were near the top, I was almost ready to suppress my contempt for their godawful techniques.

When Rory reached the last pitch from the top, he shouted up at me. "We're going over to the goiter. Why don't you come? It's easy, even for old-fashioned climbers."

I guessed that the goiter was the horizontal swelling of rock on the eastern edge of the face. It was smooth and tricky but there were easy routes all around it and I decided to go down and watch.

I climbed down onto the face again, slotting myself into an easy chimney which took me to below where the three climbers were traversing toward the goiter.

Rory went straight across, drilling and threading rope. Then when he was right out onto the most treacherous part of the overhang, he turned and motioned me casually to go along under him.

He did it with an airy wave but I looked at his eyes, peering out from under the little round helmet, and I saw just a hint of a challenge.

I looked again at my section of the rock and saw there were two difficult holds that would take me almost to the center of the underside of the massive overhang; beyond that, I couldn't see anything because of the curve in the rock.

I hesitated, then decided I would go that far but not beyond. If the holds still looked sticky, then challenge or no challenge, I would simply come back down and leave it at that.

I inched my way out, flattening myself against the swollen surface and found the first toehold, then the little crevice for the right hand, then a toehold again and I was there.

I slowly turned my neck so that I could look out along the bulge to the right and I saw that it was completely smooth; there was nowhere even for a hawk to hang its claws.

I looked up and saw Rory grinning; it was a friendly grin and for the first time since he had come up on to the peak, he looked like just any other climber you might meet in the Peaks on a weekend.

He was about twenty feet above me and as I turned to edge back, he motioned me to wait. I heard the buzz of the piton-hammer and in what seemed like seconds, he had drilled three holes in the face, in a straight, horizontal line, and threaded the rope through. Then, after putting a swift loop belay round his own shoulder he hooked himself onto the third piton and let the rope fall slack between the first and the second, so that a giant loop was lowered down to me. The loop made the move to the right, around the smooth part of the overhang, as easy as swinging on an overhead beam in a gymnasium. I reached up and tested it, and felt the security created by the counterweight of Rory's body. I grasped hold of the rope and swung out, as I had watched the other two kids do, until I felt my foot catch in the narrow little ledge right on the point of the bulge. I settled my toe into it and found a crack above and to the left, just wide enough to jam in three fingers. I let go of the rope and worked my way into balance, waiting for Rory to move farther to the right and make the next loop for me to grab.

Just for a second, he looked down at me and smiled, a funny cracked little smile, then he started to move.

With the same driving rhythm I had seen on their first ascent he unthreaded the rope, pulled it out of the three pitons, wrapped it up and started to climb upward, drilling in pitons as he went. Far to my left, the other two climbers watched also; then they too started upward and before I even had time to grasp what was happening I was completely alone on the cliff face. And I was stuck.

Without the loop that had swung me into position, I was a fly, spreadeagled on the worst convex segment of the bulge without a hold within reach in any direction. I had let them coax me into one of the nearly impossible positions in climbing; it has various technical names but what it comes down to is simply that if you make the slightest false move in any direction, you come off.

From that angle of overhang, I was going to fall outward, pitching down two hundred feet to the base of the cliff. There was nowhere to slither to, no way of sacrificing the skin on my arms and legs to reach some surface where there was something to grab at. Very carefully, I turned my head to the left to survey the rockface, looking again for any chink in the rock that might serve as a hold.

This time, my standards had changed. I wasn't looking for holds, I was looking for fingertip-size crannies, anything that would carry me back to the stance I had held before grabbing Rory's loop.

Eventually, I found one just barely within reach but it was so small that it was useless to me unless there was somewhere I could rest my left foot. I reached out with my leg, feeling the rockface, willing some little irregularity to catch the sole and tell me that I might have grip. At first there was nothing and I started to sweat and I felt despair and fury again at Rory and at my stupidity. Then, I felt something, a protrusion so small that it would barely support two toes. It wasn't enough by itself but if I could jam my fingers into the handhold and swing out far enough to put my weight on the lower hold, there might just be enough there to support the other toes as well.

It was what Jack Wescott called a "has to be" hold. Hanging there, flattened against the bulge, I could hear his laugh again, the first time I had asked him what a "has to be" was. "A 'has to be,' Philip, my son, is a hold that has to be there because if it isn't you'll fall off the mountain."

I thought about it for a second then I made my move and swung out into the new position. The "has to be" was. Just. It was probably the most tenuous grip I've ever had on a rockface, but it held long enough for me to bring my other hand across to grip the hold I had left to take Rory's rope.

I was safe and the rest of the way back was a slide on the catwalk, as easy as edging along guide rails. In less than five minutes, I was back to the clifftop where I had started from. Twenty minutes later I was down at the base again, by the easiest descent I could see.

CHAPTER 9 At the bottom of the cliff, I didn't stop to look back up, or rest, or get my breath. I started off immediately in search of Rory. I found him, still with Robin and June, talking to Peace outside one of the huts. Gellman and Michelle were there also, standing back, smoking, as if waiting for Peace to finish his conversation so they could move off.

I hit him from behind, at a run, with all my weight hunched behind my shoulder in a charge that would have had me banished from a football field for a lifetime. I hit him in the center of the back, above the kidneys and he went down with a throaty cry of pain. The blow took his breath and he couldn't gather himself immediately and I stood over him, hesitating, not sure whether to kick him or go down on top of him.

Then I heard Peace say, very calmly, "Nothing crude, Philip, please. I'll take care of it."

I started to say something but in my anger the words came out in a rush and Peace interrupted, still calm, almost casual.

"I know what Rory did. It was an experiment to test you, but if there's to be revenge, at least let there be some point to it."

He looked down at Rory.

"You'll take Kildare's place in the interrogation scenario." Rory didn't argue. He got up off the ground without looking at me, limping and rubbing his back.

"I thought discipline wasn't a characteristic of the younger generation," I said.

"It isn't." Peace formed his wispy, fragile-faced smile. "But as you know, we have scenarios to deal with people who refuse to take part in scenarios."

Then I heard Michelle say to Gellman, "You'd better watch this too," and she led us off in the opposite direction to the one Rory had taken, into the hut where I knew Peace slept.

I was becoming so conditioned that I was not even surprised to find that one of the cubicles was full of electronic equipment, with a large television screen as the centerpiece.

"Our observation room," Peace said. "For the Vikings, not for you."

He smiled at Michelle. "With Michelle you are allowed to have privacy. I hope you make good use of it."

She poured drinks from a bottle on the wooden table in the corner of the room and answered inconsequently, "He doesn't yet, but I'm working on it." She flashed me a quick smile, "If you ever feel like a blow-job just give a yell."

"Sex has certainly come a long way, hasn't it?" I said.

"Indeed it has," Peace said, "as you are about to see," and he turned on the screen.

The surprising thing was that it didn't seem at all eerie to be on the other end of the surveillance. On the screen were a group of people acting a scene in a room furnished like the one I had slept in, only slightly larger, with four beds instead of two. Peace said, "I'm keeping the sound off. I want you to guess what is happening."

I looked in silence at the figures and then I said, "I would guess they were about to begin an orgy."

Rory was the only figure I recognized but there were five other people in the room: three women, all in their early twenties or younger, and two men. They were all wearing jeans and shirts.

Rory was dressed the same way, lying back, crossways on

the bed, and one of the girls was sitting astride him, caressing his chest under the T-shirt and kissing his neck. Another girl, a heavy-bodied, vacant-looking teenager who seemed to be the youngest of them all, was caressing his thighs through the jeans, running her hands softly up and down over the faded blue cloth.

The two other men, who looked like shorter-haired versions of Rory himself, were sitting on the bed, one on either side of his head, looking down at the byplay and grinning. I thought at first they were just watching, then I saw that each was sitting on one of Rory's arms, and I realized that they were holding him in position with reverse finger holds.

Gellman was watching too, standing behind my chair, and he said quietly, "It looks to me more like he's about to be raped."

"Not raped," Peace replied casually. "He's being interrogated."

I saw that the girl on top of Rory had taken off his shirt and was no longer astride him, but kneeling beside him. His arms were no longer being held and he was half sitting up, laughing at the fair-haired girl who was kneeling on the floor between his legs, taking off his jeans.

She slid them down slowly, fingering his legs still, laughing and teasing, leaving him naked except for a pair of white underpants.

Rory seemed to be relaxed and enjoying the relief of not being pinned down, then suddenly the two men grabbed him from behind again and the fair-haired girl slipped the jeans over his head and twisted the flapping legs into a knot behind his head.

"Jeans make the perfect hood," Peace said. "Now the interrogation will begin."

"You mean you've given Rory some information that he has to try to withhold and they have to try and force out of him?" Gellman said. His voice very flat, his distaste showing in every word.

"No. This is a new technique. We call it," Peace hovered over the word, "random interrogation.

"When urban guerrillas kidnap someone . . . a company executive, security officer, a diplomat or whatever, they usually don't know what he knows that they want, so we teach techniques of random inquiry. Just like the confrontation therapy for alcoholics. The alcoholic drinks because he refuses to face reality. If he can be made to face reality, he won't need to drink. So you throw him in a group therapy session and everyone probes and prods and pushes until they find out what it is he doesn't want to face and make him bring it out in the open."

Peace gestured at the screen. "They're talking to Rory about his father. That's easy at first. Everyone can think of something nice to say about their father. Then they go on down the road probing into all the things about the father that the guerrillas really want to know and he really doesn't think he should tell them."

"And what the hell's that?" Gellman said, pointing at a small cylindrical object one of the men was holding, about the size of a collapsible umbrella.

"Watch."

The kid shook the tube and it came apart into six metal laths and each one extended into three segments. He deftly assembled them to make a pyramid, nearly eight feet to the pinnacle, he fiddled with it, and adjusted it, testing that the base was secure on the ground. The others were still clustered over Rory but his hands were free and they were holding him by crowding around him in an intimate huddle, cramping his limbs rather than pinning him down.

"That," Peace said, "is a portable interrogation frame—a whipping post if you like."

Gellman said very quietly, "Christ, these kids can't even improvise their own instruments of torture; they buy even them at a store."

I think he meant to lighten the horror of what we were seeing, but in some way that I didn't understand, the remark went under Peace's skin and he almost lost control.

He whirled on Gellman and the professional lecturing voice was gone.

"What you're watching is skill," he yelled. "These are not some dumb kids from an Argentine slum who take a Coca-Cola executive into the cellar and don't know what to do with him, so they kick him in the balls as a blow against world capitalism. These kids really know what it's about because we taught them. Look at that kid, there, the little one, Susan. Watch her."

They had Rory strapped onto the frame now, secured by little plastic loops, twisted around his knees and elbows, wrists and ankles. Behind him the girl Susan was carefully taking three objects out of a drawer and laying them carefully on the bed: a short length of chain, a piece of rubber tube and a narrow, plaited leather whip.

When she was ready, she moved behind Rory and started to draw each one round his body just above the waistband of his underpants, letting them slide across the skin.

I could only guess what Rory was feeling under the hood as the metal and rubber and leather touched his body, first on his back, then on his tightly muscled stomach.

"She's telling him who it is," Peace said. "She's saying, 'It's Susan and I know what I'm doing with these so you're damn right to be scared.'

"He knows who it is because he's seen her learn. When she first became a Viking she didn't know the first thing about pain. We told her to interrogate someone, a girl her own age, and she crippled her, not because she was vicious but because she was ignorant."

Michelle looked at me steadily as Peace spoke, then she said quietly in counterpoint to his fury, "You know yourself, Philip, how easy it is to get carried away."

"Susan was twenty," Peace said. "She'd never been hurt in her whole life; it was all new to her. So we set up a pain clinic and we taught her how to measure pain." He emphasized the words, underlining the obscene distortion of the hospital term.

"Now she knows." He turned back to the screen. "Rory is scared shitless now because he hasn't been told whether it's a white scenario or a black one. Well, let's tell them."

He picked up the tiny phone receiver beside the screen, still flaring with anger, and we watched on the screen as one of the girls broke away from the bed and picked up the telephone.

"Russell is still mad with Rory," Peace said. "You can make it a black scenario. Fifteen minutes."

I wanted to protest but Peace had turned to the screen again and his anger was beyond reach; the television show got sicker and sicker but we watched because there was no way we could turn it off.

The dark-haired girl pushed Susan aside and stood behind Rory, running her palms caressingly up his back, then she started to roll down his underpants, stopping when they were curled around his thighs.

"That's Maria," Peace said. "She's the artist. She didn't need to be taught. Watch how she caresses him as she talks. You don't know what she's saying but I'll tell you. She's saying in her gentle love-voice that she's put his underpants there to catch the blood.

"She doesn't waste anything. She can turn every gesture, every phrase into terror. She's the ultimate therapist."

"And I suppose this is to teach Rory how to withstand pain," I said. "This is the other side of the pain clinic."

"Don't be so goddam silly," Michelle said angrily. "You don't seriously believe that these kids can withstand pain, do you? The next fifteen minutes are going to be the worst Rory's ever had, but they're nothing. You've been around.

Look at any page in the files of *Amnesty*. Read Solzhenitsyn. You don't really believe we can teach kids like this to survive a Brazilian police cell? We teach them to use pain, to inflict it, to know how to measure it. If they ever become the ones under that kind of stress, we make goddam sure we have ways of disposing of them."

She was furious too now. I, like Gellman, had once again not understood the techniques and the skills. I had disappointed.

Maria had started on Rory now and he was writhing around in the frame; the other interrogators were up close, huddled around him to keep out of the way of the blows.

"This is a disposable age," Peace said. "Disposable tissues. Disposable guerrillas."

He reached down and turned off the set, then he said, in a voice of one who is tired of television repeats, "I think we've seen enough. I've seen it all before and you'll be seeing it all again. We don't want you to get bored too soon."

"Weapon training—11:30 A.M." I read the notice on the printed sheet pinned to the door of my cubicle and I saw that someone had written in pen beside it, "Russell and Gellman not to miss."

Gellman read it too, standing beside me. "We may as well go," he said. "It can't be worse than the television around here."

We went outside and strolled across the grass to the hut where we were supposed to assemble.

Instead of shaven recruits in battle fatigues and berets, there were the kids again, about thirty of them, all new faces, but the same jeans and T-shirts and sneakers, and the only variations in their uniform were in the length of hair, the width of the flare in the jean legs and an occasional fancy belt buckle.

The instructor was a girl who looked about fifteen, with

large breasts swinging loose under her shirt, an American accent and a snappy manner, like a younger, less sophisticated version of Michelle at her most aggressive.

Before we had even settled in our seats, she banged down a small tin on the bench in front of her and said, "This is body talc." Beside it, she put an aerosol can with a brightly colored label I couldn't read. "And that is vaginal deodorant spray, both manufactured by Hairy Cosmetic Company, Incorporated."

She paused for laughter, then went on, "When you mix the body talc with water, it makes a paste like this."

She spread some on the bench, kneading it into a little blob. "And now, we have a plastic explosive, fifteen times more powerful than any currently in use. The talc, though, really is talc, and if a customs officer or cop inspects it, it feels right, looks right and smells right."

She held up the aerosol can again. "I'm not going to tell you yet what this is. Aside from its real purpose, it is a deodorant, but I wouldn't use it because Hairy hasn't quite got the secondary formula together yet and you're liable to get a roaring itch."

When the laughter had faded she said, "It also comes in masculine hair fixative for the guys but I thought this one would amuse you . . . now." She closed off the laughter, drawing our attention professionally back to the white blob of plastic explosive.

"Are there problems with it?"

"Detonation, I guess . . . and where to put the stuff."

"That's right," the girl said. "The best places are often hidden away somewhere. To do real damage to an apartment building it's handy to be able to set off chain explosions, so you bury the plastic somewhere in the boiler room or the heating system. Obscure places are best for the charge.

"Now, we'll show you how we've solved the problems." She held up the can of vaginal deodorant.

"This," she said, "is liquid detonator." She took off the cap, put her finger on the nozzle and squirted a spray of fine liquid over the blob of plastic.

"It takes eight seconds to dry and then the plastic is armed and ready to explode."

Two girls in the front row squealed and drew back and there was scattered superior laughter from some of the others in the class.

The instructor smiled. "For those of you who are new to explosives that is lesson one. When plastic is armed it is ready to go off, but it doesn't go off by itself. You still have to detonate it."

She smiled again. "And all you have to do with this stuff is light it." As she spoke, she whipped a matchbox out from behind a tin on the bench, pulled out a match, struck it and threw it, burning, on top of the mound of plastic.

This time the whole two front rows cowered back and there were shrieks from all over the room. But there was no explosion.

"That's lesson two," she said, when the uproar had subsided. "An ordinary flame won't do. You need a very intense, searing flame." She paused dramatically, then strode swiftly to the side of the room and pulled a bright red fire extinguisher off the wall.

"And this," she said, "is where we get our intense flame from." She put the extinguisher down on the bench.

"Inside here is—would you believe?—paint. It's a good quality paint; if you put it on a house, it would last five or six years and look great but that wouldn't be such a good idea because the base of this particular paint is a mixture of phosphorus and napalm jelly. It is *very* incendiary."

She held it up. "But like the plastic, it doesn't go off by itself so it's safe to carry around." She grinned. "More or less . . .

"Now, we are all going outside and you are going to have a demonstration of the most *gorgeous* urban guerrilla weapon ever invented"—the adjective made her just for a second an ordinary teenager again—"you are going to see the graffiti bomb."

When we got outside, she lined us up at the back of the hut, facing across an open field. At the far side, there was a ruined stone cottage and the remains of a low stone wall projecting out from it. To the right, there were two large squares of wood on legs—targets, obviously, but with no markings on them.

The girl focused our attention then she began: "The first thing I'd better tell you," she said, "is that the graffiti bomb started because Hairy goes to movies." She smiled. "He was working on the problem of how to detonate explosive charges and he went to see a neat movie about a crazie who loved to blow up buildings.

"Okay, so the crazie used to put his explosive charge wherever it was going to do the most damage, then run a cord to someplace outside the building and make the detonator into some little target that looked quite innocent—a flowerpot in a yard or something like that. Then he'd conceal himself nearby with a sniper rifle and fire at the pot. The detonator activates—and the crazie racks up another building."

She made a sweeping gesture with her arm. "Okay, so Hairy saw this and he thought it was really neat to have the explosive buried inside and an innocent target outside that would set it off, but"—she grinned again—"he knows you by now, and he knows that all your marksmanship medals are worthless because you never practice. You'd be there half the night trying to hit the flowerpot."

She raised her hands to quiet the laughter. "However . . . all is not lost. Hairy understands. Now watch."

She turned to a big guy from the front row. "Take this fire extinguisher and go and spray both targets. Put on as much as you like."

We watched as the kid raced across the field with the extinguisher and quickly covered the whole surface of both boards with white paint. When he came back, the instructor turned to the class.

"Okay, that's what's called really playing it safe. Now, who's the lousiest shot here. I want a real loser."

She looked around, and after some murmuring, the group settled on a straggle-haired little girl called Essie and pushed her to the front.

The instructor handed her a .22 rifle.

"A bigger caliber is better," she said, "but you get into trouble carrying weapons across frontiers, and most places you can buy these things without too much license hassle.

"Okay, shoot."

The girl raised the rifle and took aim. She had a sloppy shoulder position and a poor grip, and I wondered if she would manage to hit even the huge white squares in the field.

"Hit the one on the left, if you can," the instructor said. The girl fired and the small weapon barely recoiled against her shoulder. There was a crack, then a roaring hiss and the left-hand square became a single sheet of flame, white against the blue sky.

"Jesus," Gellman said. "Isn't science wonderful?"

"All right," she said. "That was to show you how the paint works. You can spray it on any surface and set it on fire. Right. Now we're going to show you what the graffiti bomb is really all about."

She walked over to the group and stood by the big guy who had painted the targets. She pointed at the cottage and the wall projecting out into the field. "Over there is a cottage," she said. "You're going to destroy it in three simple operations.

"Come with me. . . . Now. Take the tin of talc, pour some onto the ground and add some water from this can."

The kid did as he was told and made a small piece of dough. "Make it bigger," the instructor said. "About the size of a tennis ball."

When he had finished shaping it, she handed him the can. "Now arm the plastic." He sprayed it carefully, waited for it to dry, then stood up.

"Okay. Now go over to the cottage and find a good place to hide the plastic. It's not for real, so don't worry too much. There are no boilers or heating systems, so just find a hiding place."

As he was about to move off, she said, "No. Wait a minute."

She turned to the girl who had fired the rifle.

"While he's doing that, you're going to have fun. Go to that wall there and paint graffiti all over it. Anything you like. Only there's one thing—listen carefully and get this straight: it's got to make a continuous line.

"Whatever you paint has got to make a continuous line, so once you've started, don't stop spraying; don't take the jet of paint off the wall."

As they ran across the field, Gellman turned to me and lit a cigarette. "One more thing under the general heading of knowledge I could have done without," he said. I nodded.

The kid with the plastic had disappeared inside the ruins of the cottage but outside, the girl was having fun. She quickly mastered the nozzle control on the extinguisher, then raced up and down the wall, painting crazily. She did a disarmament sign and "Yankees go home" and "fuck" and then she got bored with art and just waved the jet around making lines and splashes all over the stonework.

When the other kid came out, she stopped and they ran back to the group.

The instructor faced the class. "Okay, guessing-game time. What do we have to do to complete the graffiti bomb?"

There was silence for a moment then someone said, "Join 'em up?"

"That's right. What else?"

"Make sure there's somewhere on the graffiti that's big enough to hit."

"Great. You've got it," the instructor said. "The graffiti are to make a trail to the plastic. Obviously it doesn't have to be graffiti. If they would look too conspicuous you could paint the whole wall . . . make a really neat job of it. Inside, you can repaint a skirting board, or a heating duct, anything leading down to where the charge is.

"Okay," she said to the two who had just come back. "One more run over the field. Have you got the idea?"

They nodded and raced off again. The girl looked at her graffiti and turned the end of one of the scrawls into a huge white flower, with a solid core; then she went to the opposite end of the wall and joined the graffiti to a single line running down the side of the house. At the door, she went inside still painting the line, like a kid trailing a stick along a fence. In a moment, they were back, sweating slightly, and we all looked at the house. The instructor picked up the rifle.

"Who wants to do it?" she asked. Several hands went up and she handed the weapon casually to a girl standing at her elbow. "Okay . . . go."

The girl raised the rifle, took aim at the wall and fired. There was a hissing sound and the flower caught fire but there was barely time to realize it, because the flame seared along the graffiti at astonishing speed, turning the lettering black, and in a few seconds the sheet of flame vanished into the house. There was a pause, a split second at most, then an explosion shook the cottage, and stone and wood from the ruined frame collapsed into the empty shell of the building.

"And that, my children," the instructor said calmly, "is the graffiti bomb. Any questions? . . . No? Okay. Lunchtime everyone."

"It's lunchtime," Gellman said wryly. "I'm glad nothing is being allowed to interrupt the normal routine of our day."

"It's not because the weapons are so sophisticated that they're terrifying," I said slowly. "It's because they're so goddam right for the kids of the permissive age."

When we got to our hut, Peace, who had changed into another safari jacket, was standing by the steps again. He seemed to have gotten over his anger and no one mentioned Rory or the random interrogation.

"What next?" I asked.

"Street wisdom training, combined with a gourmet lunch in dainty old Castleford," Peace said.

"I thought you'd enjoy the quaint market-town atmosphere—a change from the space age."

We changed and drove down to Castleford in a station wagon, Peace, Michelle, Gellman and I, outwardly an unremarkable group of early season tourists in town perhaps for a break from golfing at one of the resort hotels in the valley or to buy a gift for the pretty dark-haired girl in the pale blue summer dress.

I hadn't been to Castleford for nearly two years but I could see before we had reached the market square that little had changed.

Castleford began as a country retreat for the wool barons of the North, then tried to grow into a spa but discovered the waters were nondescript and the winter climate too cold. So it settled for a middle way: a little tourism, some retirement properties, and agriculture and sheep farming on the low hills around.

The war had brought light industry. The town fathers had been greedy and wanted it but they hadn't wanted to spoil the quaintness, so they had zoned all the factories out of sight onto the fringes and pretended that prosperity was coming as an act of God.

The wealthy kids went to the tennis and country clubs and smoked dope and drove fast cars. The kids from the factories roared off on motorcycles and hung around garish all-night transport cafés on the far fringes of town unseen until they appeared in magistrates court for brawling, vandalism or speeding on the North-West motorway.

When we drove in, as if to point up the grotesque contrast with the camp, Peace chose to take us to the daintiest restaurant of all—the Lobster Trap, where the old ladies rested after a morning shopping and ate tasteless shellfish and buttered white bread and tea.

We sat down and as we ordered, Peace handed me a tiny carrot-shaped piece of rubber.

"What is it," I asked, "an earplug?"

Peace handed another one to Gellman.

"In a way," he said, "put them in and see."

I put it carefully into my right ear and I could hear voices clearly. It sounded like several people and they were saying, one after the other, "Nothing here," "Nothing here yet," "Nothing my end."

"Those are Vikings," Peace said, as he closed the menu. "I thought you'd like to listen to them as a break from the monotony of watching the ladies in the flowered hats.

"It's a scenario. A kidnap scenario. The victim is a girl called Essie—I think you saw her this morning. She's loose somewhere in Castleford. A team of Vikings is looking for her."

He saw me tense and he put his hand on my arm in mock reassurance.

"Don't worry," he said. "This hasn't got a vicious ending. This one is just to teach the kids how to move around in the street."

"Street wisdom training?"

"That's it. It's nothing dramatic. Most of the Vikings were brought up in middle-class homes and they don't know anything about streets. They're used to driving around in cars. Until we started training them they didn't walk much anywhere.

"They don't know how to spot an alleyway where someone might be hiding. If you're a kid from Harlem, being alert on

the street comes naturally. These kids have to be taught."
He smiled.

Instead of asking about how they communicated, I sat stolidly and watched Gellman make a sandwich.

It was a beautiful sight and before he had finished, he had mesmerized a group of surreptitious watchers at the surrounding tables. He had ordered tuna casserole and now he was meticulously taking out the pieces of fish, soaking them in the buttery sauce and laying them out on several pieces of thick white bread. I watched for a while as he made patterns on the slices, choosing the angles carefully, laying each piece as close as possible to the next to thicken the filling.

Peace also watched for a while, then, irritated, he turned to Michelle. "Before Gellman offers you one of those god-awful sandwiches, would you mind showing us how you swallow a radio transmitter?"

I looked in spite of myself and so did Gellman, and the Vikings were suddenly very real again, as their voices droned in my ear. Michelle dipped into her handbag and pulled out an object that might have been a large antibiotic capsule.

Cupping her hand so that no one at the nearby tables could see, she put it between her thumb and forefinger and pressed the ends. Around the outside of the casing, tiny hairs appeared, but I could see they were stiffer than real hairs, more like tiny fishhooks protruding from the capsule. Deftly she picked up a napkin from the table and put it to her mouth, using it as a shield, and put the capsule into her mouth, sliding it deep into her throat with a neat, practiced gesture.

When she had finished, Peace said, "That's what the Vikings are wearing.

"It's a complete transmitter, powered by an electro-chip. The hairs make it cling to the inside of the throat. If you need to conceal it further, there's a simple exercise which allows you to free it from the wall of the throat and swallow it, to be recovered later, of course."

Michelle grinned. "That's a very safe procedure, actually. Cops are surprisingly thorough about some things. Ever since the narcs showed the way, they've become really hip to rectal searching, but they aren't into sorting through shit."

"Charming," Gellman said, closing the last of his sandwiches. "We are all impressed, now we can eat."

Peace folded his napkin carefully. "Just one last scenario, then you're ready. You say you are impressed with the Vikings and I believe you. But they have yet to be impressed with you. Listen in your earphones."

I listened and noticed that they had gone silent.

Peace looked at his watch. "Five minutes ago," he said, "the scenario changed. There is a new squad of Vikings coming down to Castleford—they have left the camp already. The leader is Rory."

"So he's all right," I said, quickly.

"We patched him up. As a matter of fact, one of his worst injuries was the one from the blow you gave him in the spine."

He smiled. "This is a kidnap scenario. It goes all the way . . . and you and Mr. Gellman are the victims. If they catch you, shall we say, we'll see you on television."

CHAPTER 10   I stood up from the table and grabbed Gellman's arm. "Move," I said. "Right now. Don't argue. Move."

I almost dragged him out of the restaurant and on the sidewalk, and I turned right, without caring which way it was leading. I knew the theory of how you escaped from this kind of trap; I'd studied kidnaps, written about them, analyzed them, and watched the victims released, shaken and sometimes dying, to give the classic press conference under the police station lights or at the embassy door.

If I stopped to think I could scare as easily as Gellman. The only difference between us was that I knew the moves, and I knew what it took to deal with the Vikings. That was what Michelle had been talking about when she played with my frustration levels in London: I knew what it took and I had spent a lifetime turning my back on it, because I didn't want to be the kind of person who had what it took.

I *was* a romantic and I fulfilled my romanticism through Julia and through the mountains and I knew it and I was glad. But I knew too there was no place for romantics here, out in the streets, with the guerrillas loose and random interrogation at the end. I thought about it just once as we ran down the hill toward the marketplace, then I put it out of my mind and concentrated on Rory as though he were my personal spot of light in a solemn meditation.

I could hear Gellman beginning to puff; he was slightly behind me and I dragged him on roughly, pulling him forward bodily, driving him to quicken his pace.

In the square, I saw a taxi parked outside the phony façade of the reconstructed Guild Hall and I pushed him into it and told the driver to take us up the hill.

He asked, "Where?" and I said, "Just up, I'll tell you where at the top," and he grunted and moved off and I sat back and grinned at Gellman.

Gellman grinned back. "I never did like hide and seek when I was a kid. I used to prefer kiss and tell but I've gone off that since this morning."

I turned and looked at him squarely. "One thing," I said. "While we're running, laugh, joke, anything that helps, but if they catch us, think about Rory and think about that room. Just decide as calmly as you can, 'I won't go in there, whatever it costs.' "

"I'll try," Gellman said. "You lead, I'll follow."

The cab driver had started to listen and I told him to pull over to the curb. I smiled at him and offered him a cigarette.

"Are you playing some kind of game, sir?"

I nodded. "Yes. In a way. Now, listen. When you drop us some young kids may come and ask you where you took us. Right? And I don't want you to tell them."

"Right, sir. I won't. You can count on me," he replied seriously.

"Yes," I said, "I believe I can and I'm going to tell you why. The license of this cab is 465 GVH. It will take about ten minutes to get your address from the records office. If you do tell anyone where you dropped us, I'll be calling on you and you can count on a full year off work from the kicking you'll be getting. Okay?

"So close your ears and take us fast to somewhere I can buy a motorbike."

I turned back to Gellman, "Have you still got the plug in your ear?"

He nodded.

"Keep it there. Just in case. They might just come back on, accidentally or something."

The driver moved off again and he seemed to have shriveled behind the wheel.

I leaned over. "How far will you need to take us?"

"There's a bike shop at Cluff's Bridge," he said.

"Okay," I said. "Move it."

"I don't want to sound dumb, but why are we buying a motorbike?" Gellman asked.

"We need our own wheels. There are twenty Vikings in a squad. I doubt if there are more than two car-rental places in Castleford, probably both in the town center. The Vikings can easily cover them both and the station and bus depot as well. You probably can't rent bikes. That leaves stealing and buying. We steal as a last resort; we don't want cop trouble. Buying is better but it takes too long to buy a car.

"Bikes are the best bet. We should get one for three hundred pounds. If they take Barclay cards, we'll have it in five minutes . . . if they don't they can phone a clearance on a check to London in ten or so, if we can persuade them to hurry."

Gellman nodded toward the driver's back. "I have a feeling you'll find a way."

The bike shop we found had a sign—"Richardson and Sons—Motorcycles"—a window full of mini-Hondas for the teenie market and one big Kawasaki and a side lot, fenced off with wire, full of assorted British motorcycles.

I gave the driver two pounds and a smile and he was pulling away before we were properly out on the sidewalk.

Inside the shop there was an elderly man in a gray woolen pullover behind the counter and a couple of youths in leather jackets standing at the back of the store.

"Mr. Richardson?"

"Aye, that's right." He had a broad Yorkshire accent.

"How much is the Matchless in the yard; the three-fifty with the stripe on the engine?"

"You can have her for three hundred."

"Good condition?"

"Nowt wrong w'yer at all."

I pulled out a Barclay card and put it on the counter.

I saw his face drop. "I don't rightly know as how I can do it with one of those things . . ." he said. "Me son knows more about them."

I leaned over the counter. "Mr. Richardson, how many bikes have you sold this month?"

"Well, things are a bit tight right now . . . summer trade's not really started yet."

"All right," I said. I pointed to the credit machine behind the counter. "On the underside of that gadget is a phone number. You call it up and give the number on my card. They see if I'm good for three hundred quid and they say okay. They give you a number to write on the check to make sure nothing goes wrong after.

"Now if you can do that inside five minutes, you've just made your first sale of the month. If you can't, you've just lost it . . . all right?"

Before he could say anything, I turned away from the counter and started to look at helmets.

Gellman followed.

"Consumer credit selling in one easy lesson," he said. He looked over his shoulder.

"He's on the phone already."

It did take less than five minutes and when he had finished, Mr. Richardson looked really pleased with himself.

"I reckon that's all right then. The girl said it was like money in't bank."

"It is," I said. "How much for those helmets?"

"Six quid each."

I nodded. "And I want two jackets. The old-fashioned

kind. None of these fancy cross-zips the kids like."

He went into the back of the store and came back with the top halves of two sets of motorcycle leathers and put them on the counter.

"Three quid each," he said. "We don't sell too many of them nowadays."

I handed one to Gellman. "With this on, you won't look too conspicuous," I said. "There are plenty of middle-aged motorcyclists in the north of England."

Mr. Richardson went outside to get the bike and Gellman said, "Do you have a license, by the way?"

"No," I grinned, "but it doesn't matter. I haven't ridden much on roads."

Gellman smiled his wry, hovering smile. "You can ride?"

"Yes," I said. "I learned in the army. I was sent on a motorcycle course. Just before becoming a mountain-rescue instructor. Only the army could tell you why."

Mr. Richardson came back with the bike and we walked out onto the flagged pavement in front of the store and he kicked over the engine for us.

"What's that canal down there?" I asked.

"That's old ship canal."

"Is there a towpath? Can you get along there to the new part of Castleford?"

"Aye. If yer careful. It's a bit bumpy. . . . You come out by Fordings Mills."

I straddled the machine and motioned Gellman to get on behind. "They're very low and very uncomfortable on the rear," I said. "You'll be stiff tomorrow."

"I'll take my chances," Gellman said. "Just make sure that's all that's wrong tomorrow, will you?"

I twisted the throttle and pulled out onto the roadway. The street was deserted except for a car parked farther up in the middle of a row of terraced houses.

I cruised down the hill slowly to get the feel of the bike and found that it was easy. I hadn't forgotten. The instructor's pronouncement after the army course was simple: "If they didn't keep the manuals easy you'd still not know where to put the oil; but you ride all right. . . . It must be like balancing on mountains."

At the bottom of the hill, I edged the bike off the road and down a narrow lane leading to the canal I had seen from the store. It seemed to be the fastest route into the new town, where, hopefully, we could find somewhere obscure to hide and wait out the end of the scenario.

By the canal was a towpath of black gravel, badly maintained but still passable, and I set off along it, cautiously negotiating each rut and pothole as it came. After a while, old habits came back and I started absorbing the shocks more easily and reacting with less strain. I also started to go faster.

To find us, they would have had to drive fast through the thirty miles of winding lanes from the camp to Castleford, then come directly to the spot where we were, without any searching. It could happen but it would be chance. Now the problem was to find a hiding place until nightfall.

Ahead, I could see a bridge over the canal and a turnoff up onto a croft. The ground was open for over a mile and parts of the rough wasteland had been used for dumping garbage; the rest was grass and stone and bits of rubbish—the kind of terrain I was most used to on the bike. It seemed to be a shortcut to the low hangarlike buildings ahead which I guessed were the edge of the new Castleford industrial estate. Far ahead, the towpath seemed to pass under the next bridge with no access to the two-lane highway above it.

"We'd better go that way," I said to Gellman over my shoulder, pointing upward toward the croft, and I slowed to look for a way onto it. A short way along, I found a section of the fence where the wire was broken and flattened and I nudged the wheels carefully over it and started up the slope.

It was a difficult surface and I negotiated the holes and mounds cautiously, but as we approached the summit of the mound, it became easier and I looked around to study the terrain. With the elevation, I could see I had made the right choice. There were several places where we could get out and onto the road and in among the buildings.

At the summit, I stopped for a moment to choose the best of them, and I suddenly heard a crackle in my ear, then a singsong voice, "Mr. Rus-sell, Mr. Gell-man, we can se-ee you."

I felt Gellman jump, startled, behind me on the pillion. He had heard it too. It was Rory.

"Mr. Rus-sell. You were very go-od but we cheat-ed. Your ear-receiver is spe-cial. It's a homer . . . and we've found you."

Then the singsong tone stopped and Rory's Irish accent was clear and plain.

"And now," he said, "the black part of the scenario begins."

"Oh, shit," I heard Gellman say softly. It was a quiet, profane prayer. I looked around again and all at once there were six motorcycles on the croft, coming off the roadway and fanning out ahead of us. I looked back, and there were three more behind.

In the earphone I could hear Rory giving orders, guiding the machines into a net around us. I watched them move into position, slowly, circling over the slopes of the croft, disappearing then reappearing behind the piles of scrap and garbage. There was no telling who was who, or which was Rory; they were totally faceless behind black wraparound visors.

In the earphone, the orders stopped and I heard Rory say in his singsong voice again, "Mr. Rus-sell, we're nearly read-y." Then in flat tones, "Aren't we nice to give you a chance? Since you fancy yourself on a bike, we've left you a way out so we can see how good you *really* are."

I looked back and saw that the towpath we had come from was barred now by one of the Vikings. The broken stretch of fence was blocked by a motorcycle laid on its side. It wasn't quite wide enough to fill the whole gap, so the rider, a powerful-looking kid with football shoulders, was kneeling in the space that was left. He had a gun, a heavy-looking black automatic, and he was aiming it at us, with his wrist supported on his left arm in marksman position.

Behind and to the left, two cyclists were circling and wheeling and I could see they were going to be the beaters, driving us down toward the funnel made by the other four.

"You get the situation, do you, Mr. Russell?" The voice in the earphone was hard. "Watch closely and in a minute you'll see the kids by the road turn and pull away to the farthest corners of the field. If you're good, if you're very, very good, you can make it to the opposite corner and out onto the road.

"If you make it, all you have to do is to keep ahead of us for twenty minutes. Then you phone the camp and the scenario is over."

The voice became singsong again: "The number is 52345, but if we catch you, you won't need it. We'll take you back ourse-elves."

I turned to Gellman. "Take off your earplug and throw it away." He did so and I threw mine into the grass beside it.

I started forward slowly to avoid a slide from wheelspin on the loose surface then suddenly I turned the bike sharply to the right and raced back toward the towpath.

They had made a mistake, and as I roared toward the kid blocking the gap in the fence, I didn't even believe it was a gamble. The gun was the mistake. If there was a chance either of us would be killed in the scenario, the whole vicious charade since Montreal became meaningless.

When he saw what was happening, the kid in the gap froze; he had time to move but he couldn't. For a second too long he couldn't believe I was going to ride him down.

As the front wheel hit him, I didn't think about the scream and the crunch of bone. I was doing only one thing and doing it as I had been taught, as well as I could remember. This was a "controlled spin and recovery after striking an obstacle." The kid's death was a lurch and a bump and a twist of the handlebars and then we were on the towpath and we were free.

It was a mile down the canal to Cluff's Bridge where we had started. The two Vikings closest could be on the towpath before we left it but they could not catch up enough to see which way we turned when we were back on the road by the store where we had bought the bike.

The Viking bikes were faster than the Matchless; there would be no time for decisions or hesitation at Cluff's Bridge. We couldn't stay on the street in front of terraced houses; whichever way we turned we could not be out of sight before the first pursuers were up on the road also.

Behind the yard, I had seen a laneway, wider than the narrow alley leading to the back of the houses, and it had looked as though it would lead into the maze of back streets I had noticed from the taxi.

I decided that would be it. In the rearview mirror on the handlebar, I could see two bikes already on the towpath behind us; they were gunning hard, heads down, the black visors half-hidden behind the handlebars.

The exit from the towpath was easy: a twist, a little skid, a correction, then a straight run up onto the still-deserted street where we had been before. Left, right, left, into the alley and there we got lucky. The alley crossed three main roads in quick succession, each a descent into Castleford; it was all one suburb of cheap housing sprawling over the hill, and the main roads radiated out through the houses and on into the country. The Viking bikers would have to pause at every turn, guessing which way we had taken; there was not even a straight view for them down the alleyway itself, which twisted and turned between the junctions.

Our play had to be speed and the random choice of direction. I chose the third left—a bet placed arbitrarily on the board of crisscross streets. Then three more bets in quick succession. A wide loop and another twist.

We rode for fifteen minutes, then I pulled into a narrow turning between two blocks of row housing and killed the engine. I felt Gellman pushing away from the saddle to ease the cramps in his legs as he struggled awkwardly off the machine.

"I've never been on a motorbike before," he said. "My instincts always told me they weren't for me, and they were right."

The joke was a reflex; when he had stretched himself enough to get the blood circulating again, I could see him starting to think and his face went grim and he looked suddenly tired.

"I suppose we killed the kid."

"I think so," I said.

"So we've started."

"Yes," I said. "The war's begun. So far, we've only killed the enemy."

I could see he knew what I meant. He took out a cigarette and offered me one. "What now?"

"The scenario is supposed to be over, but they lie a lot."

"So we phone Peace and hope he's done his lying for the day?"

"Something like that," I said. "We'll put the bike somewhere behind one of the houses, out of the way, then we'll go into that café across the street; you can't see inside from the roadway. If they find us there, we'll have lost the gamble. The risk is no worse here and I could use a coffee."

I left him to finish his cigarette in the alley, wheeled the bike around to the back of the houses and parked it out of sight behind someone's garage, and we walked across to the café, fashioned as a pseudo-American hamburger joint.

We sat down in one of the plywood booths and ordered two coffees and got a nasty look for taking up choice seats without eating.

Gellman still looked very shaken, so I said lightly, "Peace would be ashamed of us. We're breaking the first rule of street wisdom: never make yourself conspicuous. We should have ordered two of their sinister-looking hamburgers and those milk shakes made from old tea leaves."

"I'm going to do better than that when that fellow turns his back," Gellman said. I watched fascinated as he reached into the pocket of the jacket under the motorcycle leathers and pulled out one of the tuna sandwiches he had been making at lunchtime. With a quick movement, he took a large bite and put it back in his pocket, turning his head away from the man behind the counter.

I couldn't hold back the laughter. The sight of Gellman munching a tuna sandwich in a back street hamburger joint, wearing motorcycle leathers over a blazer and slacks, was just too much.

"What are the choices?" he said, swallowing the last of the sandwich.

"None really."

I thought of Julia suddenly for the first time since my adrenaline had started to surge in the Lobster Trap.

"We can't walk out on the scenario. We can only play and hope Peace is really going to end it soon. The sooner we telephone, the greater chance he'll prolong it, hoping to see us caught; the longer we wait, the more chance the Vikings have of finding us."

"I played games like that when I was studying statistics," Gellman said. "They were called no-win situations."

"Drink your coffee and give me a cigarette," I said. "We'll just sit until we feel moved to make the phone call, as the Quakers say."

We sat for a while and smoked. I saw the counterman was getting impatient so I bought two hot dogs to pacify him and put them between us in the booth.

The telephone was in the back of the café and I went to check that it was working, but I didn't make the call. I came back and sat and thought about Peace and wondered whether he was bored by the scenario yet or whether he was inventing a new one; or whether finally we were going to be set in motion, like clockwork toys to run his campaign of terror, whatever it was.

I thought about it for a while then I put the thoughts aside and watched the customers, checking each one, sizing them up as adversaries, looking for signs that anyone was looking, searching.

It wasn't difficult because there were so few customers and they were mostly older people, obviously living nearby, and the kids who came in and out were mostly too young to be Vikings; in a few years, I thought wryly, there may be juvenile Vikings; we're almost there, but not quite yet.

Then a girl came in and as soon as she stepped up to the counter, I knew that she was a threat. There was nothing particular about her that was wrong. I just knew that she worried me. I knew the kids in suburbs like this and she could easily have been one of them. She looked right but she still scared me.

She wasn't looking at us, and she didn't seem to care about anything except the cheeseburger she had ordered in a northern British voice. She was sitting casually at the counter, waiting for it to cook on the heated slab of metal behind the counter. Nothing was wrong but I could almost see the transmitter, the tiny capsule clinging in her throat.

She had her face away from the booth and I could imagine her mouthing words into the invisible transmitter. Did you have to be a ventriloquist or did you just mumble to yourself?

All I knew was that I felt I could see the transmitter as clearly as if her throat were transparent. Was it instinct or paranoia? I didn't know, but I could see the counterman walking toward the back of the shop. If she was a Viking, if there was a transmitter, she would be free to speak into it.

I touched Gellman's arm hard to warn him to turn, and

in the same instant I slid out of the booth and took the two strides to the counter and grabbed the girl.

I whirled her around and brought her face up to mine and she stared, horror-struck under the curls as I gripped her arm in a vicious, biting hold. I looked at her face and there was no way of knowing. I hesitated just for a second then I hit her hard in the stomach, then seized her by the hair and twisted her head downward and thrust my fingers deep into the throat.

She writhed and retched and suddenly the transmitter was there on the counter, a ladybug in a pool of vomit.

She stared at me, terrified, and I dragged her upright, twisting her hair and slamming her back against the counter.

I could hear the counterman coming, running, shouting, " 'Ere what the Christ do you think . . . ?"

The words were cut by the bowl of brown ketchup Gellman had slammed into his face. It was a beautiful moment of exquisite comic relief but it wasn't enough. The slimy brown syrup blinded him but it didn't stop him. He faltered, flung his hands to his face to try to clear his vision, and I knew he was going to come on.

I tightened my grip on the girl, pinning her against the counter with my thigh to free one hand to fend off the raging bulk that was now only a few feet away.

But there was no need. Gellman reached over the counter and slammed a stool across on his head before his eyes were clear enough to charge and he fell, heavily, behind the counter.

The girl screamed and I pressed my knee hard into her groin and held her face close.

"Have you called them yet? Where are they?"

She squirmed with the pain, then she gathered just enough strength to move her head from side to side, despite the grip I had of her hair. It was a shudder of the head more than a shake. She wasn't saying no. She was refusing to answer.

I stood back from her, holding her by the arm. She was a slim, wiry girl, twenty years old at most, and I could see the relief in her eyes that her defiance had been enough.

"Come this way," I said, leading her toward the booth and I could see the relief growing. She was thinking, "We're going to wait; then they'll find me and we'll have won." I felt her arm relax, her body loosen after the tension of the struggle and the pain.

Gellman was at the counter watching, uncertain, not knowing what I was going to do. I paused midway between the booth and the counter, then without warning, at the moment when she was most relaxed, I scooped her bodily off the floor and threw her over the counter. Before she could collect her limbs and try to get up, I was over with her and I grabbed her again, and as she screamed I pushed her face down to within a foot of the open plate of the stove.

I held it there, grotesquely suspended over the smoking black fumes and the sizzling oval of meat and I yelled at her, close into her ear, "Where are the Vikings?" I could feel the heat of the stove on my arm and feel the trembling throughout her body. I twisted her head upward again, to give her a chance to speak, and as I turned I saw Peace standing in the doorway.

"It's all right, Philip," he said quietly. "You have been deemed to have escaped. The scenario is over."

CHAPTER 11 "I don't understand why you're letting me do this," I said as we came out of the Blackheath music store and started to walk down the hill. "I don't see why you're letting me have dinner with the Wescotts."

We had been back in London only one day and the order from Peace had come as a complete surprise.

"Peace decided it was easier this way," Michelle said, as we walked toward the corner where her little green Renault was parked.

"While we were at the camp, Wescott started to make a real nuisance of himself. He made five or six attempts to contact you. Then he invited you for Jane's birthday. He was very insistent. He made it clear this will be your chance to explain your behavior. If you refuse, he'll try to see you alone. It could become a real drag. At dinner, the surveillance will be total. We already have an electronic lariat in place."

She paused. "And don't forget the catch. You have to break off your friendship with Wescott, tonight."

"Yes," I said bitterly. "You told me that part. It'll be fun after over twenty years. . . . He's the closest friend I have."

As we walked, I tried again to decide whether I dare take the risk I had planned on the flight back from Derbyshire. We were obviously nearly ready to begin the operation. I had to try, somehow, to convey to someone that my new life was a black charade.

Of all the people I knew who might be made to understand, Wescott was the quickest thinker and he was the one who knew me best; and the dinner party looked like the last chance I would have to try, before the Vikings went into operation.

I had sweated over the thought all the way down from Derbyshire and I had cringed with shame at my stupidity at the funeral. But I knew that the way was still to use some kind of code based on the experiences I had shared with Wescott.

Wescott and I had been friends for nearly twenty years. He knew me better than any other person except Julia, and we had shared experiences that could not possibly all be known to the people who had prepared the dossier for my kidnap.

I had decided that I would try and devise a code, and at the music store I had found a gift which could, if I was careful, set the evening's conversation in a context that Jack would understand but which would seem harmless to the experts manipulating the surveillance system.

The gift was a blue guitar, a beautiful classical guitar, stained with a soft blue eye, ingrained into the exquisite wood. It was a suitable, original gift for Jane, who played the guitar well, but it was the color that was important.

At Cambridge, Wescott had read English and American literature and he had done a thesis on the poetry of Wallace Stevens. By Wescott's standards, Peace and Hairy were, I was sure, barely literate. I was gambling that Peace had never read the Stevens poem with the line, "Things as they are are changed upon the blue guitar." If I introduced the idea correctly, Wescott would get it immediately. After that, I had somehow to guide the conversation so that I could convey the rest of the message.

If I played the game well, I was sure I could win; my great fear was that I would remember Julia and what the stakes were and lose control when everything hung on the subtlety of a phrase.

I thought about it again as Michelle drove in silence down into the older, more elegant part of Chislehurst, below the institute, where Wescott lived. By the time we had reached the house, I had decided that I would try. As we pulled up at the curb I said to Michelle, "I know there'll be cameras too. Do we have to have the whoring widower number, too?"

Michelle looked at me steadily. "Yes," she said. "Peace won't be happy unless you break with Wescott. That's why he's letting you go to dinner. You are not to part friends. . . ." She hesitated, and I saw the faint hint that she and I could be on the same side.

"If you can't bring yourself to do it, I'll come and wave my bra in Jane's face."

I smiled at her and got out of the car.

"You won't need to do that. I'll manage. Anyway, just seeing you sitting out here will set the evening off on a stirring footing."

I walked down the drive, carrying the guitar case, and I wondered suddenly whether I would even get inside the house. I could imagine Jane opening the door, seeing Michelle and saying something that no friendship between Jack and me could stand against.

But it was Jack who opened the door. He saw Michelle sitting in the Renault, lighting a cigarette, watching me. I watched his eyes and I could see he was confused. I had accepted his offer to make peace and now I seemed determined to offend.

As he put out his hand, he said, "She's very pretty."

It was a make or break moment. I thought of the surveillance team but I knew I had to get in.

I said as warmly as I could, "Jack, I'm sorry. My car broke down. There was no other way."

He nodded and I stepped quickly in before Jane could appear and see Michelle.

The first hurdle was over but there would be so many more.

As Jack took my coat, I wondered if I could even manage a whole evening of word games with the stakes this high. I had no gambits prepared after the blue guitar and I felt all my confidence rushing away. Then, in time, Jane appeared and the game was on.

I lifted the guitar case up and handed it to her. "Your present," I said, "for a very happy birthday. I hope you'll take it as if it were coming from both of us."

"From Julia or from your new girl? . . ."

It was a bitchy reflex and I guessed that she had snapped the words out despite a promise to Jack not to open with a scene.

"We'd better go inside, Philip," Jack said. "Jane, why don't you check on the dinner? I'll get us all a drink."

It was a very obvious maneuver to head off a confrontation but he said it very firmly and Jane turned and went back into the kitchen.

Wescott led me into the living room and I saw that he had laid out dinner in the way I liked it best—informally, sitting around the old-fashioned fireplace. The room was furnished with antiques; Wescott's private passion was collecting and he had had many tussles with customs on his return from newspaper assignments abroad. His pride was the pair of lamps, with Chinese porcelain bases, that cast a soft, yellow light over the whole room.

Without asking me what I wanted, Wescott poured me a whiskey over ice and brought it to me as I settled in one of the deep comfortable armchairs.

In normal times, it would have been an exquisite moment of relaxation, the first savoring of the pleasures of the evening. I enjoyed Wescott's company more than that of any other man, and we had spent countless days and nights, talking, arguing or simply chatting idly about mountains, skiing or cars.

I sipped the whiskey and wondered, as I looked at Wescott, if we had really stored up enough shared experience to defeat the invisible watchers and listeners. But he had barely settled himself opposite me when Jane came back into the room. I could see from her eyes that she could not let matters rest. She had not wanted this dinner; she had done it to please Jack and she was determined not to let me use our friendship to run away from what I had done.

"I'd better look at my present hadn't I," she said, and sat down very formally in the third armchair. I smiled and handed her the guitar case that was resting beside my leg.

She undid the wrapping silently, then unfastened the clips and pulled back the lid of the case. Just for a moment, her eyes showed real pleasure, and she began to say, "Philip, it must have cost a fortune . . . it's so beautiful . . ." Then she let the words tail away, as though she had read a line from the wrong script.

I was determined not to waste the lapse so I said, "Look, Jane, it is my way of saying sorry. I wanted to do it in some way that would make you both understand."

I looked at Wescott. Would he rise to the hint? He looked at me quizzically.

"I still don't play, you know," he said, "but it is a beautiful guitar."

I laughed. "Well if you still can't play, you can enjoy the color."

It was done, and as I sipped my whiskey again I could see a look coming into Wescott's eyes that I knew so well. He was still the "fastest man on the intellectual draw" as Julia had once called him.

He had understood.

Jane put the guitar back into its case. "You must realize, Philip, that an apology doesn't fix everything," she said. "I know it's none of our business . . ." She tailed off again and I said quickly, "I could have stopped all this by saying it wasn't anyone's business, but I know you cared very much for Julia and I did too."

Jack got up and said, "Look, I'm going to make a suggestion. I want a truce. I think Philip wants to talk about all this, but this isn't the moment. Let's chat for a while . . . we can get to it later."

"That's a bit artificial isn't it?" Jane was angry again but she could see that Wescott meant to have his way.

He said, "Perhaps it is, but I care for you both too much to have you tearing at each other's throats this early in the evening."

He turned to me and then settled back in his chair. "Philip, why don't you tell us about the new job."

"It pays well," I said, "that's the first thing you can say about it. Forty-five thousand dollars a year plus fringes . . . a lot of them."

We had always been frank about such matters and he did not find it strange to hear the actual salary figures.

"I can see why you would want to say goodbye to the academic hustle for a while," he said. "That's a lot of temptation. Is it a long contract?"

"Two years, with a renewable option." I had seen an opening. "Whether I stay will depend on how the first block of research goes; it's going to be on the effects of urban violence on the economies of cities."

He had the lead and if he took it, I was ready with the next part of the message.

"What about your book?" He said it very casually and I could see he knew this was where I wanted to lead him.

"I've postponed publication for now," I said equally casually. "As Bob Allen used to say: Every piece of academic work can be improved with a little delay."

Wescott grinned. "Yes," he said, "I'm sure he's right." As he said it, I could feel the relief pouring through me. He was on the right wavelength.

Bob Allen had been our tutor at King's, an irascible little man who believed that all literature had been primarily created to be dissected by critics. He also believed that anyone of any competence could do anything quickly. If there was one man in the whole of England who would not have approved of postponing the publication of my book it was Bob Allen, and Wescott knew that as well as I did.

Jane said irritably, "If you two are going to get back into your university days that quickly, I'm going to get back to the kitchen to bring dinner. With any luck you'll have finished with skiing before I get back."

Without realizing it, she had given me another good lead. I said quickly, "Have you done any lately, Jack?"

"Not much," he answered. "We managed a week in Switzerland after the last Zurich conference. Jane flew out to join me. What about you?"

"So so," I said. "I'm going off downhill. I'm thinking of switching to cross-country. It's a sign of age, maybe."

Wescott was too smart to let it show but I knew that he must have been shocked by the remark. He knew better than anyone that I detested cross-country skiing. I felt safe saying it because I was sure the Vikings would not have discovered that. In ten years I had never even mentioned it to anyone. But Wescott knew from our university days that I thought of it like golf, as a retirement sport.

"Are you going anywhere special to start?" he asked.

"I thought I might try Finland."

The country was his clue; my only fear was that there were two inferences and that he might take the wrong one. He knew I disliked Finland; as a student I had had a brief holiday there which had included a disastrous love affair and a broken ankle. He would take that as a sign, again, that I was lying, that something was wrong, but there was a much more precise reference, if only he would remember it: Finland was my code word for Ivor Pearson.

We had both known Pearson in Rome when he was, outwardly, commercial attaché at the British Embassy. A cautious man about his covers, Pearson had done brilliantly in his commercial duties and when his new posting was announced, as first secretary in the British Embassy in Helsinki, we had roared with laughter at the ineptitude of the intelligence service. As a listening post for eastern Europe, Finland was a massive assignment; as a promotion for a brilliant commercial attaché in Rome, it was ludicrous, and for a while, whenever either of us had done something we were proud of, we had adopted the catch phrase, "Be careful. You'll get a promotion to Finland."

Would Wescott remember? I drank some more whiskey but I need not have worried. The reply came back immediately.

"Finland? I hear it's okay, but even there, it's getting a bit commercial." I was halfway there. Wescott knew now that there was something seriously wrong and he also knew that I wanted Ivor Pearson involved. What I had to convey now was that I wanted to be put under surveillance.

Then, just as I was wondering whether I dare risk a less cautious remark, Jack took the lead for me.

"Forty-five thousand dollars a year," he said thoughtfully. "That's a helluva lot of money. . . . Do you need any help at the institute?"

I could imagine the listening surveillance team tensing up, waiting for my reply.

"I'm afraid not. There are no vacancies at all. About the only person we could use right now is some dreary statistician who can count lost jobs and broken drainpipes and relate it to urban violence in Northern Ireland. Someone like old Doug Bell."

Wescott's look left no doubt that the message was through. We both knew what the Vikings could not have known: that Doug Bell was not a statistician but an obscure physicist back in Cambridge who studied the composition of raindrops. He also had acquired a nasty habit that irritated everyone in our college beyond measure: that of spying on people from behind the curtains of his rooms.

Wescott could not have forgotten and Peace could surely not know.

Now, for the hardest part of all. I had to offend Wescott and somehow at the same time make him understand that it was not my fault. If I wasn't convincing to Peace, everything I had achieved at dinner would be lost.

I was dreading the moment. If I could not find an ambiguous context before the night was out, I would have to do it brutally. I dared not do otherwise.

I knew Wescott was watching for me to make some other move. He handed me a third whiskey and Jane came back, bringing a huge tray of what she always called "pick and savor" foods: delicious tidbits of meat and fish fried with heavy spices that we would take from a tray between us in front of the fire.

We chatted about skiing again and for a while, it was like old times, but before long, Jane handed me a piece of ginger chicken and said, aggressively, "Look, Philip. Tell us honestly . . . about Julia. Tell us what happened with this girl Michelle."

As she said the name, I suddenly saw how the evening had to end. Wescott would understand it; only Jane would be offended more deeply than I dared to think about.

I hesitated, then I said very carefully, "It was a coincidence: one of those hateful ones that you wish would never happen. I was having an affair with Michelle in Canada; it had been going on before. I think it would have ended in a divorce . . ."

I saw Jane tense and I said, "Look. You asked me to be honest. I'm trying to be. . . . Then there was the car crash. A coincidence. I could have given Michelle up but there didn't seem any point . . . that would have just made it a double tragedy."

I said the words slowly, hesitating over each one.

"A double tragedy for you perhaps. But what about Julia's name? Couldn't you at least have waited awhile, even a few days after the funeral?"

She had given me the opening.

I turned to Jack. "I know I should have. But it was a sex thing. I admit it. It's the kind of thing you only feel once in a lifetime. Even now, tonight, I just can't wait to get back to her."

I looked at Jack, pleadingly. "You know how it is . . . remember Miranda, how you couldn't keep your hands off her?"

Jane lunged out of her chair and yelled, "For Christ's sake, Philip, what the hell do you mean by a remark like that? Do you have to drag in some woman Jack's never even told me about to excuse yourself?"

Wescott got up too. "I think you'd better leave." The voice was very cold. He put his hand on Jane's arm. "You'd better wait upstairs. . . . I'll see Philip out."

In the hallway, he handed me my coat and I said, "Jack, I'm sorry if I've spoiled so many good memories. I'm sorry I blurted out about Miranda . . . I know how Jane feels about that sort of thing . . . but it is just how I feel about Michelle."

He looked at me squarely. "I understand," he said. "But you'd better not come again."

He said it very calmly but sadly and as he closed the door behind me all I could think about was what a superb actor he had turned out to be. That was the moment when he could have ruined everything. But he had been perfect.

I thought of the night Wescott had come into my room in Cambridge to tell me about Miranda. She was a trim, sexy girl, one of a crowd of apparently older girls from the town who enjoyed picking up younger students. I could see Wescott's face, white as he told me about the invitation he had received. He was more scared than I had ever seen him, even in the toughest mountain pitch.

"She sent me an invitation," he said, "to a birthday party. Incredibly it's only her fourteenth! I've been sleeping with her since she was thirteen. She's the very worst kind of jail-bait."

I had said, "What are you going to do?" and he had looked

at me and replied, "I have to go. She's threatened a scene if I don't. I don't think I've ever been more scared to go back to a woman in my whole life."

I walked down the drive to the gate, with no idea how I was supposed to get back to Blackheath. As if by invisible stage direction, the green Renault appeared, with Michelle driving.

"You were superb," she said. "I'm glad it went well. Peace was delighted."

"I'm glad he's glad," I said bitterly. "I really enjoyed breaking up a twenty-year friendship."

I went to bed more confident than I had been since Montreal, but when Michelle woke me the next morning, I knew from her behavior that something serious had happened in the few hours I had been asleep.

She glanced at her watch every few minutes and seemed to be timing every gesture I made. She made breakfast while I dressed and shaved and then watched me eat, and I had the feeling that she might push the eggs down my throat if I took a couple of seconds too long to swallow them.

Finally she left the room and went into the bathroom, and when she came out I could see she was making a conscious effort to pull herself together. By the time the Rover came just after 7:30, she was almost herself again—professionally relaxed, detached, cynical.

Driven by a young chauffeur I had not seen before, we went to the institute and picked up Gellman. He got in and slumped beside us, without commenting on why he had been told to be there.

Gellman's state seemed to disturb Michelle again. It was barely perceptible but I sensed that she wanted him to be bright and cheerful and was worried that he should be so morose and vegetable-like. To me, it was no surprise; I knew Gellman functioned like an automaton for the first hour or so after getting up, but I could understand Michelle being irritated by it.

I asked her a couple of times where we were going and she refused to answer, but when we were through Bermondsey and turning over Blackfriar's Bridge onto the South Embankment, I said: "Which is it, Chelsea or the airport?" and she said shortly, "The airport, Heathrow. But we're not flying anywhere."

"If we're not going anywhere," I said, "I presume this monster production has something to do with finding out what our target is."

"We're going to meet Peace," she said.

"To find out what the target is?" I persisted.

"I don't know," she said. "That's for Peace to decide."

The lie was obvious as she must have known it was, but she seemed too preoccupied to bother covering it up.

Beside me, Gellman stirred.

"Good morning," I said. "Good to have you awake."

"What the hell is going on, anyway?" he said. "All Peace said was, 'Make sure you bring your driver's license.' "

"I can't talk about it," Michelle said. "Why don't you just talk to Philip and stop worrying?"

Once you looked outside the car, it was difficult to be depressed. It was the first really fine spring morning there had been and the air was bright and sharp, and I decided to let the issue rest and try to clear my mind for whatever was coming.

We were already close to the airport, and over the suburban rooftops, I saw a Boeing 747 beginning its approach pattern. As always, it was a sight that lifted my spirits. For me, so much excitement had begun at Heathrow.

Then I saw the motorcyclists parked along the perimeter of the airfield. I had no idea whether they were Vikings, but the cycles and the leather-jacketed figures were indissociable from the training camp and the chase.

Outwardly, they looked like plane spotters, and I thought suddenly how easy terrorism had become. What if they were Vikings? What if the rectangular black boxes on the back of the cycles were not radio receivers, but devices to transmit interference patterns to disrupt the all-weather landing systems that were used nowadays, even on a clear day?

With the right electronic toys, one of the kids could bring down a 747, or even force a midair collision. A flick of a button and there could be seven or eight hundred corpses spread over the tarmac and shining grass.

As we passed the last of the motorcyclists and turned onto the last exit road leading to the Queen's Building, Gellman's frown lifted slightly and he said, obviously thinking aloud, "I wonder why I need a driver's license."

"You'll know shortly," Michelle said. "Peace is waiting for us at the international arrivals in the Queen's Building."

Then, as the car turned into the unloading bays, I saw Peace standing beside the special pickup zone, and I knew immediately that there was going to be no point in asking him questions.

He was an actor, already well into a play. He was wearing what I had once heard Gellman call "post-hipster money clothes," the kind of flamboyant uniform that rock stars wear to financial conferences.

"Alan, Philip, good morning," he said jovially as the car pulled to the curb and we stepped out. "Michelle. Hi." Her name was an intentional afterthought, reminding me of the little verbal tricks with which he had tried to establish his authority at the cabin in Quebec.

But she was completely composed and showed no sign of irritation at Peace's manner.

"What do you want me to do with my driver's license?" Gellman asked bluntly. I could see the directness was an attempt to cut through Peace's sidewalk theatricals, but Peace was not going to be sidetracked before the big soliloquy.

Peace pulled his flared sheepskin jacket round him in a

gesture indicating that we were to move on. "I want you to rent a car," he said shortly. "Hairy will tell you why . . . in fact you can go and join him now. He's over there."

As Peace pointed toward the Middle East Airlines counter I saw Hairy standing beside it, wearing jeans and an odd-looking Indian tunic.

Without arguing, Gellman turned and set off toward him.

Peace smiled. "It's time for you to learn some more about our little campaign," he said. "I'll fill Alan in later. He has rather an important little job to do first. Come this way." He grinned. "It's finally time for you to take a look at our target."

He turned and we walked up the long moving ramp leading to the observation area of the Queen's Building, but at the upper level, instead of taking the main corridor leading to the long arc of glass windows projecting out over the runways, we walked down to the end of the building, which looked out over the back of the airport complex.

When we stopped, my eyes followed his outflung arm across the blocklike shapes of the cargo buildings to a slope right on the edge of the complex. The huge building was shaped like a single steel and glass half-moon, laid on its side, and along the top edge in giant letters was the word INTERMARK. Below it, pinned by invisible supports to the glass façade, was a company logo—five red circles, pierced by a single arrow rising vertically toward the sky.

The target was to be the Intermark Corporation, third largest multinational corporation in the world: a huge, almost limitless conglomerate whose tentacles reached into everything from oil, natural resources and transportation to food, hotels and correspondence courses.

"So that's our target," I said. "Intermark. Just like that."

"Yes," Peace said. "Just like that."

I stared across at the building and tried to remember what I knew about the company but one persistent image kept blocking out all the rest: the huge, bearded face of Peter

Sabara, an American, the president of Intermark.

Peter Sabara had been nicknamed by the media "the Pirate," and the Intermark style was naked aggression. A New York journalist had given him the name because "sailing is his hobby and plundering his greatest love." Privately, Sabara was known to relish the sobriquet. He had let his beard flourish and once, at a party in Paris, he had even worn a single gold earring.

Intermark's world sales exceeded $23 billion. It owned three hundred companies, making everything from oil tankers to cosmetics, but as Sabara often said, "Our business is not making things, it is making money."

Of the top ten conglomerates, only one other, Globex, was so diversified. Journalists loved to contrast the styles of their presidents. At least once a year, every financial writer had to do an article about "the Pirate" versus "the Accountant," contrasting Sabara's extroverted heartiness and massive, muscled body with the rimless glasses, slender frame and obsession with figures of Martin Axton, the president of Globex.

As targets for the Vikings, Globex and Intermark were about the most vulnerable of the big multinationals because of their diversity.

There was frequent speculation in the financial media that they shared too many markets and areas of activity for both to survive in the top ten, and the vicious rivalry between them was one of the constant features of international commerce.

If you were determined to wreak radical vengeance on only one, Globex would probably have been the more logical choice, as it was, if only marginally, the more ruthless, but I guessed that the Vikings had chosen Intermark because, given Sabara's stature in the world of business, it would be a stunning victory—if the Vikings won.

"You know all about Intermark, of course, Philip," Peace said as we stood by the glass picture windows. "Do you remember what they called that building a year or two back?"

"The glass trap," I said. "The Pirate's glass trap."

"Good. So you remember how Intermark got into the car-rental business."

"Yes," I said. "Doesn't everyone?"

Intermark had been in the middle of a big expansion of its British operations. They had come "company-shopping," as Sabara called it, and had spent $150 million in less than a year. One of the companies they had tried to buy was Wilson Car Hire, a long-established, slightly old-fashioned firm, with headquarters in London. Wilson had resisted; the takeover bid had failed and Peter Sabara did not like failure.

Put simply, in noncommercial terms, he had decided to have his revenge.

Intermark had started to build the airport car-rental terminal and announced that it was entering the field exactly nine months hence. Then it had leaked to the financial press the news that it had not acquired any car fleet or plant and equipment. The building was being constructed as an empty shell—and the message was not long coming through what they intended to put inside.

The media, quick to sense the drama, had coined the name "the glass trap." Using every trick in the City's black book, and ruining the reputation of an old-established merchants' bank in the process, Intermark took over Wilson one week after the building was completed. They used rumor and whisper and barely legal stock speculation against the company and when the deal was done, they fired every director and two thirds of the senior staff, leaving them to fight for compensation in the courts. Then they had set out to prove—with depressing ease—that the public really didn't care.

Pcace turned away from the window. "They have some very good architects," he said, "very good at carving messages in glass and stone. They've put the offices of just enough other Intermark interests in to give the impression of solidity and power—but not too many to overshadow the rental business.

"Now think about this, Philip." He smiled. "Altogether, it took Intermark nineteen months to build up that car-rental operation; we're going to destroy it for them in twenty-four hours."

He started to walk back down the observation area corridor. "We're going to open the war against corporate power with a techno-guerrilla campaign against Intermark Car Rentals—what the commercial people call a demonstration project. Not a big operation, just enough to let the world know who the Vikings are, to let Intermark know that they have an enemy with some class for a change and to work the bugs out of our own organization.

"Twenty-four hours after we start, I guarantee that no one will step into an Intermark rental car, anywhere in England . . . and I wouldn't think there'd be too much enthusiasm for their fleets in the States and Canada either."

He began to pick up speed and strode on toward the moving ramp.

"We're going over to the Intermark building now. I thought it would be a nice touch to brief you in their own building. Do you think the Pirate will like that?"

I did not laugh. In the communications age, all it took was a combination of technical know-how and moral mindlessness. The Vikings had both.

Peace led us back to the Rover and gave instructions to the driver. Michelle stayed silent, withdrawn. Peace made a point of having her sit up front with the driver.

"Now," he said, when we were settled inside, "you know enough about terrorism, Philip, to know that the campaign is going to have to be pretty spectacular.

"No one has heard of the Vikings. There are a lot of people competing for media space and, of course, we have to impress Intermark. The rental car thing is strictly a warm-up.

When we come back for the next bite, we want to make sure that Intermark will take us *very* seriously."

"Tell me something," I said. "Why Intermark? They're a bunch of bastards when you look behind the logo and the image, but they don't have a corner on corporate bastardy. Why not Globex?"

"It was a completely random choice. We decided to concentrate on one multinational corporation to make more impact. The others will get the message. We can't afford to dissipate our thrust."

It was plausible, yet it didn't sound quite right. . . . But there was no time to think about it then. We were close to the Intermark building, approaching the ramp which led under a sign marked: GENERAL INQUIRY—PARKING.

The approach was formed in two horseshoes—a big one under a smaller one. The bottom one carried up to gigantic garage doors where rental cars entered and left. The upper one led into a convoluted reception area for the main offices, where cars could be handed to company drivers to be valet-parked on the far side of the building.

Peace smiled. "We'll have coffee and I'll show you the plans we have for some changes in Intermark's operations."

The restaurant was on the mezzanine, projecting out over the main floor like a theater balcony. The hallmark of the interior style was a series of small glass scenic elevators which joined the various levels at high speed.

We took one up to the restaurant floor, found a table near the balcony edge and ordered coffee.

All the electronic toys—the computer terminals, the interbranch Telex units and the like—were very visible, in the latest corporate style: sharing with the customer, no secrets behind the desk. It was all designed for the illusion of freedom and swift flow, giving the impression that anyone could effortlessly walk into the hallway and walk away with a $5000 car.

When we had poured the coffee Peace carefully took a

135

little too long to put cream and sugar in his and then he said, "Philip, do you remember what the phrase 'in association with' came to mean in the Intermark context?"

I nodded, remembering the final press conference after the Wilson takeover.

Peter Sabara had announced with deliberate blandness that the Intermark Corporation, "in association with" Wilson Car Hire, was going to offer travelers a new concept in vehicle rental. It would draw on the best of both organizations and would be called Intermark Car Rentals. The chairman of Wilson had sat beside Sabara through the humiliation ceremony, then stood up and resigned, to have it accepted calmly, just before the Intermark president turned to the press to ask, "Any questions?"

The press had picked up the phrase and "in association with" had become synonymous with death by suffocation in the palm of a corporate giant.

"Now look at this," Peace said, reaching inside his coat and pulling out a slightly crumpled leaflet, printed in black on white, but with the red Intermark logo in one corner and a red Viking helmet with twin horns on the other.

"Intermark, in association with the Viking Guerrilla Organization, proudly announces Rental Excitement—another new concept in vehicle hire," the leaflet said.

> Are you bored with the humdrum routines of business?
>
> Would you like to know the excitement of international travel without ever leaving the ground?
>
> In the belief that citizens of our present-day consumer society are starved for excitement, Intermark is presenting a series of "guerrilla weeks" which will allow its customers to enjoy some of the biggest thrills of the present age.

Are you man enough—or woman enough—to deal with urban guerrillas? What would you do if you found your car was booby-trapped? Have you ever been hijacked? Test your personal survival skills with Intermark. Face murder, beating, arson, kidnap. This concept will allow every commercial traveler to know the excitement enjoyed by the Elizabethan merchant adventurers of glorious times past.

During guerrilla week, one car in every ten rented by Intermark will be designated as a target-car. Viking guerrillas will become your adversary. Your days of boredom will be over.

"Jesus bloody Christ," I said. I looked at Peace. His smile was beatific. "Is it a scare-threat or for real?"

"Philip," Peace said quietly. "You know how we operate. We deal only in realities. We'll be starting quite soon."

He picked up his coffee cup. "The final preparations are being made. Though Intermark doesn't realize it, they have had nine Vikings on their staff for the past six months. We have a few details left to settle, especially on the booby traps. We have a number of people doing studies on how long it takes to get cars out of the rental building and down onto various parts of the surrounding freeways."

"Is that what you've got Gellman doing?" I said sharply.

Peace nodded, sipping the coffee.

"For Christ's sake, why? You didn't kidnap a man with a mind like Alan's to make him a time and motion expert. What the hell are you playing at?"

Suddenly, icily, I knew.

"You've started the guerrilla campaign! You've started it, you bastard, and you've got Gellman down there in it."

Peace slowly put down his cup again. "Yes," he said. "You got off too lightly at the camp, Philip. That's why I put Gellman down there. You're learning about the Vikings with your head, but you haven't grasped them with your gut yet."

I jumped up and peered over the rail, searching the lines for Alan.

"He went through about ten minutes ago," Peace said. "While you were pouring your second cup of coffee. But don't worry. He's supposed to be very lucky and he has nine chances out of ten to survive."

The line of cars moving out of the garage was lengthening. Every minute or so, activated by an internal signal, the garage doors slid smoothly upward, moving so swiftly that they were clearly controlled electronically rather than mechanically. As soon as the opening was high enough, a rental car would pull out, pause briefly at a stop sign on the rim of the apron, then nose its way into the line wending downward toward the perimeter motorway.

As I watched, a trim orange Ford Capri with flashy black stripes down the side pulled out and stopped at the sign, then stalled, just as it was about to pull away.

We could hear no sounds through the glass, but the single figure of a young man behind the driving wheel was visible clearly enough to see that he was pulling on the starter, obviously without results.

A minute passed and another car pulled out behind him, blocking the retreat back into the garage, as there was no room for either vehicle to turn around.

The driver of the Capri got out and for a moment it looked as though he would open the hood of the car. He hesitated with his hand on the catch, then thought better of it and ran back into the garage through a small door farther along the wall.

I leaned forward in my seat, hands tensed. I couldn't take my eyes off the car. The driver came back and with him was an older man, wearing Intermark overalls and carrying a long gunmetal-gray toolbox. The mechanic went around to the front of the car and the driver, obviously afraid of dirtying his smart gray business suit, stood slightly back, looking over his shoulder.

The mechanic paused and put his hand on the hood with a gesture that seemed to mean the engine was hot, then he leaned down, pulled a lever under the radiator grill and swung open the hood.

You could only guess at the screams and the hissing, but the terror on the man's face was visible even as he tried to protect his head with his arms. A cloud of steam exploded out of the engine, enveloping the whole of his upper body, precipitating into scalding droplets of liquid all over his face and arms. The young driver was caught too, only slightly less directly, and staggered back, choking and stumbling.

Inside the terminal, people ran to the glass show-windows, and all around customers were standing up in the restaurant and upper level offices, craning for a better view.

Peace stood up too. "I suppose we'd better stand up," he said. "We don't want to seem too blasé even though it's quite a small accident. So easy to arrange too—a couple of chemical pellets in the radiator to make the cooling system overheat like crazy, and a little adjustment to the top pipe so it comes loose when you open the hood. Just like a champagne bottle that's been shaken too hard."

Two more mechanics had come running from inside the garage. One tried to help the injured men and the other tried to approach the engine from the side. Suddenly the whole engine seemed to explode in his face. When the smoke had cleared, the frame of the car was still intact but the man was on his knees, cradling his head in his arms, with his forehead almost touching the ground.

"Not steam that time," Peace said quietly. "We added just a touch of CS-18 anti-riot gas. You aren't supposed to go that close to it. It hurts the eyes and skin if you do."

Before I could speak, Peace had turned and put his hand on my wrist. "The message of that little trick was, 'Don't try

139

to interfere when an Intermark car is in trouble. It spoils the game and it's very dangerous.' There is a lesson there for you . . . and for Julia.

"Anyway. We got a lot of the ideas from you. Don't you remember your book? That little section 'Ingenuity in Terrorism.' It really set us a challenge."

Peace sat down again and picked up his coffee cup. "Accidents happen in garages all the time," he said. "Think about the manager. He's really got problems."

He glanced down at his watch.

"Just about at this moment, every newspaper, radio and television station in London is receiving messages about Guerrilla Week at Intermark Car Rentals. When you first read it, it looks like some kind of sick joke. No one is going to take it literally at first.

"The manager will get the flyers too. They've been sent to the Intermark head office on the Embankment and they'll be Telexed through. If you got one of those on your desk, would you pull out every stop and ask the police to declare an emergency and start trying to get all your cars back?

"He won't be sure enough. The first accident had a nice natural look about it. That was intentional too. When the media people start calling up . . . what will he say? What can he say? . . . That the whole thing is ridiculous. Yes, we've had an accident out front. Two of our employees were burned while they were trying to repair an overheating engine.

"He'll get away with it . . . until the next accident, which is due quite soon."

He pointed out over the apron. "Isn't random terror really intriguing? At this moment, I honestly don't know which cars are booby-trapped and it really doesn't matter. The Vikings who are rigging the cars in the garage don't care. They never see who gets into them. Anyone with a credit card can play."

There was nothing to say, nothing to be done. I couldn't

stop anything. All I could think about was Gellman. "You're insane, Peace, you're absolutely insane," I said through clenched teeth.

"That, Philip, is one of your truly silly remarks," he said. "You know perfectly well I'm not insane. You've written books about terrorism. You're just seeing it from the inside, that's all. You're not watching a lunatic. You're watching a terrorist who knows his business.

"In a minute you're going to see a little booby trap that was thought out especially with the televiewer in mind." He gestured toward the apron. "In a minute or two, some lucky Intermark customer is going to find that the interior of his car is starting to fill with tear gas. It won't hurt him if he thinks quickly, keeps his car under control and pulls over to the curb real fast.

"But if he should lose control, then the result is pretty spectacular, because if he bangs into anything, it's going to detonate a phosphorus grenade under the hood."

He broke off suddenly. "There," he said. "Down there . . . I think someone's number is about to come up."

I looked out and all that was happening was that something was going wrong with the patterns playing on the windows of the Intermark building. At first the cars were in loops and curves as they were supposed to be: two arcing lines down the ramp, two cloverleaf-eights at either side of the airport and, in between, four lanes of freeway traffic into which the rental cars were filtering. Then suddenly, the pattern became distorted.

A black Mercedes of the kind I had seen advertised in the Intermark literature was swinging out of lane, weaving— crossing and recrossing the main traffic lanes.

I pictured the driver, choking, panicking, holding desperately onto the wheel, pumping the brakes.

The pattern had gone haywire now as one of the following cars nudged a concrete buttress under the overpass and spun round, careening into the center lane where it was hit solidly from behind by a small open-backed truck. The driver of the black Mercedes was still holding on, slowing now, but as he veered one last time, a family-size Ford behind tipped the rear bumper.

There was a single flash—white first, then red, then black and the Mercedes was suddenly the charred base of a firework that was sending a plume of whirling flames and smoke into the air.

Without the noise and screams, it was a pure, beautiful image against the blue sky. There was no death or suffering, just a pattern of color, rising with clean lines compared to the tangle of metal on the highway below it.

Peace reached out and touched my arm again and this time I could feel his excitement.

"Now you can see that we're for real," he said. "The games are over."

Then with a movement that seemed to come almost in slow motion, he sat back in his chair and turned his face away from the direction of the window.

"That's enough of the brutal side for the moment," he said, resuming his cold, deliberately tantalizing voice. "That wasn't Gellman. I told him to rent a midpriced car. So you can relax. It's just another road death.

"We call our style of technological terrorism the Viking Process. The Viking style is subtle, beautiful, like an Oriental martial art. Think of it as technological judo: using the strengths of an organization against itself.

"Right at this moment, the management of Intermark Car Rentals is beginning to take the Viking threat seriously. They've realized that if the leaflet is only half true, they're going to have a lot of deaths and violence. So they must contact the drivers of the vehicles.

"But they have a problem. When Intermark took over Wilson Car Hire they put in the most sophisticated customer credit and billing system available at that time. At the core of it is one data storage drum. On that drum are the names of everyone who has a credit card, everyone who has ever rented an Intermark car, and using lists they've bought from agencies specializing in that kind of thing, they've put in everyone who might be a potential customer.

"Every minute or so, when a customer takes out a car, his data are flipped up onto the screen, to check his status in the car-rental universe. When he has his car, details like his home and business telephone numbers, his family contacts are all added to the store." He paused and opened his hands.

"About five minutes ago, that data drum unfortunately got erased. At this moment, Intermark has no idea who has their cars—or even who might have them."

He smiled nastily. "However, all is not lost. We didn't want to leave them completely in the dark, so before we erased the drum, we did one or two things to help them.

"Using all those neat multidestination telegram systems the Post Office has nowadays, we sent information about Guerrilla Excitement Week to all of the customers' homes and offices. So at least there's a fair chance that some of the people will call in to say their loved one or revered boss is currently in an Intermark car and are they all right.

"That should take care of the Intermark switchboard for a few hours. In fact, they'll probably have to pay to get some new lines in a big hurry.

"Incidentally . . . all the car radios in the cars that went out this morning have been doctored a bit. If the BBC starts broadcasting warnings, it will rather depend on whether you're in a roadside café having a coffee at the time.

"But there won't be any warnings yet anyway—because all that silly language on the flyers will still be having some effect. The security people will have been called in and they'll have read the Viking literature, and if I'm not mistaken, a lot of arguing will have broken out. In police work they have all kinds of fancy language for stalling like 'Put all units on standby.' All in all, I think it will be a while before we get full-scale countermeasures, don't you?"

He was exalted now, the prophet triumphant. "And there's just one last thing," he said. "We've been careful to see that not all the problems come from booby traps. Some of the violence is a bit more personalized. . . ." He lingered over the word.

"Some of the target cars really are going to get hijacked and the drivers are going to actually fall into Viking hands. That will personalize the Vikings, make them real.

"I have a feeling that by tomorrow there are going to be an awful lot of cars stuck in odd places around England that no one is willing to drive anywhere—even if the police have checked them out."

He looked down at his watch. "Now," he said, "sometime within the next five minutes, we shall know whether Gellman has been unlucky or not. I told him to be back here by eleven o'clock. He must be just about ready to come back up the ramp."

I leaped to the rail and stared down at the cars flowing around the building. The traffic had speeded up again on the motorway and the Mercedes and other burned-out shells had been moved onto the shoulder. Peace got up and stood beside me.

"He didn't get a car with a gas pellet," he said calmly. "And the hijackings are all going to happen well away from the airport. So he's got just one hazard left, the straight, old-fashioned bomb in the car. It's exciting, isn't it? Just think how many relatives and loved ones will be going through what you're going through before the game is over."

As the hypnotic lines and circles weaved, I let my eyes go out of focus and I thought of Alan. I had a silly image of him in my mind's eye, eating a sandwich in a restaurant in a tiny West African state.

The image of Alan was there when I saw the car explode on the freeway, and I knew with all the certainty the unconscious mind can possess that he was inside it.

The explosion was instantaneous. I couldn't even see

what kind of car it was. There was no plume of smoke, no break in the weaving patterns of traffic.

In a single instant, a ball came into existence—a huge black ball out of which sparks seemed to be showering into the wind. The ball expanded. It became a balloon rolling down the center of the freeway. I closed my eyes but the image was still there. The ball. The flames. Then the image lost its shape and all that was left in the darkness was the formless but absolute certainty that it was Gellman who had been killed.

PART

CHAPTER 12   When I opened my eyes, I threw myself across the table at Peace, grasping for any part of his body that I could break or crush.

I didn't think about killing him; it was just a total blind desire to hurt him, to put my pain at Gellman's death onto him, but there is no doubt I would have killed him if Michelle hadn't managed to get between us.

Reconstructing it later, some of the details were clear and some were hazy. I remembered the feeling of having my full weight against his leg as I pushed him back against the balustrade and trying to break it, as I groped for his throat and eyes.

Then there was Michelle's body, thrusting between us, and then I felt someone else on my back and we all went down onto the restaurant floor.

I didn't remember exactly when the drug went in, but I knew it was Michelle who had grabbed my wrist and managed to put the needle in while we were thrashing around on the floor.

Just before I passed out, I knew I had enough leverage on Peace's arm to dislocate his shoulder if I could only get it up high enough, and I remember thinking how fragile his bones seemed as I tried to maneuver his arm out from under the table to twist it upward.

After that, there were only fragments of images, like snatches of a drunken brawl.

When I came to, I was lying on my back, in bed at the

Blackheath house, naked, under a single sheet and blanket, staring at moonshadows on the ceiling.

I heard footsteps and Michelle came into the bedroom. She was wearing a blue sleeping robe and her hair was untied, but there was nothing casual about her look; she might as well have been wearing a hospital white coat.

She reached down and rolled back my eyelids and there was no sensation as her fingertips touched them.

"How do you feel?" she asked.

"I don't feel anything." My voice sounded remote and had the wrong timbre. "Is Gellman dead?"

"Yes."

"Just go back to sleep and dream of Julia."

I felt no pain or sorrow. Nothing registered and I closed my eyes and drifted into sleep.

When I woke up again it was daylight and Michelle was sitting at the foot of the bed, dressed in a brightly patterned silk shirt and an expensive-looking beige skirt.

She let me come fully awake, then she said, quietly, "You have some color back. How about feeling?"

"Yes," I said. "I can feel. And I feel like shit. You're very nifty with a needle."

"When you work around crazies, hitting a vein fast is a basic survival skill," she said.

"What happened to Peace?"

She smiled slightly. "He has a lot of bruises and a very sore shoulder. You were very rough with him."

"And Julia," I said. "What about Julia?" In my head, it seemed like a desperate, anxious question but I realized that my nerves were still partly anesthetized by the drug.

"Nothing has happened so far."

"You mean there have been no sanctions?"

"No," Michelle said. "There's no point in talking about sanctions for something like trying to kill Peace. I've persuaded them that Gellman's death put you under exceptional and unnecessary stress."

The drug made the words acceptable. With my emotions stilled, they seemed simply an odd tag, attached irrelevantly to the death of a friend.

"Why did you help me?" I asked.

She got up from the bed, turned away, brushing aside any hint of collusion. "I've spent over a year preparing you for this project. I'm not going to have it all wrecked by one of Peace's ego trips. But it's lucky for you they need you."

When she left, I lay staring at the ceiling again and thinking, "Yes, it's lucky, but why do they need me still?"

It couldn't be to help with the planning. They had lied about that. I was sure they wouldn't start the campaign against the car rentals if the rest wasn't ready. The follow-up would have to be swift.

So why did they want me? The best guess I could make was that I was to be sacrificed at the end of the campaign. I would be the leader—the one who was arrested or who died, dramatically, in a hail of police bullets, conveniently closing the case. And it would work. If Peace, Hairy and Michelle all dropped away, the authorities would be left with me and a group of Vikings who had acted on orders coming out of the Institute for Social Change—my institute.

There was no longer any doubt that there was someone else behind Peace. Michelle had talked about convincing "them."

But what kind of radical guerrillas needed a front man? If the Vikings did succeed in destroying Intermark, why would their leaders want to stay in hiding, leaving a straw man to take the credit for such a spectacular revolutionary coup?

A familiar nagging doubt returned: What if they were not radicals at all? I tried to go carefully over the options and thought of a dozen bizarre possibilities from a CIA plot to discredit radicalism to a whim of some millionaire crazie who wanted to be different and destroy the right instead of the left.

The CIA idea was the most likely but I could not bring myself to take it seriously. I had only intuition to go on, and ten years' experience of watching the CIA at work, but the feel of the Viking operation was not right for them. But if the Vikings were not radicals and not government, then who were they? As I pondered, Michelle came back.

"You'd better get up and go into the garden for a while," she said. "The air will help you get yourself together."

She left before I could argue, so I got dressed and went outside and stared at my favorite Tree of Heaven in the garden instead of at the ceiling, trying not to think about the giant balloon of fire rolling down the freeway with Gellman inside it.

After a while, I heard the telephone ring. I heard Michelle answer it, then I heard her hurrying downstairs.

As she came into the garden, she looked worried. "How do you feel? Is the dope through your system yet?" she asked, then added, "I only gave you a tiny dose," as if willing me to say I felt better.

"I'm surviving," I said. "The best I can describe it is like coming back into the real world after a long illness."

"Well you'll have to manage," she said. "Peace just called. He's back at the institute and Jack Wescott has been there, looking for you. Apparently he made a nuisance of himself and he's determined to see you. Peace is going to get in touch with him now, and tell him to call you here, at the house." She hesitated, as if knowing that she was saying something that should not be said.

"Peace says you've got to stall Wescott for at least two weeks. He's alerted the surveillance team and you'd better make sure you do it right."

Out there, beyond the house, wheels were turning that might help me out of the cube. Perhaps I had been put under surveillance by Pearson's security people already. Perhaps someone was beginning to understand.

I should have been thinking calmly about devising a code for my contact with Wescott, instead of having to fight off the effects of a drug that had been given me because I couldn't keep a grip on myself.

I went upstairs to wait for the call and when it did come, I picked up the receiver with the leaden feeling that I had blown a chance to reach outside the cube. Then I heard Wescott and I felt a rush of relief.

I had made no preparations for the call. But Jack had. Though the words were harmless I could tell from his tone and I was sure too that the surveillance team would not know.

"Philip," he said.

"Jack, how are you?"

"Not so good, thanks to you, you bastard." There was faint, rueful mock heartiness in the voice that would, I was sure, sound plausible to the surveillance team. But I knew it simply wasn't Jack.

"I'm sorry about the dinner," I said. "I seem to have made rather a mess of things."

"I'm getting over it, but Jane isn't. I'm in the doghouse along with you, over Miranda."

Doghouse was a word Wescott would never use. I knew that but would the listeners? I hesitated.

"Look, Jack, maybe it will all blow over. Maybe we should leave it for a while. I don't want to mess everything up with Jane."

If he agreed, I knew I had lost my chance, but I knew I dare not say less.

"I think so too," Wescott said. "But I still want to hear about it all. Maybe we could go climbing. Talk about it away from Jane.

"Look, Andy Johnson is coming back from the States. He wants us all to get together. Can you make it?"

I hesitated again, trying to find exactly the phrase to tell

Wescott I knew what he was trying to do. "I'd really like that," I said, trying to sound disappointed. "But I can't get away. Not right now anyway. I've got a helluva lot of work to catch up on that won't wait."

"There's no hurry," Wescott said. "Let me know when you're free. I'll set up a meeting with Andy. Try and make it sometime, though." There was a pause. "We can't just let it all go to hell like this."

"I'll try as soon as I can," I said. "And thanks for calling. Good luck with Jane."

"I'll need it, you old sod. Next time, stay away from sexy ladies, will you," Wescott said, and hung up.

As I put down the receiver, I heard Michelle's laughter from the top of the stairs. "Chauvinists of the world unite," she said. "Jesus Christ." But despite the sarcasm, I could see she was relieved.

"Do you care," I said, "as long as the Lord Peace is satisfied?"

"No," she said. "That was okay. Now I must get back to work."

I heard her go back into the bedroom and I went back to the garden to try to calm myself down. I had the message I wanted from Wescott and I was sure no listeners could have spotted it. I could think of no way that Peace could know that Andy Johnson was dead, that he had died in a rockfall when we were still students together.

The name was Wescott's code word for a place. He was suggesting a rendezvous and I knew that if I could only find a way to get out of my cube for just a few hours, Wescott would be waiting there, ready with help. The place was the Barbary Tower, a strange Victorian folly in St. John's Wood.

One night after a dinner of the Cambridge Mountaineering Club, the three of us—Andy Johnson, Wescott and I—had climbed it. Building climbing had been a fad among mountaineers when I was at Cambridge and we had done the Barbary Tower at crazy speed, still drunk from the dinner and the mountain talk.

The message was clear. There was a chink in the cube and I knew I had two weeks to find a way to use it.

CHAPTER 13 "The next scenario is based on sex, not violence. Hotels and sex go so well together, don't you think?"

We were standing in the entrance of the London-Intermark. As he spoke, Peace pointed to a huge banner strung across the hotel lobby, suspended between two fake marble pillars.

"We're just going to have some fun with the natural urges of these good people."

I read the sign. INTERMARK HOTELS WELCOMES THE MEDIA EXECUTIVES OF NORTH AMERICA.

"Sex not violence," Peace repeated. "You can relax. This is one you can enjoy."

The scene in the lobby was no particular surprise. The London-Intermark was primarily a convention hotel, which in practical terms meant it had been designed to cater to that inexplicable American desire: to travel without moving.

If you wanted to visit London without leaving Chicago, this was the hotel for you and the Media Executive delegates were clearly completely at home.

They were all dressed in convention uniform—business suits and dresses to go with business suits—and wore large, colorful name tags on their chests. As we came in, I had passed close enough to read one which said, "Hi. I'm Hal. Glad to meet you," with the crest of the Media Executive Association.

"Did you ever see such a bunch of jerks?" Peace said as we walked through the lobby. "It took Intermark's convention people two years to get them here. There are three hundred of them and they meet once a year. It's their first time in an Intermark hotel. They've been given unbelievable concessions on rates. Half of their stay has been written off against the hotel's PR budget. They're supposed to be 'target material' for spreading the Intermark message across the States." He smiled his irritating, cool smile. "We thought they'd be ideal for spreading the Viking message, too."

There were three times the usual number of security men in the lobby, stationed in twos behind pillars and next to the check-in counters and information desk. Peace noticed them and smiled. "Sabara has flown in from New York. He'll be here shortly. The Pirate is very upset." Peace chuckled at the thought.

"You know how he likes to pretend that his cars are an extension of his own hospitality. He even says things like 'Why don't you borrow one of my cars?'" Peace smirked. "Well, he can't say that any more because the rental-car operation was closed down officially this morning. They've got a hundred cars stranded all over southern England. No one will touch them. The police have had to put them in special pounds until the bomb squad goes over them one by one.

"Ninety percent of their reservations cancelled out." He smiled. "The other ten percent must be the blind and the deaf and the ones who don't watch television. There's been panic in the associated companies in the States and Canada too. We've helped it along with cables saying 'Good news. Car-rental excitement coming to your territory soon.'"

Peace gestured around the lobby.

"Mr. Sabara also likes to say to hotel guests, 'Welcome to my home,' but I think he'll have stopped doing that by tomorrow."

I noticed that Peace said it with special intensity. He was clearly relishing the thought of Sabara's anguish and was seeing the enemy as a person as much as a corporation.

"Here they come," he said. "The Pirate and his court."

We stood back beside one of the pillars and watched as more than thirty people entered the lobby, moving quickly and decisively toward the elevators. It was hard to tell who was who, but the general rule seemed to be that the body-guards were bigger than the corporate courtiers.

However, there was no mistaking Sabara. His thick beard and massive muscular frame stood out even above the inner circle of bodyguards packed close in around him.

"Christ, he looks angry," Michelle said, "and he's got a lot of the brass with him. There's half the 'quarter-of-a-million club' there."

Sabara had made it well known that he paid himself the highest salary of any corporate executive in the world— $950,000 a year. Beneath him, there were six regional presidents who were paid $250,000 a year, and it was said that they enjoyed their status in the "club" as much as the money.

"Yes, he does look angry, doesn't he?" Peace said. "But not nearly as angry as he's going to be when the next scenario is over."

"You're not going to attack Sabara?" I said. "You're not that crazy."

Peace smiled. "We're not going to attack his body. Just his mind. We're going to destroy his entire beloved hotel chain and he won't even know it's happened . . . until it's too late."

He saw me tense slightly and said quickly, "Don't worry, Philip. There aren't going to be any bombs . . . no terrible scenes of flying glass and broken bodies in the swimming pool. That's not our style this time. We made our point in the car-rental scenario. We know how to be vicious. Now we can afford to be subtle."

I was already beginning to feel uneasy. He was protesting too much, I was sure. But I could only wait and watch.

I noticed Michelle was looking hard at him and he hesitated. I read the exchange as meaning that I was not to be upset, and I wondered again how much of the truth they would tell me about the hotel scenario. I was to be nursed along. But I had decided already that I would be their puppet for as long as I had to, to find out what was behind them. And who. Until then, I would accept whatever I had to accept.

"We're just going to use sex to convey to the media executives that staying in an Intermark hotel isn't a very good idea," Peace continued.

"We have a scheme that's really worthy of the communications age. We're going to turn Intermark Hotels on its ear and we're going to use just twenty guests and we won't even have to gather them in one place. There'll be nothing for any security guard to see. It will all be done by mirrors—or rather cameras."

He smiled a mock conspiratorial smile at Michelle. "As Philip discovered in Montreal, it is possible for a hotel room to be very private and very public at the same time."

The room Peace had rented in my name was 1106 and it was the kind of room that could have been slotted into a hundred different hotels in twenty countries, without anyone noticing the difference. It was comfortable, antiseptic and tasteless, or rather it was decorated with the basic American nontaste that was international hotel style.

Peace let me look around for a few moments, then he said, "There are really only two things you need to look at: the lock and the television set."

He walked over to the door and put his hand on the inside knob. "As you see, it's one of the latest electromagnetic locks. No key. Just a plastic card which is issued to the guest."

He put his hand into his pocket and pulled out a metal cube, not much bigger than a golf ball. "You hold this next to the lock, press this button and zap . . . until further notice you can forget about opening the door, either with the guest card or the hotel master cards. The lock is stuck, period. Until you unscramble its brains by reversing the process.

"Now . . ." he came back into the center of the room, "item two—the television set."

"This," Peace said, pulling a small brochure from his pocket, "is a very interesting document which is sent to the management of every big convention hotel by Hotel-View, the pay-TV company with most of the concessions for the full-length movies that you pay to watch in your room, without commercial interruptions, as they say."

He flipped the pasteboard pages over and held the last one out toward me.

"Do you know what this tells us? Well, it tells us in statistical form something we know already: that a lot of people have dirty minds and like to watch blue movies."

He pointed to some figures in red in a little box on the last page.

"If you look at these figures," he said, "you'll see that whenever that ultimate flesh-and-lust epic *A Night in Rio* is shown as a late-evening feature, about eighty-two percent of the guests in each hotel stay in their rooms and pay a special six-dollar fee to watch it. Pretty impressive when you consider that most of them have made a transatlantic flight to get here. You'd think they'd want to be out 'seeing London' or some such nonsense but *Night in Rio* wins every time."

"And it isn't even any great hell of a sex movie," Michelle said with a little sneer. "People's frustration level is just unbelievable. It's just a male-oriented fantasy with a lot of lingering looks at the female in heat. Even the camera work is lousy."

"Anyway," Peace interrupted, "all you need to know for our purposes is that a very large number of guests will be in their rooms while it's on . . . and we can be extra sure because we know from the convention manager's records that the Media Executives carefully avoided having any of their social functions at a time that might clash with it.

"Now," he went on brusquely, "hotel TV sets are always sealed so you can't tamper with them and they are always in a commanding position in the room.

"When color television was first introduced, people stole the tubes like crazy. One chain lost two hundred tubes at sixty dollars each within a week of going to color. So the hotels got the TV manufacturers to design guest-proof backs." He smiled. "Which means that once a TV set has been doctored Viking style, there's not much a guest can do about it, except smash it to pieces, and people are surprisingly reluctant to do that.

"As for the commanding position, now, most hotels make sure that you can't move the TV set . . . and that it's somewhere it can be seen from all the key places in the room." He flashed a quick, humorless grin.

"Which means, of course, that if you add a little camera to the set, it can see you in all the key places in the room.

"So you now have all the elements for an interesting do-it-yourself project.

"The Media Executives of North America like to watch blue movies. We're going to help them to make their own blue movie."

"What do you mean, make their own?" I asked, although my mind was already racing ahead and I knew what they had in mind.

"Tonight at eleven o'clock about twenty executives from the media convention who have been carefully chosen for their interesting bedroom habits are going to take part in a live, closed-circuit TV show, substituting for *A Night in Rio*," Peace said.

"What about the hotel security system?" I said. "What happens when the people in the rooms realize what's going on and start panicking?"

"Philip, you must give us credit for thinking about all this rather carefully," Peace said, returning to his maddening, casual tone.

"We're limiting the scenario to about twenty people—with some actors in reserve in case some go out. Remember it will be eleven o'clock. They will have settled in for the night. They will lock their doors and most of them will not try them again so they won't know they are locked in. They will find out as soon as the fun starts, then they will start to phone out. But unfortunately, their lines will not be connected. We've already doctored the main switchboard so that twenty lines can go dead without any sign of it showing up to the hotel operators. No one will be surprised if they dial in and get a busy signal. It's blue movie time. As you'll see, people do some interesting things during blue movies. It's phone-off-the-hook and enjoy time. There is no room service. They can get everything—ice, drinks, food—from the computer toys.

"The security people will see nothing, of course. Most of the surveillance is done by video monitors but they don't have cameras in the rooms"—he grinned nastily—"only Vikings can do that. So the rent-a-cop security people see mostly the hotel corridors. The doors are virtually soundproof. The monitors will see the occasional hotel employee circulating on the upper floors.

"I have the feeling that the occupancy rate is going to take a rather spectacular nosedive. We're going to make the glossy life of international expense account living just a little less glossy."

He paused, waiting for me to comment.

"That's all true," I said. "But why Intermark? Why not Globex? They'd be a more obvious target for this scenario. They have more hotels and an even nastier reputation for exploitation than Intermark."

Was it my imagination, or did Peace hesitate just a second too long before giving his stock answer?

"As I told you before, Globex and the rest will come later. We have to show we have the power to destroy one multinational corporation. We mustn't dissipate our strength.

"Come on downstairs again. I have to show you the rest of the technical side of do-it-yourself blue movies."

As we walked to the bank of elevators and descended to the lobby, I looked at the hotel in a new light after Peace's monologue, and I realized just how automated hotel management had become. Peace was quite right. You could isolate twenty rooms in a thousand-room hotel without anyone knowing until it was too late. All it took was a handful of Vikings and they were already in place.

We left the hotel in the Rover and drove through a succession of side streets and alleys to a cul-de-sac about a mile away.

Parked at the end was a three-ton van, painted in subdued colors. WESTINGALE'S TV REPAIR, it said on the side. "Customer service—all makes."

Peace opened the rear doors and ushered me inside. Michelle followed and closed the doors behind us.

Inside there was enough space for us to stand facing a triple row of TV monitor screens—nine in all—along one wall.

"There's nothing special about this rig," Peace said. "You could mix a modest TV show from it. It's a bit better equipped than the average outside broadcast van, but not much."

There was one very small chair facing the panel and Peace sat down in it, leaving Michelle and me standing behind him.

He touched what seemed to be a master switch on the control panel and nodded toward the clock above one row of screens.

"It's twelve o'clock," he said, "so there's just a chance some of our actors will be in their rooms changing for lunch. Let's have a look."

He started playing with the switches, and onto the screen, in sequence, came the images of several hotel rooms similar to the one we had just left.

They were all empty and the camera eye stared at the un-ruffled beds and newly tidied surrounds.

"Let's see if our big stars are in," he said. Michelle laughed. "You'll like our male lead. He's Clarke Boorman. He publishes a chain of small-town newspapers in the Southwest. Pillar of virtue. Prominent in one of those Bible Belt chapels. Has a two-minute speech he will give before any audience of suitably worthy-minded people about the need for America to return to the old-time virtues."

Peace laughed. "And he likes conventions because it gives him a chance to leave all that shit back home and screw around with a chick called Molly Cassidy."

He adjusted the image on one of the screens. "We're in luck. There she is."

On the screen was a room bigger than the ones we had seen before, and in the middle of it was an attractive but artificially beautiful girl of about twenty-three. She had the figure of a hometown beauty queen, with monstrous breasts and hips that jutted out through a skimpy mini-dress.

"She's quite a sexy little thing actually," Michelle said, "but Boorman is like a drunken whale. He weighs about two-fifty and has no idea how to handle himself in bed. He has some very funny little tricks, but she puts up with him for the sake of an apartment in Phoenix and a lot of time when she doesn't have to see him."

As Michelle was speaking, the girl was standing at the closet, looking through a row of dresses. Despite myself, I could feel my excitement rising, and I suddenly felt Michelle's hand on my neck.

"You're flushing," she said. "You're discovering the joys of personalized voyeurism." She laughed. "Think of it as the poor man's seduction. When you watch a girl like this, it's a cheap version of a beautiful moment when you're in the middle of a seduction number and you suddenly realize, 'My god, she's going to. I'm really going to see that beautiful body and touch it and penetrate it.'

"This is a watered-down version. See but no touch . . . but it's better than nothing."

From the row of hangers, the girl chose a blue dress with a skirt slightly longer than the one she was wearing. She put it on the bed and started to unfasten the narrow leather belt round her waist.

As her fingers touched the top button of her mini-dress, Peace put his hand on the switch.

He waited until she had unbuttoned it almost down to the waist then he flicked the switch and the screen went blank.

"That's enough of a trailer, Philip," he said. "We wouldn't want to spoil the show scheduled for tonight."

When they took me back to the van that night, they put me inside, locked the doors and left me alone. Peace dropped me there at exactly ten minutes to eleven. He looked inside briefly to see that the panel of monitor screens was switched on, but he made no attempt to tell me how it worked.

"You'll be able to figure it out for yourself," he said, when I asked. "It will keep you amused until showtime. Just don't try to damage anything. This is only a monitor van . . . the control panel is somewhere else. Whatever you do here, you can't change what's happening in the hotel. So just sit tight and see how a white scenario works."

When I was alone inside the van, I checked over the screens and found that I could work out easily what they were all for. On the main right-hand monitor was the regular program going out over the London-wide hotel pay-TV network. On the screen was the end of a popular first-run musical film about horse-racing, and the final credit titles were just rolling. When the credits had finished, a pretty blonde-haired announcer came onto the screen and urged viewers in a mock-sexy voice not to miss the special late-night adult presentation of *A Night in Rio*.

The clock on the monitor panel showed two minutes to

eleven and the rest of the screens were still showing vertical color bars.

At thirty seconds before eleven o'clock, the central monitor came alive and I recognized with a little shock that the girl on the screen was Maria, the girl I had seen during the random interrogation session of Rory at the camp, the one Peace had described as a natural sadist.

She was naked except for a pair of white bikini briefs with little bows at the side and her black hair had been carefully combed so that it fell into symmetrical showers of ringlets on each shoulder.

She was standing in front of what looked like the set of a television game-show with, on one side, a huge wire cage in which numbered Ping-Pong balls were bouncing around and, on the other, a large TV screen that was blank.

As the second hand moved toward eleven o'clock, she was obviously composing herself to be live and on camera. Meanwhile, on the right-hand monitor, the credits for a *Night in Rio* were beginning to roll and I guessed that I was now looking at two circuits. The *Night in Rio* film was going out normally to the majority of the rooms on the network and Maria to only the twenty people Peace had chosen as targets.

"Good evening, ladies and gentlemen," Maria said. "My name is Jennifer, the Intermark girl, and I'm here to welcome you to a very special gala screening of a *Night in Rio*, with our own special premovie contest.

"Tonight, Intermark Hotels is pleased to announce a special contest with as first prize—yes, ladies and gentlemen—a night in Rio. So let me begin by introducing tonight's contestants who have all been chosen from among our special guests at the London-Intermark, the Media Executives of North America."

I had stopped thinking about the mechanics of the operation now. My eyes were fixed on the control panel, and suddenly on the monitor next to the one with Maria on it, another screen came to life.

On one screen I could hear Maria saying, ". . . let me introduce our first contestant, ladies and gentlemen . . . Mr. Clarke Boorman, the newly elected international president of the Media Executives of North America and his lovely companion, Miss Molly Cassidy."

As she spoke, the camera moved onto her studio monitor and suddenly the images on the two adjacent screens in the van had become identical.

They showed a man sitting on a sofa, obviously directly in front of his hotel TV set. He was wearing green and white striped shorts which reached almost to his knees and hung, rumpled and baggy, around the layers of a grossly flabby body.

His whole body was white and soft and there were big pads of fat wherever there should have been muscles. He had close-cut gray hair and a heavy-set face which would probably have made him look fairly imposing when dressed, but naked he was an unimpressive sight.

Across his knee, lying on her back, was Molly, the girl I had seen earlier in the day. Her shoulders and head were disengaged from Boorman and rested against the arm of the sofa. It was as if her body was made up of two independent halves. The top half was watching TV and eating an apple. The bottom half was offering itself to Boorman, whose hands were groping inside a pair of high-waisted ballooning pants that were obviously part of a "birthday present from boyfriend" nightdress set.

When they both saw their own picture on the screen they were watching, they started, but the effect of Boorman's reaction was to throw Molly off his knee and onto the floor. Despite the horror, it was impossible not to laugh, especially as Boorman actually stepped on her on his way to peer at the screen, as though he would understand more clearly what was happening if he could look inside the set.

As his face came into grotesque close-up, the camera switched to Maria, who was saying rapidly, ". . . and our second contestant is . . ." and pointing toward the monitor screen.

Without the battery of monitor screens recording the whole cueing pattern, I saw that it would take several minutes of indescribable confusion for people in each room to figure out what was happening. As they did so, they were treated to a series of rapid-fire images: a room-by-room tour to meet the other "contestants" in a series of unforgettable pictures.

The twenty had been chosen, as Peace had promised, to give the whole spectrum of sexual permutations: male on male, male on female, female on female, couples and odd numbers—the whole panorama of hotel bedroom sexuality down to the man in shirttails alone with his TV screen.

The cameras were cued to each room only once and I could only guess at the reactions of each, after they had seen themselves on the screen. But what could they do? Shout and scream unheard, pound on the magnetically sealed soundproof doors, rattle the receivers of dead telephones, weep, cry, scream . . . all in the computerized anonymity of a giant hotel. Most, I guessed, would rush back to the screen where Maria was back on camera again, standing beside the cage full of numbered balls.

"And now, ladies and gentlemen, the draw," she said, "but before we pick the lucky room number, let me tell you a bit more about the grand prize.

"In the interests of broadening international understanding, Intermark has kindly agreed not to send the winning contestants for a conventional night at the Rio-Intermark, wonderful though that would be.

"Instead the winners will be enjoying a most unusual prize. They will be able to experience a night in Rio as it has been experienced by hundreds of freedom fighters, struggling against world capitalism and the power of the multinational corporations.

"Ladies and gentlemen, our grand prize is an authentic simulation of a night at Rio's Sierra Detention Center . . . and the lucky winner is . . ." She pressed a button and the machine projected a ball out onto the stage. She let it bounce, then ran after it, picked it up and held it in front of the camera.

"Ladies and gentlemen, number fourteen thirty-two. Mr. Clarke Boorman and Miss Molly Cassidy."

The camera flashed back immediately to the Boorman bedroom where Boorman was standing beside the bed, shouting frantically into the dead phone. Molly was standing at the closet again, making a frenzied search through her wardrobe, rejecting item after item as though her choice of clothing might in some way mitigate the horror that was coming.

Before she had chosen a garment, there was a sound of hammering on the door. I imagined how it would look from the corridor. Two or three hotel employees answering what . . . ? A TV repair call.

Then the door burst open and I saw that they must have been hiding in an adjacent room because their costume was so bizarre that it could not have passed for any kind of hotel uniform, except in a quick dash across the corridor.

The first figure to enter was a man who came in backwards, pulling on a mask as he did so. When he turned, Molly Cassidy screamed, and I saw that it was a grotesque fright-mask, on top of an all-black security force uniform.

There were five Vikings in all: three male and two female versions of the same police state nightmare, and with them they were dragging what looked like a room-service trolley, covered with a white tablecloth.

Before they were fully through the door, Boorman had found the courage to try to block their entry. He leaped over the bed and threw all his weight against the first man, clawing at the gargoyle face under the peaked cap. The man side-stepped effortlessly, brought up a truncheon from the side of his leg and smashed Boorman across the naked stomach, sending him to the floor, wheezing and crying with pain.

Molly turned from the closet and tried to get around the bed but another masked figure jumped after her, truncheon raised. Instead of swinging at her, he leveled the club like a sword and thrust the end hard below her rib cage and she fell, sobbing, to her knees beside the bed.

As she fell, the cameras switched back to Maria.

"Now, ladies and gentlemen, you are going to see an authentic interrogation, using equipment manufactured by Intermark-Electronics, a little-known subsidiary which supplies high-quality instruments of torture and interrogation widely used in Vietnam, Greece and a number of Latin American countries," she said, and the camera panned back to the hotel room.

The Vikings had erected two pyramid-shaped whipping frames of the kind they had used in Derbyshire and hung Boorman and Molly, one on each.

"The Intermark auto-interrogator we are using tonight incorporates all the latest developments in bio-monitoring technology and electro-torture," Maria's voice continued as the Vikings moved swiftly around the two figures, attaching adhesive electrodes to their temples, chest and wrists, with wires leading to a panel of dials and switches, revealed now that the cloth had been removed from the serving trolley. "With the auto-interrogator, breathing, heart rate and pulse are monitored and reduced to a single life-indicator and displayed on the little screen you see to the left of the victim. The monitors are linked by minicomputer to the source of the current so that the maximum charge that can be withstood by the victim at any given moment is measured and automatically applied."

She smiled sweetly. "The unit even comes with interchangeable sets of electrodes to fit all parts of the body."

The camera cut close to one of the female Vikings who

was holding up a pair of claws and a pair of three-inch spikes with rubber bases and slipping them on and off the ends of the wires, like an air hostess demonstrating the emergency oxygen equipment before takeoff.

Although the audio levels were obviously being adjusted in the control room, Maria's voice was almost drowned out by the screams of Molly Cassidy as a Viking attached a wired claw to her left shoulder, then fixed a second claw at the top of Boorman's spine.

Then, for an instant, there was no commentary, only the shrieks and the sobbing, as one of the men pressed a small lever at the side of the unit.

Boorman screamed too and both bodies twisted in the frames and sweat began to pour from their skin. On the display screens a line of red blips raced across the bottom segment, rising upward toward the green life-indicator, then falling back down again.

"And now a quick look at our other contestants, as we may yet need a lucky runner-up to fill in, should Mr. Boorman and Miss Cassidy not feel able to enjoy the interrogation long enough to fill the time allotted for your viewing pleasure," Maria's voice intoned.

CHAPTER 14   After that the screens went dead. I tried to get out of the van, but the doors were still locked and there were no sounds in the street outside.

I sat in the dark and forced myself to let the images of the scenario play back in my mind. Even allowing for the mock television-contest heartiness, it had sounded odd. It had the same feeling to it as when an advertising copywriter used the "ecological message" or the "women's liberation message." This was the "freedom fighter message" and there was something too cold and cynical about it that I couldn't fully understand.

I was becoming more and more certain now that they were not genuine radicals. I tried to cast the problem in the form of the classic question in the politics of war: who gains by the conflict? But I was too tired to concentrate and eventually I let myself fall asleep.

When I was wakened by the sound of the engine starting up, it was already half-past eight and I could see daylight through the crack between the doors of the van.

I hammered on the partition next to the driver's cab but I got no response. We drove for nearly half an hour and then stopped and it was Michelle who opened the door.

I knew immediately that we were playing some kind of game again. She was smiling and relaxed, dressed in typical suburban housewife's casual garb.

"I thought I'd take you shopping," she said. "Take your mind off the Vikings for a bit."

I looked around and saw that we were in the parking lot

of a supermarket. FOODWAY CITY, the peeling lettering read, ALL YOU NEED TO EAT UNDER ONE ROOF. The checkout counters were visible through the glass front; they had old-fashioned cash registers. Though the store had only just opened, there were already a hundred or so shoppers, most of them women, pushing carts along the aisles, some with the inevitable children perched in the basket seats.

"Where the hell are we?" I said.

"Lewisham." She smiled. "It's a pretty dingy sort of supermarket but it's the nearest one to Blackheath and I'm American enough not to like shopping for food in a hundred different little shops."

Was this some kind of test? I followed her inside, we took a cart and started off up the first aisle. She pushed the cart firmly on ahead and started to choose packages quickly from the shelf.

I followed her and said quietly, "Did you watch the scenario last night?"

"I don't need to. That's not my part." I sensed immediately what she was doing. She was gathering her psychologist's detachment around her like armor.

"Did Boorman get around to his paddle number last night?" she said. "You know he puts that Molly chick across his knee and whacks her with his wife's sorority initiation paddle. He brings it to every convention, wrapped in a blue cloth bag so it won't get scratched and his wife will notice when he puts it back. Jesus, people are weird. If only they'd bring all those fantasies out into the open. Make use of them. Stop pretending they believe in such antiquated sexual codes."

She meant it to sound contemptuous but she said it too loudly.

She pointed angrily down the aisle to where a young woman in an ultrashort pink miniskirt, with a child in a stroller beside her, was reading a magazine at the display counter.

173

"Look at that chick," she said. "Nice little respectable young housewife and mother, dutifully doing the morning shopping before going home to change and feed her nice new infant. Now look at her face. Do you know what's on the centerfold of that magazine? It's a guy with a cock like an elephant's sitting in a barber chair with a woman hairdresser scooting around, symbolically castrating him by snip-snipping at his hair."

She laughed suddenly and I could see the thought had relieved some of her own tension. "But you should never be surprised at young mummies, though. They get married and they get initiated. Then they have a kid and once you've run a kid through the reproductive system you find out the equipment isn't as fragile as you thought it was, so you start getting interested in some real action.

"Meanwhile, daddy is getting all tender over the kid and starts projecting all kinds of tenderness and fragility onto her. Result, one superfrustrated young mummie looking for excitement. I have really great success with young mummies at my club."

"What club?" I asked. I could see she was being carried away by her tough-sexologist routine but I had never heard her mention anything before that didn't seem to have to do with the Vikings.

She laughed. "My club is something you really aren't ready for," she said. "It's a sex club. It's the most advanced sex-research project currently in progress. It's what I'm really into."

I didn't see much chance but I knew I had to try. If the sex club was a real club, with a building, and it didn't come under Peace's control, I had to see if she would take me there.

"How do you know I'm not ready for it?" I said, as calmly as I could manage.

"Actually, the club is designed for people just like you,"

she said, in a mocking tone. "People who are starting to come unglued in the permissive society.

"Like the husband who is finding lifelong monogamy a heavy trip and looks up every skirt that passes, then plays around, gets divorced, abandons the kids, looks up some more skirts, then crumples into a heap because he finds out he really can't deal with permissiveness. He doesn't have the skills for it."

The pride in her voice now was unmistakable. "There are better ways of organizing sex in a society. That's what the club is for. To toughen people up sexually, so they can handle sexuality without rigid structures."

She laughed. "You'd be the perfect candidate. I'd love to work with you. But you'd need a lot of getting ready."

"How do you know when people are ready?" I said carefully.

"I've found a neat method," she said. "I show them films —films of the club. They're some of the best blue movies ever made, actually."

"Would you let me see them?"

She stopped short suddenly, as if realizing how far she had let herself be carried away.

"Don't be ridiculous. All that stuff is outside your little cube. If you're looking for escape routes, you'll have to think again."

I noticed that her hands were no longer clenched. Her mood changed suddenly. "Come and help me find some meat. We have to hurry. Peace will be here in a minute."

"Peace? Why is he coming? Did he tell you to bring me here?"

She saw my look and said indifferently, "Don't start getting uptight. He just wants to talk to you. He knew I wanted to shop so he told me to do it here and he would join us. Stop worrying. It's not a scenario."

But when I saw Peace standing outside the checkout lines, scanning the shoppers, I knew that either Michelle was lying or this was a scenario she had not been warned about.

He was wearing jeans and a dressy version of a blue fisherman's sweater which made him look slender and elegant and set him apart from the Lewisham shopping crowd.

When he spotted us, he made a sign to indicate he would wait outside until Michelle had checked through the groceries.

Outside he nodded to Michelle. "Put that stuff in the parcel pickup. We'll go and have a coffee."

"There's a half-decent-looking café down there," Michelle said, pointing to a little row of shops that had been grafted onto the older supermarket as an obvious afterthought.

"Oh no, my dear," he said. "When in Lewisham, do as the locals do." Under the sneer, he was obviously enjoying some private joke, but I couldn't see what it was, so I let it pass without comment and we followed Peace back between the iron posts that marked the supermarket entrance.

In the corner was a tiny lunch-counter with windows looking out into the store. Without asking, Peace bought three coffees, served in polystyrene cups.

"The coffee is probably evil," he said, "But the atmosphere is so atmospheric."

I could see he was making a point of not mentioning the scene at the hotel and I decided not to indulge him.

"How is the hotel business?" I asked. "Has the Intermark occupancy rate taken a satisfactory nosedive?"

Peace made a little mock bow toward Michelle. "My, he is becoming blasé," he said. "You really are doing neat things with his head."

He turned to me. "Everything is chugging along nicely, thank you. Officially, Intermark won't close the hotel, but it's pretty much empty except for a few diehards who are making a big production out of 'not being pushed around by those damn radicals.' We'll fix that this afternoon with a few phone calls." He mimicked a little girl voice: " 'Hello. Viking Productions here. Would you care to take part in one of our contests?' The media side is rolling nicely. Everyone has clips from the video tape and there are stills for the papers. It's amazing how much is getting shown. The BBC had some on this morning. Tits and asses covered up of course. You know the rules. Electro-torture, Si. Nudity, No.

"We've sent cables to all the Intermark hotels saying 'Good News, etc. . . . . Viking Productions announces big contest coming your way, very soon,' and we've sent the word to American Express and all the big travel agencies . . . and so far, it's gone to the convention bureaus in about sixty cities. These multidestination Telex messages really save so much time."

He said it all with a cold, wary smile, looking into my eyes, watching to see how far I would let him go.

"Now we can get on with the big one."

I saw that Michelle was looking intently at Peace. She wasn't going to say anything but I could see she did not know what he meant.

"Would you mind telling us about it now," I said, "so we don't have to stand here drinking any more of this godawful coffee? You've set your little stage. The homely suburban supermarket will be a nice contrasting setting to point up all the power and soaring vision of Simon Peace and his Vikings. Just get on with it, will you?"

He made an effort not to show his annoyance.

"There's a little more to it than that, Philip," he said carefully. "The next scenario has been thought out with particular care. We've really only been playing around up to now . . . but everything is working nicely. The Vikings are in good shape. I think we're ready to go ahead."

"With what?" I had the feeling that I was saying it only a second ahead of Michelle.

"With our big scenario," he said blandly. "Actually there's a little warm-up first. But I'll tell you about that in a minute. First, let's talk about weapons. . . . You've done a lot of studies of terrorist weapons, so we won't have to spell things out too much for you, will we?"

"What kind of weapons?" I said.

Peace smiled. "Big weapons," he said. "Big weapons that do a great deal of damage."

He saw me hesitate and tapped his fingers together mockingly. "Not quite so tough-minded suddenly, are you?" he said. "Never mind. I'll do the talking instead."

He opened his palm and tapped two of the fingers. "So far, we've done two operations. They've both been near perfect successes, and as they say in the military, we've 'taken out' two of Intermark's nicest little operations.

"But we're still having to struggle for space in the media. So far there have only been thirty deaths and some injuries. The Palestinians killed that many this morning with a single explosion.

"We're up in the headlines because our scenarios have been rather more original . . . but in the long run, people don't really appreciate finesse." His voice hardened suddenly.

"You have to really scare them shitless . . . and that, I'm afraid, means a *lot* of casualties."

I listened to the words and watched his eyes and I couldn't see anything that could be measured as insanity. He really was, as far as I could tell, the prototype new age sadist. Amoral. Indifferent to suffering to the point where his own cleverness gave him more pleasure than the sight of the suffering it caused. It was all a game, a contest to find the levers that made people move in the communications age and manipulate them with whatever technology seemed most appropriate.

"Get it up front," Michelle snapped suddenly. "What casualties? How many?"

"I don't think we can put a number value on it yet," Peace said. "Let's just say that we have our eye on the record books."

"What is the record for that kind of insanity?" I said. "I haven't seen the figures lately. Five hundred, a thousand, or what?"

"You're in the right kind of ballpark," Peace said menacingly. "But a lot depends, don't you think, on the quality of the injuries? The style, if you like."

"Jesus Christ, stop fucking around," Michelle said angrily. "What in hell are you talking about?"

There was no doubt that the reaction was spontaneous. Whatever the new scenario was, I could see she knew none of the details. This was not an act.

"The point is really very simple," he said calmly. "The death toll for the average plane crash is running somewhere around the three-hundred mark. Five years ago, that was what the media so charmingly called a 'major disaster.' Now it's just 'disaster,' or possibly a 'tragedy,' or even just an 'air crash.'

"The first time urban guerrillas bombed a hotel, it was 'wanton slaughter of innocent bystanders.' Now it's just a rather draggy story which photographers and cameramen don't like because blood and gore always look the same and when you've seen one caved-in building you've seen them all.

"So there are two ways you can go. You can either go up and up and up . . . until the figures just become unreal and you get bogged down in the earthquake league . . . or you can put a little style into it . . . throw a few scares into people that touch some really dark corners of the mind.

"I think we can say we've found a way to do that."

He picked up his coffee cup.

"People are scared of unusual weapons," he said. "They've

grown used to bombs and rockets and things like that. So we've had to look around in the finer print of the weapons manuals. Some of it isn't even classified as weapons."

He reached into his pocket and pulled out a crumpled piece of paper. It was a photocopy of a newspaper article which looked as though it had been taken from a library file. He spread it out in front of me on the table.

COMMISSION FAILS TO HALT CHEMICAL SCARE, the headline said.

It was written in a formal *New York Times*-like style and the lead said the United States commission dealing with the transportation of hazardous substances had failed to agree to ban the transportation of something called Haldoxicon.

Peace let me read the first few lines, then he said impatiently, "You don't need to read all that. All it says is that the lucky householders who live along railway tracks in the United States are going to go on being in danger of being sprayed with a particularly nasty substance that rolls past them every day in refrigerated tanker cars. The reason there isn't going to be a ban is that the chemical manufacturers' lobby managed to convince the commission that they shouldn't ban railway shipment of the stuff unless they can come up with an alternative way, and since there is no safe way to ship it, the commission decided to cop out and put the problem 'under special study.' "

The languid, game-playing voice was gone now, and his tone was cold and hard.

"We have a large cylinder of Haldoxicon that we've put in one of Intermark's installations, one we've chosen very, very carefully. It's a place where a great many people gather, to buy things and enjoy themselves. It's one of those showplaces that multinational corporations love to have, so they can impress everyone with their power and put all their wares on display.

"When the time is right, we're going to explode the Haldoxicon and the result is going to be nasty enough and spectacular enough so that we won't need to keep on repeating our message anymore. When it's over, people will know that the only smart thing to do is to stay away from anything owned by Intermark—forever."

"When?" I said. "When?"

"I don't think it's very prudent to tell you when . . . or where," Peace said. "Not yet. First we have the warm-up. We're going to create a little panic in the boardroom of Intermark. We're going to send a little private message to Sabara."

He smiled viciously. "Right now the Pirate is trying to put together his own counterterrorist force. He's hiring professional security people to come after the Vikings. But we're going to show him it's too late.

"Sabara has only himself to blame. He built Intermark's security along all the wrong lines. He was too proud of his own toughness. He wasn't afraid of being attacked like this. But he felt intellectually inferior, so he put all his security resources into stealing other peoples' ideas—ripping off patents, buying away people. He's never been hit by terrorists so he never studied terrorism properly. Now it's too late."

As he spoke, I had the feeling the words were an echo and that I recognized the lines but I couldn't remember from where. An interview? A magazine article? Somewhere I had heard or read this same contemptuous assessment of Sabara made by somebody else, a public, known figure. It was as if Peace were parroting phrases, like an underling who has learned his boss's prejudices and repeats them, almost without being aware of it.

He picked up his coffee cup again, crumpled it in his hand, and threw it into a basket beside the table.

"It all seems very unreal, doesn't it," he said, "when you talk about it here in this quaint little supermarket? But it's real. Very real. It's Hairy's masterpiece.

"Do you remember Derbyshire? Do you remember our neat little weapon system . . . with the funny little phosphorous paint trails?"

"The graffiti bomb?"

"Yes. That's the one," Peace said. "It looks a bit primitive when you see it first, but it has a lot of advantages. Did you know that since terrorists started to be so generous with their explosive packages, the world's security agencies have started getting very sophisticated at devising ways of tracking down things like remote-control detonators? They have a toy now that can sweep a building as big as a theater in a few minutes and see if there is anything electronic about to do something nasty.

"They have another toy that came out of NASA that can listen for ticking mechanical gadgets and can spot them even through crowds and noise by an amplifying and filtering process.

"But they haven't developed anything that tells you when a trail of paint is about to be ignited. . . . It just hasn't seemed necessary up to now."

"What does Haldoxicon do?" I asked.

"When the row about transporting it started, one of the more sensational papers called it the 'Frankenstein' chemical—it creates monsters out of everything it touches. It does blister and burn rather badly, and a little goes a very long way. That's why we're sending Intermark a more graphic message.

"It won't be a Viking operation this time. It will just be an accident. In an obscure corner of the Intermark empire that no one bothers much about."

He gestured with his hand.

"I mean, Jesus. Foodway City. What a name. No wonder Intermark doesn't let on it's one of theirs."

I was so used to Peace's theatricals that I hadn't realized how carefully he had measured the words.

Before there was time to do anything except whirl around,

there was a hissing sound, loud enough to be heard even inside the luncheonette.

Instinctively, I looked up and it was all there, as I knew it had to be.

Suspended from the high metallic barn-shaped roof were a series of heating ducts and pipes and metal stanchions. They were all painted brightly in the familiar penny-pinching style of architecture that colored the brickwork instead of putting on real facing and tried to make the roof supports look as though they were meant to be exposed instead of covered.

Then the change of color started and it went so quickly that it was almost impossible to keep up with the trail.

The heating pipe that had started out as orange was turning black. The trail fizzled and hissed and then it reached an intersection with a yellow metal roof support and that too started to turn black.

At the head of the black trail, the heat had created a dancing cone of sparks that was racing now, inexorably toward a bulge right in the center of the crisscross beams. When it reached it, there was hiss like steam escaping from a huge pressure boiler; then there was a flash and the air above the supermarket was filled with a delicate tracery of white particles, like some esoteric firework, designed specially for some gala performance.

Within seconds the spray started to sink downward, cascading onto the crowd below, and as I watched, all I could think was, "Oh God—their eyes—they're all looking up."

CHAPTER 15   "Just lie back in the cushions and relax. Watch the screen. Let yourself be aroused. Don't think. Feel. I told you they're some of the best blue movies ever made."

I tried to do as she said but I couldn't. Her own tension was so great that it was impossible not to be affected by it.

She had become an almost grotesque caricature of her own professional image since the explosion at the supermarket. It had started slowly at first. There had been a car waiting at the side entrance and we had left immediately, without seeing the effects of the Haldoxicon. We had heard the screams and the crying, but we had not seen the burning, blistering skin. I didn't know how many people had been disfigured, and as soon as we were driving away, she had started talking about it as an abstraction. "Vietnam brought to London suburbia, courtesy of the Vikings."

Then, when Peace had dropped us at the Blackheath house, I thought she had been putting on an act. She had started talking about letting me go to the sex club and I thought that I had won. It seemed as though the horrors of the Haldoxicon had finally got to her and she had decided to help me find another escape route.

But then she had started telling me how she would prepare me for the films, and I realized that it was not settled, that I must still take the test, to see if I was ready.

Slowly, I began to see that she was wound so tightly that it would need only a wrong word or look to push her beyond all reach and control.

As far as I could judge it, she was trying to feel remorse

and could not. She had told me enough about her training for me to know that her hate words were "bleeding heart" and "compassion." Looking at her now made me think of a phrase from Catholic dogma. Invincibly ignorant they said of someone who could not be touched by faith, and I wondered if her training had made her invincibly indifferent.

During the afternoon, I could see the pressure building up and as it did, the more gaily and boldly she flew her professional colors.

At one point she ran upstairs to the bedroom and came back with what looked like a silk scarf over ten feet long. "When you were at Cambridge," she said, "you studied medieval literature and courted Julia and climbed mountains. One day, you'll hang your ice-axe over the fireplace and I shall hang this. This is my symbol of what I did at the university."

I asked her what it was and she roared with laughter.

"It's a bondage tie," she said. "You use it to pinion a man or woman—though I worked on men—to increase the intensity of their orgasm by playing on their fear of being powerless. For my thesis I practiced fellatio on 40 male volunteer subjects and I recorded over seven hundred orgasms on an orgasmometer. I became so good at it that no one in the entire psych school could match my readings. They used to say in my class that when I'd finished, you had to wipe the ceilings."

By the time she was ready to show me the films, I had gathered that she did not know herself whether she was going to take me out of the cube.

I had gathered that the sex club was the very center of her professional existence.

She turned down the lights and prepared the video machine. As the tape spool started to turn, I felt the sweat gathering on my palms and I tried to dry them surreptitiously on the fabric of the armchair.

"That's right," Michelle said, curling up on the floor and

resting her shoulder against my knee, "just let your male anticipation take over. Let your body loosen up. Just watch and enjoy."

Then the screen was filled with a picture of a small bedroom, cozily furnished in blues and yellows, in the manner of a country hotel: a bit chintzy, with a rosewood dresser, lamps with crinkly shades and a high double bed.

On the bed was a young woman in her early twenties, dressed in a plain black minidress. She was sitting upright, her back resting against the headboard, supported by two pillows. She was drinking what looked like a cocktail and reading a magazine.

"She's just rung for Mahlke," Michelle said. "If you look at her closely, you can see she's a little tense and excited. Not too much, because she's had Mahlke before; she's been on the project four months now."

"Who's Mahlke?" I asked. My voice sounded a little hoarse and unnatural.

"Mahlke's my greatest find. She's the ultimate artist of the vibrator. She's bisexual herself and she works equally well on men and women. In this film she's working as a preparer."

Mahlke came on the screen. She looked about forty and slightly dumpy and she was dressed in a white housedress with just a hint of the hospital uniform in its cut. In the side view, her face seemed craggy and masculine, despite long frizzy black hair.

"The girl on the bed is called Jose," Michelle said. "She's arrived at the club for the evening and she didn't feel in the right mood so she called Mahlke. Mahlke will prepare her by getting rid of the day's tensions—get her ready for sex, if you like."

Michelle pointed to the screen. "You'll have to look closely," she said. "She uses a tiny vibrator, not much bigger than her hand. Isn't she beautiful with it?"

The camera moved in close and followed Mahlke's hand, moving slowly about under the girl's dress.

"She doesn't usually bother to undress anyone," Michelle said, with a kind of proprietary pride. "During these preparation sessions she only goes a little way, of course. Not far enough to waste any of the juices. But in a full vibrator session, I've seen her take quite a frigid woman into a soaking orgasm without even taking off her pants."

I listened for some hint of humor but there was none. For Michelle, Mahlke's skill was a technological marvel.

As we watched Mahlke turn the girl this way and that, stroking the crevices of her body, Michelle told me the model number of the vibrator—it could be had for less than twelve dollars on direct importation from West Germany—and how long it took a woman to learn to use one, on herself or on someone else for "vibrator therapy."

"When Mahlke applied to me for a job, I told her to give me the greatest experience she could with a vibrator," Michelle said.

"She put me in what she called the birthing position— naked with my legs up on one of those metal frames they use to hold you apart during childbirth. I've never felt so naked in my life. She worked on me for two hours. She nearly drove me mad. I'll never forget it. It was a week before I even thought about having a man again, and at night I used to dream about the humming of the vibrator. She is just an artist."

The video tape segment ended with a haunting image of Jose spread across Mahlke's knees like a naughty child, her body squirming under the strokes of the massager.

Michelle let the screen go dead, then she said softly, "I showed you that first to get you in the mood. Now we'll go back to the beginning and show you what the club is like."

It was the kind of house the first generation of Victorian would-be aristocrats had built over a period of fifty years, but only a few had survived, half-hidden in small grounds surrounded by high walls.

"We've managed to make forty bedrooms," Michelle said. "Amazing isn't it? Mind you, they're all about the size of the old servants' rooms. The group rooms are all below and there's a kitchen and an office." She paused, waiting for a new image to come onto the screen. "Now, look at that very carefully."

The camera moved in to show in detail what appeared to be the main entrance. There was nothing special about it. It was just a gate with an iron grille and a short path leading to a heavy wooden door. The camera tracked through and the door opened to show a small lobby, rather like the entrance to a family hotel. There was a small counter and, behind it, sets of keys on a pigeonholed board.

"It's really two houses back to back," Michelle said. "What you saw first was the men's entrance. This is the women's."

"How quaint," I said. "Isn't that a bit coy for the age of future shock?"

"You'll see how coy it is," she said, smiling broadly. "Watch the woman checking in."

On the screen we watched a woman about forty years old, dressed in a smart black business suit, taking a key, leaving the lobby and going upstairs, apparently to one of the rooms.

"There are no advance bookings," Michelle said. "She's been given a randomly selected key. On the other side of the building, a man will be given the same key, probably sometime within the next half hour. Or she may find a man there already when she gets to the room.

"She will have no idea who it will be. Neither will the staff. Both sides function completely independently. It's totally random matching."

"The commercial traveler's dream," I said. "The great male travel fantasy come true."

I regretted the words as soon as I had said them. But I

had said it too quickly and it had come out as a facile put-down.

"What you're watching is a whole generation of screwed-up people getting used to the endemic availability of sex," she said angrily, "and all you can call it is a commercial traveler's dream come true."

I saw it was a bad mistake. I had changed her mood with one phrase.

I said humbly, "I'm sorry. Does it work? Or do the couples get stage fright?"

"Some of them do." Her voice was still sullen but I knew she did not want to break off the session.

"Random matching is only the first step toward building people's sexual security," she said. "When all the experiments are finished, we will have resolved definitively the conflict between work and sex. It's something old-guard corporations like Intermark will never understand. But once they're out of the way, we can really get on with projects like mine."

Then she explained it to me, kneeling at my feet in the darkened room, and all I could think of was "How can this possibly fit in with any radical vision of the universe?"

In that instant I saw finally, beyond any doubt, how perfectly she fitted into the pattern I knew so well: the radicals who come in out of the cold of the streets, into the security of the corporate world. She was a natural sell-out, I thought, just like Peace. I knew now that I had the answer to the Viking puzzle but I dared not ask the questions that would give me the confirmation I needed. A wrong move now and I would lose the only chance I had of breaking out of the cube.

I forced myself to listen, without probing or attacking. She called her project Future Sex—a sexual value system for the age of future shock, and I could almost smell the intensity of her obsession.

She saw it as nothing less than a complete reworking of

the entire family system and social structure of the Western world to make it compatible with the growth of a global economy. Future Sex recognized that as corporations grew larger and spread across the world, they were creating a new generation of nomads. The corporations needed rootless people: men and women who could travel at a moment's notice without being worried by regrets at neglecting spouse and family.

Without such ties, travel itself could be a reward and an incentive, instead of a source of stress and tension. For stay-at-homes, Future Sex offered a cushion for divorce or an alternative to marriage and a set of temptations to help marriage breakdowns along.

"We're absolutely nonchauvinist, though," she said proudly. "Whatever we offer men, we offer to women equally."

At the bottom end of the hierarchy, Project Future Sex helped make shift and weekend work palatable.

"Young kids hate working Saturday nights because they never get to dances and they're afraid of never getting laid," she said bluntly. "In Future Sex we show them Sunday morning is just as good a time for sexual experience as Saturday night. Sex is always available."

Her vision of corporate sex was all-inclusive. It went beyond pension to the grave: for the lonely final years, there would be unlimited access to sessions with Mahlke.

She touched my arm gently. "Do you remember Montreal? I laid out for you a classic little male fantasy. I offered you a night of sex without responsibility. There isn't a man alive who doesn't dream now and then about uncomplicated sex. Funsex. Sex without context.

"But when a man took a night off from his responsibilities, he always used to risk the three Victorian bugaboos—detection, infection and conception. In Montreal, I offered you the ultimate bait: freedom from all three. A night of sex you didn't have to work for—or pay later for—or so you thought.

"And now," she said, "I'm going to show you how we make sex universally available. It's time to see the Room of Darkness. The place where you can do exactly as you want without pressure or fear of failure."

I felt my mouth dry and I knew I must let her see that I was aroused.

Michelle turned on the video player again, then I felt her come back and kneel beside me, her shoulder against my thigh.

"That," she said, "is the room when it's not in use." I looked at the screen and saw a large empty room with a dome-shaped ceiling and no furniture of any kind. The floor undulated gently in a series of hummocks, and the material covering the floor was divided into nine different segments.

"There's silk and leather and down and vinyl and fur and four different kinds of soft spongy material with different textures," Michelle said.

"Some of the textures are warm and some are cool. Sometimes we put in a dozen huge pillows made of very soft material but mostly we leave it empty, especially when there are a lot of bodies; the pillows interfere with the skin contact. We've come a long way since the original idea back in the fifties."

"Was it your idea?"

I expected her to say yes but the answer surprised me.

"Oh, no," she said, "I just refined it. The original Room of Darkness was put together in the psych school of the University of Vienna.

"A bunch of really bright students designed it because they were finding the sexual psychology course a really heavy trip. They found they were all getting too self-conscious. Every time they went out with someone on campus, they found they were analyzing their behavior and worrying about technique and response and all that stuff. They decided they needed a place where they could really relax.

"So they got a room in one of the student houses and blacked it out and put mattresses all over the floor. And they arranged that anyone could go in, dressed or undressed, and just be free.

"No one knows who you are and nobody cares. It's just a pile of bodies. You can do what you like, ball anyone, ball everyone. If you don't perform okay, that's cool. No one knows who you are. You're not being judged, and if the person you fucked wasn't happy, they can stick around until they are.

"It's sex, total sex."

She was quite carried away now, exhilarated at the idea of total sexual abandon. Then she started to talk about how she had designed her own room of total, hermetic darkness.

"We use it to teach new sexual techniques without people even realizing they're being taught," she said proudly. "We send in a therapist who can recognize people easily by touch alone.

"But mostly, we use it as a do-it-yourself sensorium. In the darkness, you have a chance to make everyone perform better by stripping off their inhibitions. Darkness is a great leveler. Watch now."

I looked and suddenly the room was no longer empty. First the screen went completely black, then there was a pause and it lightened again, only this time to the purplish hue I recognized as the color produced by the latest infrared photographic systems.

There was no transition. The video tape had been edited so there was blackness one instant then a screen full of naked bodies, writhing, crawling and twisting; shapes coupling, recoupling, joining; everywhere hands, mouths, genitals groping, searching, offering, the flesh all livid under the infrascope.

"That," Michelle said proudly, "is an orgy for everyday people. You don't have to be beautiful or a Don Juan to enjoy it. It's the sexual escape of the future. You and Julia try to create timeless moments. You're looking for echoes of the divine, which is another way of saying you're looking for oblivion."

She pointed to the screen. "Well, this is oblivion too. It's sex reduced to total, beautiful sensation." Then she paused, as if making up her mind, and said, "I'll take you there tomorrow night."

CHAPTER 16   The sign in the hallway read: IF YOU DON'T FEEL SEXY, STAY AT HOME. NO ONE IS FORCING YOU.

By the evening, I was almost wishing that Michelle would change her mind, but as she dressed she had talked about how she had convinced Peace that no special surveillance would be needed that night and she had bragged about how "they" trusted me more in her hands than in his. It was infuriating to feel so close to being able to ask who "they" were, but I knew that I dare not.

She had put on a slinky minidress, bright with splotches of Art Deco colors, as though preparing for a night of abandon, but I knew that she was close to breaking point.

I had decided what I was going to do. I had the equipment and I was sure I could get out of the club, but I had to act before she came to an emotional crisis.

At the club Michelle took me to a room like the one I had seen on the video clips. When we were inside she locked the door, sat down on the bed, silent, waiting. I was just about to make my first move when there was a knock on the door, softly at first, then insistently.

I nodded to Michelle to open it and stepped quietly into the bathroom. "No crowds," I hissed at her. "I'm not in the mood yet." Michelle unlocked the door and opened it and a man walked in.

He was dressed only in a pair of leather trousers, held up by a broad belt, studded with shiny metal shields. He didn't look more than about twenty-five, and even with partial vision through the crack in the bathroom door, I could see that he spent most of his time lifting weights and building his tanned body into a shape that pleased him. His simpering look and posture suggested that he spent the rest of the time admiring the results in a mirror.

"I heard you come in," he said, in a slightly effeminate upper-class English voice, "and I thought Michelle can't be going to play twosies . . . that's so old-fashioned."

He sat down on a chair by the bed. I couldn't see Michelle clearly but she seemed to be backing away, and I realized suddenly that it might only take a few wrong words to push her into a full-blown psychotic break.

"What about a nice little game of threesies?" the man said teasingly. "You look so nice tonight." He giggled. "What are you wearing under that gaudy little dress? Can I have a look?"

"Not tonight, Stephen," Michelle said. When I heard her voice I knew I had to move quickly. Normally, she would have been able to deal with idiots like this with a wave of the hand and a flick of the skirt but she sounded strained and desperately ill at ease.

Through the door, I tried to size Stephen up. There are two kinds of bodybuilders—those who like to fight and those who would do almost anything to avoid one, and I couldn't tell which type Stephen was. But if there was a fight and it was noisy, other people might come and the situation could get completely out of hand.

But I was much more worried about Michelle's mood. She was balanced on a hairline. I decided to act quickly and take the risk. I stepped into the bedroom and smiled at Stephen menacingly. "No threesies tonight," I said. "I have a date with Michelle."

He giggled again. "Oh come on, Michelle's terrific in a group. And dates are so old-fashioned."

I smiled at him. "Stand up," I said. "And let me look at you."

He stood up and posed to let me examine his smoothly oiled muscles.

I stepped in very close and said quietly, "Stephen, I'm really old-fashioned. When I go to the beach, I kick sand in people's faces."

For a second I thought I'd misjudged him and he was going to swing at me. I moved closer and let him feel the edge of my shoes on his bare toes.

He backed away quickly and opened the door. As he left, I heard Michelle gasp slightly, then she just stared at me as if knowing that the next move was also mine.

I gripped her arm, encircling the wrist and squeezing hard enough for her to flinch, but she didn't try to draw away.

"If you cry out, I'll break your jaw," I said. "It isn't worth it. In this place it would just sound like heavy foreplay."

Her eyes gave me the reaction I was expecting. She wasn't surprised. She knew this was why I had wanted to come to the club all along, but in her mind there had to be no sense of complicity. She wanted to be forced, to have her conflicts resolved for her. She could not bring herself to help but she longed to acquiesce, to help without helping.

She watched as I pulled out the hypodermic already loaded with the sedative she had used on me at the airport. Finding her stock at the house had been easy and now I had only to unsheathe the needle.

I squeezed her wrist harder and she winced.

"I need three hours," I said. "How much juice is that?"

"Half." She didn't hesitate but the word came out hoarsely.

I edged the tip of the needle toward a vein in her forearm and for the first time she tried to resist.

"Not there. Lower."

She didn't ask where I was going but there was a whole unspoken dialogue between us. She had spent enough months studying me, reading me; she knew that the Haldoxicon had pushed me beyond the point where I could hold back, even for Julia. The Haldoxicon was over her emotional limit, too, but her conditioning was too strong for her to admit it. The needle was the release she wanted.

I found the right spot and pressed the plunger. When the cylinder was half empty I hesitated, wondering whether to trust her estimate, but I decided to take her word. I was sure it wasn't a trick and I might need her awake as soon as I got back.

When I withdrew the point she lay back on the bed. It was a gesture of dismissal, telling me to go, so she would have no more responsibility.

I put the needle on the bedside table where it would be visible if anyone came into the room. Then I strode to the window.

I couldn't pause to check whether the drainpipes were secure in their fastenings or whether the mortar holding the windowsills was cracked by the weather. I had to assume that everything on the side of the mansion was as it should be. As I went down, I discovered that it was, and I found too that even after so many years, I was still as at home on the outside of a building as I was in an elevator.

Nor did the perimeter wall present any problems. It took less than three minutes to find handholds and footholds in the brickwork and the ivy, slip over the token barricade on the top and slither, in two quick stages, down to the street below.

On the sidewalk, I just kept moving, not caring whether anyone in the couple of passing cars had seen the descent. I found a taxi almost immediately, gave the address of the Barbary Tower and was driven there in under seven minutes.

I wasn't sure what I would find when I got there. I was trusting that Wescott and Pearson had made some arrangements to find me. If they hadn't I would do whatever was necessary to find them.

I knew the tower had been converted into expensive apartments, but since London is not New York, I guessed there would be no special security arrangements at the entrance and the tenants would probably rely on glass doors and a speaker phone system to guarantee their privacy.

I arrived ready to disturb every tenant in the tower if I had to, until someone let me in, but there was no need even for that.

When I had paid off the taxi driver and stepped onto the sidewalk in front of the tower, two men got out of a car parked a little way up the street and one said, in an overloud policeman's voice, "Are you Philip Russell?"

They drove me across London very fast but very discreetly in an unmarked police car and within fifteen minutes I was inside a drab Whitehall office, in a nondescript building I guessed belonged to some obscure branch of the Ministry of Defence or the Foreign Office.

It all went so smoothly that I felt exhilarated, yet let down. It was like climbing out of a deep, dark pit and finding that you can see properly and still have the use of your limbs.

I had made it out of the cube. I had reached friends, and between what they knew and what I knew, the picture was finally going to come together, I thought.

Instead, I walked into a tough, angry confrontation, with four of the six people present determined to arrest and interrogated me immediately. Pearson and Wescott were there but they were my only allies, and Jack was barely allowed to greet me before he was pushed to one side and warned to keep silent.

Pearson was in a scarcely stronger position and it didn't take long to see why. He was Foreign Office. This was England and they resented his intervention, especially on my side.

The four who wanted to arrest me came from four different security agencies: New Scotland Yard, the Home Office, the SIS and a newly formed antiterrorist unit, responsible, I gathered, directly to the Prime Minister's office.

Through the shouting and arguing that broke out as soon as I arrived, I gathered quickly they believed my coded message at the dinner had been a trick. The institute had been under surveillance before the dinner. They believed I had known this and was using Wescott to cover my tracks.

But at least they had only circumstantial evidence against me. The Vikings had given them nothing on me yet. That would come later. From their own surveillance they had gathered only that I was always in the right place at the right time. I had the skills to lead the Vikings and enough knowledge of terrorism to plan the campaign. I had left the Defence Institute in suspicious circumstances. I had become more affluent than I had ever been before.

But as I listened, the real message coming through was that they were desperate for a suspect. They were under pressure and they had nothing against anyone else.

They knew about Gellman and about Peace and Hairy and Michelle, but they had me marked as the leader, the director of the institute who might be—had to be—behind it all.

They had search warrants for the institute, and only Pearson's standing in the intelligence community had blocked the arrest thus far, but he was obviously in quicksand and I was sinking with him.

When we were finally all seated around a battered wooden conference table, which shone in the flat barrack-style lighting, the man from Scotland Yard threw an open packet of photographs onto it, letting them skitter across in front of me.

They showed faces, dozens of them, blistered and disfigured, some of them so badly that only the clothing at the neck reminded one that they were human beings.

"The results of your latest little coup," he said. "Take a good look at them."

I looked down at the photographs then back at him. "What evidence do you have that I'm responsible for that?" I said.

"Enough to hold you until we've rounded up those insane hoodlum guerrillas of yours," he shouted.

"On the assumption, I take it, that while I'm inside they will be leaderless and therefore powerless and will allow themselves to be picked up just like that. Tell me," I said, "how many do you think you could lay your hands on in the next hour . . . or the next twenty-four hours for that matter?"

"Don't get smart with me, you vicious bastard," he yelled. "We'll keep you as long as we goddam well need to."

It wasn't difficult to visualize the dialogue that could go back and forth for hours, leading nowhere.

There was only one man in the room I saw any hope with and I decided that I would ignore the rest and work on him.

Charles Norton represented the special antiterrorist squad. He was a huge man, heavily muscled and burly and well over six feet four inches tall. There was stillness about him that suggested power and controlled violence, and he had a nasty look about the eyes that belied his black suit and discreet gray tie. He looked like a man who would wear a bowler hat to work and carry an umbrella, then hang them carefully on his hat stand before going into the back room to smash the face of some IRA suspect with his huge knuckles.

He had a totally humorless face, with deep, grim-looking frown lines. I guessed he was in his early forties, but his face looked older than his body, which had the set of a natural athlete.

Norton sat like a young man, spine upright, shoulders supporting themselves easily. I had the vague feeling that I had seen him before somewhere, but I couldn't remember where and there wasn't time to think about it.

I waited for a break in the row, then I said to him as

calmly as I could, "I presume that since Jack Wescott is here, you don't totally disbelieve his story."

Norton grunted but said nothing.

"And I presume," I went on, "that Pearson has told you that he has no reason to suppose, after knowing me for several years, that I'm a sadistic terrorist crazie who has been nursing a secret desire to kill or maim half London."

This time he nodded, but still did not answer.

"And did you know that my wife Julia is not dead?"

"Wescott told us he suspected that," Norton said carefully. "But we have no evidence of that at all. Suppose you show us some. If she's alive, where is she?"

"As far as I know, she's somewhere in England, being held by the Vikings," I said. "She was kidnapped the week before the so-called funeral in Greenwich. They used her as a lever to make me work for them."

"Then you've killed a lot of people to keep her alive," Norton said sarcastically. "Do you want us to weep for her now or later?"

I turned to Pearson. "Ivor," I said, "Norton doesn't know me, so he's going to have some trouble believing what I have to say next. So before I say anything else, I want you to take him out into the corridor and talk to him. I want you to convince him that if he arrests me now as leader of the Vikings, two things will happen. First, he will probably be responsible for one of the worst horrors in the history of terrorism. Second, he will win for himself a place in the history of intelligence work as the fool to end all fools."

I looked around the room then added quietly, "In fact, why don't you all go outside with Ivor and listen to him, before it's too late for you, too?"

There was complete silence in the room but only for a second, then Norton got up and said to Pearson, "You'd better do as he says. Come outside and convince me."

They all went out into the corridor, taking Wescott with

them and left me alone with one of the men who had brought me in the car. I smoked a cigarette and stared at the drab green walls, and then they came back inside and I knew I had the breakthrough I needed.

"I'll listen to your version," Norton said, and I noticed that he made no attempt to spread any of the responsibility around.

"I believe the Vikings are not real radical guerrillas," I said. "I believe there's someone behind them who wants to destroy Intermark for some entirely different reason."

"What reason? Who?"

Norton had obviously been through too many interrogations to show any surprise.

"I don't know," I said. "I just know that there are too many signs that the people behind the Vikings have nothing to do with radicalism."

I wanted to go farther, to guess out loud. But I knew that what I was thinking was too outrageous for this group. They weren't ready for it . . . except for Wescott, and Pearson possibly. I wasn't sure about Norton. With the others, I would only lose what little credibility I had established. It wasn't worth the risk.

"And you've been set up as a decoy to mislead us," Norton said.

"Yes. There were two of us. Alan Gellman was the other one. Gellman was to appear to be the economic strategist. I was to be the guerrilla commander. Gellman is dead. That was an accident, but he'll probably still be framed when the time is right."

Nobody else spoke and there was no way of telling from Norton's face what he was thinking. He put his hands and forearms on the table and leaned slightly forward. "And this horror that I'm going to be responsible for. Tell me about that."

"The Vikings have got a large quantity of Haldoxicon.

Enough to do several hundred times the damage they caused at Foodway. They have put a canister of it in one of Intermark's installations and plan to explode it, using the same kind of graffiti trails they used in the supermarket. The devastation is to be big enough and horrible enough to ensure that it wrecks Intermark's business worldwide. No one will go near an Intermark building of any kind after the explosion."

"Oh, Christ," Pearson said.

"What installation?" Norton asked with no apparent emotion.

"Again I don't know," I said. "Peace has dropped hints that it will be a shopping complex. The biggest one in London is the Battersea Mall. It's owned by Intermark. Peace must have known that I would jump to that conclusion. It may be a trick or he may have wanted to impress me with his power; he is prone to that."

Had it not been for Norton's face, I knew there would have been pandemonium in the room, but everyone seemed to know that you didn't interrupt a Norton interrogation.

"When will this happen?" he said.

"I don't know. But I believe we have a little time. Not much, but a little."

"Why?"

"The Vikings have not so far officially taken credit for the Foodway blast, have they?"

"No. And the press are cooperating. They're not linking Foodway and Intermark. It's being called an accident."

"That's how it was planned," I said. "Peace said it was to be a warning. A private message to Peter Sabara. I believe there's more to it than that."

"What?"

For the first time, I thought I could read real interest in Norton's tone.

"The explosion at Foodway City was supposed to be a

warning to Intermark that the Vikings have the Haldoxicon and aren't too squeamish to use it. But a warning really makes sense only if the Vikings want to do some kind of deal with Intermark. If they want to wipe Intermark out totally, why wait, and risk the security people getting closer? I think there'll be an approach soon, for some kind of negotiations. I don't know how long that gives us."

"It gives us about four days," Norton said. The air was electric suddenly and I saw he was giving away information no one else in the room had.

"Peter Sabara told the Prime Minister yesterday that the Vikings want to talk to him. A meeting has been set for Friday. Today is Monday, that's four days. It could be longer, but they could set the blast immediately if talks break down."

Norton sat back in his chair. "Sabara is trying to play for time. He's hiring security men who specialize in counter-terror. It could become very messy."

"Yes," I said, "Peace told me about that."

"Did he tell you where they tried to find people?"

"No."

"They went to Globex. They already have an antiterrorist unit. They put it together after the South American kidnappings. Sabara tried to buy them away. They wouldn't budge."

"No," I said. "I'm not surprised."

Norton looked at me steadily. "And we don't know for certain that it's going to be in the Battersea Mall. That's the most likely but it could be a red herring, or they could change their minds and put it somewhere else. Intermark owns cinemas, theaters, god knows what else.

"So we need information," Norton said.

"Yes. When you're ready to move, we'll have to pick up everyone we can find and screw it out of one of them. Peace and Hairy are the most likely to know. I don't see any other way."

"We would have to make very sure that we did get it out of them," Norton said thoughtfully. He looked around the room. "The questioning would not have to take too long."

No one spoke and I could see that a silent bargain was being made. Norton would do the interrogation; the others would not interfere and would not be responsible.

"What about you?" Norton asked.

"I want to go back," I said. "I'll try to find out what I can but the real reason I want to go is to try to save Julia."

There was no point in lying. Norton didn't need instruments and dials. He had stared at too many people across too many tables in dingy rooms.

"You will have to go back," he said quietly. "We're not ready to move yet. But you'll have to convince me that you aren't going to mess everything up by a show of heroics." He made the word sound nasty and unclean.

"How long do you need to prepare before you pick up Peace and the rest?" I asked.

Norton didn't answer and I could see he was calculating, slowly and carefully.

"When we find out where the stuff is hidden, we've got to be able to move a strike force in to the installation immediately. That means we have to put together, in total secrecy, a force that can blanket Battersea, or move to the other side of London if need be.

"We shall need police, fire services, ambulances . . . ladders, equipment, everything. We don't have enough time to do that properly but I can be as ready as I'm going to be by Wednesday morning."

"Then I shall try to get to see Julia tomorrow night," I said. "I believe I can persuade them to let me spend a night with her. Set your deadline for six o'clock Wednesday. I'll get her out before then."

"No," Norton said. "That's out of the question."

I didn't argue. Instead I said, "Then make me a better offer. You owe me some chance to save Julia."

Norton sat for a while and I could see he was calculating again.

"We don't owe you a goddam thing," he said finally. "But I'll go this far.

"We already have the main suspects under surveillance. We will keep them that way and we'll pick them up at six A.M. on Wednesday morning.

"If you can get them to take you to your wife on Tuesday night, we will try to tail you—if we can do it without arousing suspicion. When we have all the suspects, we will try to get you out. But don't expect miracles. You've seen the red book. You know the statistics."

He looked hard at me across the table. "And I don't have to tell you that if you move before we do, you'd better have a damn good reason."

I looked at my watch. I had been gone an hour.

"I must go back," I said.

"Tell me one thing," Norton said to me. "What makes you think they'll let you see Julia after all this time?"

"I got here tonight with help from Michelle Foxton. I think I can get her to convince Peace that I'm becoming unstable to the point where I may try to wreck the whole operation unless they let me see Julia."

"You can't wreck the operation," Norton said dispassionately. "They'll simply kill you."

"They might," I said. "But if they kill me, they lose a front man, and I'm betting that Peace has enough sense to realize that he's the next in line."

CHAPTER 17 To take me to Julia, they put me in the trunk of a car and the preparations were the only thing I had ever seen upset Hairy.

Peace was not there. "He's doing Julia," Hairy said, obviously angry that I was being allowed the meeting.

Michelle had carried the message to Peace that I was becoming seriously unstable because of the frustrations and tensions of living within the psychological confines of my cube. She had hoped the sex club would help but it hadn't; only a reunion with Julia would bring me back to reality.

She had, of course, harped on Gellman's death as the original cause of my deterioration and, at my instruction, she had told Peace that if the situation got any worse, I might have to be killed. As I had predicted, that had been the clincher and Peace had agreed. Michelle had brought back the news and the arrangements had been set in motion.

When it came to the loading, Hairy almost could not bring himself to do it. It was not that he feared I might run short of air or suffer cramps in the trunk. It was, I decided, because he was offended by the primitive way of ensuring secrecy.

In forcing me under the lid of the trunk, he banged my shoulder. When I resisted, I discovered for the first time how strong he was; it was like pushing against a truck. I recognized the kind of musculature and flesh texture that is almost impervious to normal pain.

I had not seen Michelle since she had driven me to Blackheath after I had climbed back into the sex club. She had agreed without argument to arrange the meeting with Julia, and Peace sent word back that he had agreed. I had made as much of a show of instability as I dared, and I had no idea whether it had been convincing. From inside the trunk, I had no way of knowing either whether Norton's men could pick up my trail.

It made a grotesque beginning to the meeting and when they finally did bring me to Julia, the actual moment seemed completely unreal.

I had dreamed of the meeting, daydreamed about it, and thought again and again about what I would say when I could hold her. When it happened, all I could say was, "My God, they've turned you brown."

"It's a dye," she said, putting her arms around me and squeezing me as she buried her face in my neck. "I chose the shade myself, do you like it?"

Her voice brought me back to reality. I had always loved the laughter in it, and under the unfamiliar brown skin-tone, I could see her eyes were crinkling with relief. We kissed for a long time without speaking, then we separated and she held my hand and said: "Let me show you our love nest. They've given us one night together."

It was an apartment, furnished in the very comfortable traditional English style I like most, full of chairs and sofas with deep, goose-down cushions and discreet darkwood side-tables. On one table stood a huge bowl of thickly massed flowers, tangled in carefully designed casualness against a thicket of climbing leaves.

"It's a beautiful room," Julia said. "But they didn't design it for us. Peace told me the Vikings have been using it to transact their 'business negotiations.' It's totally exposed to sound and film surveillance."

"You know Peace then," I said.

"Yes. I haven't talked to him much but I've seen him. He

comes and goes in the places they've been keeping me."

"Did they treat you well?" I asked gently.

"Yes. I was ill once . . . some kind of fever. They treated it and it got better."

I remembered Greenwich and my clumsy attempts to evade surveillance but I couldn't bring myself to talk about the funeral, so I squeezed her hand and smiled and said, "I'm glad." She led me over to the double windows, which rose from a low sill nearly to the ceiling behind light green damask drapes.

"Look where we are."

She held the drapes apart and I looked down and saw that we were overlooking Leicester Square, right in the heart of London, barely a block from where we had once extravagantly rented an apartment ourselves in the early days of our marriage. I squeezed Julia's arm and I thought suddenly how much happiness we had shared and how the joy of being close to her never seemed to lessen. I was as much in love with her now as when she had first enchanted me at Cambridge and, standing beside her, I felt the same thrill of excitement as in those first crazy days.

"They told me that, before anything else, I have to explain the security arrangements to you," Julia said. "I've been here for half an hour. They have shown me everything."

She told me and it was frighteningly simple. The brown body-dye and black hair color were to ensure that whatever happened, no one could recognize her without making an almost medical examination. The apartment was on the fifth floor of an old building above a merchant bank. There were Vikings outside the door and in an adjacent apartment.

"Peace said that from the time surveillance noticed something wrong, Vikings could be inside the apartment in less than forty-five seconds. Their orders are to kill me immediately, but they'll take you alive. Apparently Peace doesn't want you killed."

"I know why," I said. "Go on."

She said that Peace had been very specific about the window because they all knew about my climbing skills.

"They have left the window open as a kind of taunt," Julia said. "The wall outside is nearly sheer. You could perhaps make it down, they said, but there is no way on earth you could carry me, and they know that I can't climb onto a kitchen table without going dizzy."

"So if I try to climb out and tell someone you are here . . ." I said. I let the words tail off.

"Peace said he almost hoped you would. There are Vikings in the street below. They will watch you come down, take you alive and bring you back up to show you my corpse. He said that I would be dead before you were one story down."

"So that's that," I said.

"Yes. Let me make you a drink. To give us a little time to put that out of our minds."

She lingered over mixing the drinks as if to set the talk of death and escape apart from the night to come, but when we did sit down together on one of the sofas, the strangeness between us had still not gone completely.

Tracing the laugh lines around her mouth with my fingers, I said, as gently as I could, "You know, brown skin suits you."

"I've always secretly wanted to be dark, very dark. Now I'm nearly black . . . and it goes all over too." She smiled. It was the first hint of sex between us; the kisses had been from tenderness. Then, for the first time, under the strange black disguise, I could see her developing what we had so often called, in laughter, her bedroom look.

But we both sensed that it was not the right time; neither of us mentioned the cameras or the microphones, and I did not know how used she was to being permanently exposed to hostile eyes, so I didn't bring it up and we talked instead about the old days.

The reminiscing began as a kind of retreat to neutral ground where neither of us would have to think about what was happening to us; but before long, we both began to sense that our shared memories were more than just loving chatter: they were a very real shield against the electronic prying of the Vikings.

We started to use our courtship and marriage just as Wescott and I had used our youth, as a dimension of our lives that neither Peace nor Hairy nor the watching, listening technicians could penetrate: a code they could never crack.

We talked about the Himalayas and about Thyangboche and the climbing trips to the Alps, when Julia had sat, a mountain-widow in a pretty-pretty wooden chalet, playing solitaire and looking up at the mist circling peaks, wondering if the weather would change. There, in the yellow light of the alabaster lamps, she confessed fears to me that she had kept to herself through all my expeditions.

"I tried to be the perfect climbing wife," she said. "But God, I loved you so and I prayed so much."

After a while, Julia made some food in the little kitchen and we ate, sitting in the dining room again, and Julia lightened the mood by talking about the Mediterranean and the holidays we had had, as she used to say, "at sea level," when she had managed to entice me away from the mountains.

As we talked, I realized suddenly how incredibly strong she had become. There had been many times during our marriage when I had been surprised by her strength, when I had glimpsed, under the day-to-day worries, what a composed and whole human being she was.

She was controlling the conversation now; she seemed to know that she was my greatest weakness. She did not need psychological readings to know that she was the Achilles heel through which I could be brought down. She knew how afraid I was for her, how I hated her to be in pain. She was

211

talking to give me the strength not to think about anything outside the room, and later she sensed exactly the moment when she had talked me out of my anxieties. She said, "There's a bedroom next door." She smiled. "Now's your chance to have a black girl."

At the door of the bedroom she squeezed my hand and said, "They tried to spoil this for us."

"What do you mean?"

"Just before we came, one of the technicians showed me the cameras and the infrared lenses they use for photographing rooms like this in the dark. Then he showed me some sex films they had taken, to show me all the details they would see, if we made love."

She must have felt my hand twitch. I couldn't control it and she laughed. "They weren't films of you. Don't worry. I know they have some of you. They've been dropping all kinds of nasty hints."

She put her arms around me. "You always pride yourself on knowing whether I'm telling you the truth. Well look at me as I tell you, 'I don't give a tuppeny damn.' "

She whirled away from me, laughing, and pulled her dress over her head.

"Be it known," she said in a loud, strong voice, "to all surveillance technicians and all terrorists that I have dreamed of this moment on many lonely nights and no one is going to spoil it for me."

And then she fell on me, literally dragging me to the bed and tickling my back until I laughed with her; then she smothered the laughter with a kiss and held me with a strength I never knew she had.

We made love with the lights on and it was as private as our conversation had been. It was the union not of two bodies but of two human beings and the cameras and the Viking-eyes saw nothing that would help them to understand.

Later, we turned the lights down and lay very quietly together, not speaking at all, just sharing the sensations of each other's bodies breathing in unison.

Eventually Julia said, "I'd like to sleep now. Why don't you make some coffee for yourself? I know you like that after sex."

She kissed me and turned on her side. As she did so, she touched my hand. "You know why I want to sleep don't you?"

"I know," I said. "If we lie awake we shall talk too much and it will be spoiled."

"Yes," she said. "They've given us until eight o'clock. Wake me at six. . . . You always were the family alarm clock. I have some things I want to say to you then . . ." She smiled. ". . . and do to you. I love you . . . and that was wonderful, wonderful, wonderful."

"I love you too," I said, and left her as she wanted.

There was nothing I could say about the escape. I dared not give any hint. Sometime between six o'clock and eight o'clock Norton's men would try to break in . . . if they knew where we were . . . and if they had arrested Peace and the others.

There was no plan I could make to match his. I did not know whether he would attack from the hallway or the windows. I didn't know where we should be, or what I had to defend her against. I had no weapons. All I had managed so far was to locate three or four places in each room that would give some protection against weapons fire. But not much, and none against grenades or explosives or whatever else the Vikings might use.

I could only watch and wait and pray that Julia could move quickly enough when she saw the moment coming.

I remembered Norton's words. I had seen the red book—the top secret analysis of hostage situations which had been circulated to the Defence Institute. I knew the statistics. Ninety-five percent of all victims in hostage dramas die, unless released by their captors after successful negotiations.

If they are not killed by their captors, they are killed in the shoot-out, when the helicopters and the snipers and the assault squads close in.

But I could not let Julia die. I had said I would face that, but I could not. Nothing was worth that. I had always loved Julia irrationally, extravagantly. Falling in love with her had been the most beautiful thing that had ever happened to me; marrying her the one act of my life I had never regretted; and nothing that had happened with Michelle had changed that. To risk her life even to destroy the Vikings was unthinkable. I tried to think about it on and off for the rest of the night, sometimes pacing the room, sometimes sitting half-dozing in the chair.

Then for a long time, I just stared out of the window, watching the lights go out along Leicester Square as the first daylight lightened the sky.

I woke Julia before six, pleading impatience. I could not refuse to make love without alerting the surveillance team, so I let her pull me gently into bed beside her and talked drowsily about her sleep and her dreams, then we made love gently, tenderly, in a way, as she had often said, that would make sure she woke with sweet thoughts.

Afterward she went into the bathroom and I wondered if I dare dress, and decided that the risk was too great. Julia would find it odd and would make some comment, even if only a joke, and I dared not warn anyone now, at this very last moment, that something was wrong.

Julia slid between the sheets and nuzzled up beside me and said, "Philip, will you indulge me?"

"Yes, of course," I said.

There was something odd in her tone but I thought it was just the tension of waking to the realities of the morning.

"I want to plan the way we part. Because I love you so terribly much. Will you let me?" I didn't know what to say, so I pulled her closer and kissed her gently.

"Do you remember," she said, "how you used to leave me

in the mornings when you were at the mountain school in Grenoble . . . how you used to go off very slowly and quietly and I used to pretend I was asleep?" She drew in a breath softly.

"Would you do it that way . . . very slowly and quietly, so I don't know you're going?"

I lay very still and I could feel her gripping my arm tightly so that my reflexes would not betray me with a start. She was doing what Wescott had done: using a private memory to give me a message.

"I remember," I said. I wanted to try to let her know that I understood and yet tell her that she must stop. She mustn't make a move of her own. Not now.

"I remember very well," I said. "A nice, calm, quiet way to slip away from you."

I thought of the little village outside Grenoble and in that instant the scene came back so vividly that I could smell the Alpine air and even the scents of dough from the bakery under our bedroom window.

I had spent a month as an instructor at the mountaineering school at the invitation of the French government. Each morning at exactly six o'clock, a bus rolled into the square below. It went from village to village picking up climbing students to take them to where we would begin the day's ascent.

My departures had begun as a joke. On the first morning we had been making love right up to the last instant and the driver, in his impatience, started hooting loudly enough to disturb the whole village. For fun and for bravado, I had climbed out of the window and down the side of the chalet at breakneck speed and leaped into the bus while the driver was still staring impatiently at the front door.

The students had loved it, and in the silly way such things develop, it had become a tradition.

By the end of the month, I had learned the holds so well that I could get from Julia's arms to my seat in the bus in barely a minute, and I could still remember rolling off through the square, sorting my gear from the knapsack beside me, with the smell of her body mingling with my own.

"Do you think you could do it like that, just to please me?" she said. "Just get dressed and go very slowly, so I don't have to look at you."

Her voice sounded natural. Only I could know that it was not. This was what she had been working up to, all through the night.

She knew we could not both get out. She was trying to build my courage, to make me leave her and escape down the outside wall. It was already nearly seven o'clock. Norton's men could be here at any moment. I had to find some way to stall.

I dressed as slowly as I dared without arousing the suspicions of the surveillance team, then I went back to the bed and put my arms around her.

"I can't leave you," I said. "Not yet. We still have some time together. It's too precious to waste."

"It won't be a waste," she said gently. "I want you to go. I'll be fine. You don't have to worry about me." She smiled. "I won't even get pregnant. I've been taking my pills while we've been apart. I forgot last night, I was so excited, but I remembered this morning, just in time, like Zelda."

She knew the effect the word would have on me and she gripped me suddenly in a tight embrace. All the cameras would see was another gesture of love, but she was using all her strength, her fingernails digging into my back, to stop me trembling and she was smothering my face to stop me from crying out. The cameras couldn't see the tears welling in my eyes and blurring my vision.

Zelda was her last code word: the end of the message she was trying to give me.

It was the name of a young Tupamaro guerrilla we had known in Uruguay, when Julia had gone with me to South America. Zelda had been born a Catholic and like many other young guerrillas she always carried a circle of birth control pills as a symbol of her rejection of the church. She called it her anti-rosary, and one pill was a poison capsule, to be taken rather than face the torturers of the state police. She had given one to Julia.

"A souvenir to remind you of what our country has really become," she had said. Julia had told me she had thrown it away, but looking now into her eyes, I knew that she had not.

"We haven't long," Julia whispered. To the cameras she was only counting the minutes until our separation, but I could feel her heart already starting to beat faster than normal against my chest and I knew it was too late.

Sensing that I could not bring myself to leave her, she kissed me gently, then pushed me away suddenly.

"I love you so much, my darling," she said. "And there's been so much evil done in the name of our love. I couldn't bear to let them win. Please don't let them. For me."

She must have rehearsed the words, knowing they would be a clear danger signal to the surveillance team. She had known I would never have the courage to sacrifice her and she had found the courage for me. With the kiss and the words, she was releasing me, and there was nothing I could do to change it. She was forcing me to escape, and I had forty-five seconds to survive.

Without daring to look at her, I leaped off the bed, raced back into the other room, and hurled myself at the window.

CHAPTER 18 I don't remember how I got down the wall. It was as though all my years of climbing experience took on a substance of their own and made the descent for me. It was the first time I had ever gone out on the face of anything without worrying about finding secure holds and the right balance. Part of my mind was above, with Julia, and I didn't care what happened to me; another part was below and was telling me: the Vikings are down there but they have orders not to kill you. I don't even know how long it took me to negotiate the overhanging cornice which divided the upper floors of the building from the offices below. All I knew was that when I hit the street, they would be on me, and I had to break free whatever it took.

I didn't think about Norton's men; if they were there, I would know soon enough; if I started to look for them and they were not, then I was lost.

Two Vikings must have been right under me because I felt them grasping at my legs even as I braced myself for the drop onto the sidewalk. I let myself go limp and as they encircled me, I started to lash out, going for their eyes and hair. I have never been a skillful fighter but the years on the mountains have given me a resistance to pain that stood instead. When giving in to pain means losing your grip on a ledge halfway up an ice wall, you learn not to give way.

As they weren't allowed to kill me, they tried to hurt me into submission and they couldn't do it quickly enough. One of them tired and let me free and I kicked and smashed and twisted with my fingers and thumbs, tearing at any skin I could feel or see, ignoring the blood I could feel on my face and the pains in my shoulder. Then one of them went down and I stamped on his face. I didn't hit him squarely but my heel gashed his cheek and his scream made the other one falter long enough for me to kick again, forward and backward, lashing out for any limb I could find.

Then suddenly, there were six bodies locked in the tight configuration on the sidewalk instead of three; Norton's men had arrived and they started to take the Vikings off me as cleanly as with a paring knife. They broke the holds and undid the tangle of flesh and in seconds I was standing free on the sidewalk and they were wrestling the two Vikings back toward the doorway.

My first instinct was to head back up the stairs to Julia but one policeman—a tough-looking youngster with a squat once-broken nose—motioned me toward a police car parked up the street.

Then I heard a shout from inside the building: "The woman's dead. Kill Russell." Before I could react, there was a shot and one of Norton's men staggered out of the doorway and fell at my feet. Inside, the Viking he had been holding started to run up the staircase. The second security man dragged his Viking to the ground and was using him as a shield as he tried to draw his weapon. I wasn't armed and there was nothing I could do in a firefight up the staircase, so I held back, covering myself against the outside wall of the building. I could hear scuffling inside the entrance, then I heard the Viking on the ground shout: "No. For God's sake no."

There was a scream, then an explosion, and I realized that someone had thrown a grenade from the top of the staircase. Instantly the entrance hall was a mound of wood and plaster and through the smoke and fumes I could see the four bodies: the Viking and the security men intermeshed. There was nothing to tell them apart.

I heard someone coming down the staircase but the noise was drowned out by the roar of cars behind me. If I hadn't known they belonged to Norton's forces, I might almost have guessed it from the ruthless style of their attack. The first car raced across the square, and instead of stopping at the curb, it bumped over it and crashed over the mound of debris, right into the lobby of the building. The two following cars skidded into a V-shaped barricade at the entrance, and about eight plainsclothesmen jumped out and crouched behind them with pistols drawn.

Through the doorway I could see that the windows of the first car were open, but no one was visible inside. Instead I could see the sleek metal surfaces of two antiexplosive shields. Before any attack could develop from above, someone inside the car fired two gas canisters up the stairwell, using what sounded like a miniature grenade launcher. As soon as the canisters exploded, I knew there would be no resistance from the staircase. The smell was unmistakable. The police were using Ct-75, an anti-riot gas that had been banned even in Vietnam because of its devastating effects. I had seen a demonstration once in an ultra-secret Scottish testing ground, and I knew this was one of an arsenal of new antiterror weapons that were being held "in reserve" for the inevitable time when terrorist horror would become so great that counterhorror would become acceptable.

Ct-75 didn't linger; there was hardly any smoke to obscure the target and the users did not need to wear masks. As the canisters exploded, the gas dispersed under great pressure, stunning and paralyzing everyone within range; then the fumes disappeared almost immediately, leaving the victims visible and vulnerable to a close-up attack or a burst of weapons fire.

Confident there would be no shots from above, I tried to move into the doorway, but a young policeman stepped toward me and pinned me against the wall. "Wait," he said tensely. "Not yet."

As he spoke there was a burst of automatic weapons fire from the bottom of the staircase, then the sound of crashing feet. On cue, the policemen outside poured through the doorway, and this time I ran behind them.

On the second landing, the bodies of three Vikings were sprawled at the entrance to the apartment where I had been with Julia. Two policemen smashed open the doors, and as I ran up the stairs, I heard one of them shout, "Look out, they're next door. And up there." After that, the fighting became a blur of background noise and I could think only of Julia. I forced my way into the apartment and I found her in the bedroom where I had left her; she was lying unreally still, and she might have been sleeping but for the strange, awkward set to her mouth.

I knelt beside her and seized her hand as though the gesture would somehow revive her but I knew it was just a pointless reflex of tenderness. The death pill had worked quickly, and I realized that her last gesture must have been to pull the covers over her nakedness and compose herself calmly for death. I knew she would have prayed at the final moment, and I tried to think of what her words would have been and I started to cry as I squeezed her arm fiercely. For weeks I had willed myself not to think of this moment and now I felt sick and afraid and helpless, and I sat, with tears pouring down my face, staring at Julia, not able to believe that there was no way of changing what she had done.

Then Norton burst into the room. I didn't realize at first who it was. I heard the door open, and it was just a remote, unimportant sound until he roared, "Get out of this bloody bedroom, damn you. Get the hell out of here."

Before I could protest, he strode across the room and seized me by the shoulders, dragging me to my feet. I tried to resist but I've never felt such a powerful grip, and his fury made his strength seem awesome. He swung me around, using his body to block my view of Julia, and hustled me across the floor, shouldering me forward, pushing and elbowing, forcing me brutally through into the main room of the apartment. He almost threw me onto the sofa, kicking the bedroom door shut behind him.

"She killed herself to release you," he snarled. "What the hell use are you to her or us, wallowing there in your grief?" He made the word grief sound like an obscenity.

"I need you to help me root out the Vikings. You're no use to me as a blubbering husband. Now either you pull yourself together, or I'll give you a pounding."

As he spoke, he raised his arm as if to strike a sweeping backhand blow. The gesture focused me even more than the words, and I leaped off the sofa, using all my weight to strike at his body under the arm. Norton turned, blocking the move and his face relaxed a little.

"That's better," he said. "That's much better."

Instead of helping, the remark infuriated me even more.

"Don't humor me," I yelled at him. "I'm fucking sick of being manipulated. My wife is dead. The Vikings have destroyed the one human being that means more than anything else in my life. What the hell do you think I'm made of?"

Norton stepped back, pushing me away with the flat of his hand. "All right," he said. "I won't humor you. I'll give it to you straight. You're going to put Julia out of your mind. I'm going to have her taken away and put on ice somewhere, and when this is over, you can do what you like with her. You can weep over her or you can bury her or you can scatter her ashes over the Himalayas if you like.

"But until this is over I don't want to so much as hear her name. If you mention her, I'll put my boot into your groin until you forget her. I've lost three men trying to save her. Now, we have to go after Peace, and if we don't get him— and the Haldoxicon—we could have the worst holocaust since the blitz. There's no time for private grief. Is that clear?"

Looking into his eyes, I could see it wasn't just a speech

222

to take my mind off my sorrow. This was Norton dealing with his own reality. The face showed no signs of humanity, yet there was no cruelty there either—only a kind of solemnity that was more frightening than viciousness would have been.

Without letting me say anything, Norton started to push me toward the door. There were no longer any sounds of firing in the rest of the building; only feet thudding on the wooden boards of the landings.

We went downstairs and Norton paused to give orders to a young policeman who looked incongruously elegant in a slim-fitting blue suit. I didn't listen to the words. I didn't want to hear the instructions for having Julia transported to some cold-chamber somewhere to be tagged and numbered and stored until the crisis was past.

But that was the reality, and Norton was right. It had to be so. Outside, the streets were blocked off toward both Piccadilly and Covent Garden, with barricades so heavy that the early-morning onlookers attracted by the noise would be able to see nothing to explain the gunfire and the confusion of vehicles sprawled in front of the building. We got into a black police Jaguar, and we were pulling away from the curb before the doors were closed. In a moment we were through the roadblock and heading northwest.

"Are you ready to help now?" Norton said sharply.

"You mean have I stopped being a blubbering husband?"

Norton nodded stiffly. His face didn't relax. He would not make the mistake of humoring me again.

"Yes," I said evenly, "I'm ready." The words came out with unnatural coldness, but Norton could see beneath the surface calm. He knew that from that point on I would do *anything, anywhere,* to destroy the Vikings, but I would control myself and do it his way. I would play any part in the counterterror that had to be played.

Norton leaned back in his seat. "Then we'll go and get Peace. He's holed up in a house near Primrose Hill. And on the way you can tell me who you really think is behind the Vikings."

I looked at him sideways.

"What do you mean?"

"You held back yesterday. Why?"

"Because I didn't think that particular group of so-called intelligence experts would believe me," I said.

Norton nodded. "Try me. I'm not a group."

I hesitated, but only for a second. "I believe it's another multinational corporation that is using the Vikings to destroy Intermark."

Norton's response was an odd sound that was almost a sigh. My answer was obviously not a shock. He seemed satisfied—relieved, almost.

"That's what Sabara thinks," Norton said carefully. "I was at his meeting with the Prime Minister. He didn't come right out with it either, but that's what he suspects."

"Did you gather which corporation he suspects?"

"No. What do you say?"

"My bet is Globex," I said. "I've no evidence, except that they stand to gain the most from the collapse of Intermark. They would virtually inherit control of twenty-odd billion dollars' worth of markets; no one else could move in fast enough."

"But you have no evidence," Norton insisted.

"No. But Globex is ruthless enough, and they've been studying terrorism and counterterrorism ever since they were hit by guerrillas in South America. They have the experts who could have dreamed this up."

"We'll need more than that," Norton said thoughtfully. "The best thing will be a very quick confession from Peace."

As he said it, I had a sudden flash of the hotel bedroom with Boorman and Molly Cassidy suspended in the frames. Terror and counterterror: the two faces always ended up resembling each other.

224

. Then the radio in the front seat crackled. The driver picked up the receiver and said to Norton, "It's Inspector Wales, sir."

"Put him on speaker."

The driver flicked a switch and a voice sounded clearly in the car. "We've cleaned out the Leicester Square building. Eight Vikings have bought it. I'm sorry about our three men."

"It's all right, Bill," Norton replied. "It was a helluva spot to break into. Let's hope the Primrose Hill place is easier."

The voice on the radio sounded reassuring. "You'll make it easy, Chuck. You'll make it easy."

At first the words didn't register; then I felt a sudden thrill of recognition. I turned to Norton.

"Did he say Chuck? Are you *Chuck* Norton?"

"I was," Norton said grimly. "But that was a long time ago, and they've changed the rules of the game."

I didn't say anything for a moment. I sat studying the face, searching the grim, stony lines for some reminder, but there was none. It was true, and yet it couldn't be. It just didn't seem possible that this could be Chuck Norton, one of the greatest rugby players there had ever been—the man who had been the symbol of English sportsmanship when I was a student. I tried to see him as the handsome, rugged, devil-may-care youth who had captained first Eton, then Oxford, then the Combined Services and finally England. But there was no echo of all that in this man.

Norton saw what I was thinking.

"Some other kid is captain of England now," he said. "My game is national survival. It's not played the same way." He paused, cutting me off. "I don't want to talk about it. We get out here. It's time to change cars."

We turned into an alleyway somewhere on the southern fringe of Swiss Cottage and I saw two vans parked out of sight of the main road. One was a huge removal van with

SIMPSON AND SON—WE MOVE ANYTHING stencilled on the outside. Beside it was a smaller panel van marked WEMMER'S INTERIOR DESIGN LTD.

Norton got out of the car and rapped on the double doors at the back of the bigger van. "Sergeant Denning," he called, then stood back to let the doors swing open.

They opened smartly and a figure stepped out. His uniform bore some slight resemblance to that of the metropolitan police, but in most respects he was a soldier. I could tell from his legs that he was a lean and probably youthful man, but his upper body was distorted by a bulky flak jacket and his face was barely visible under a blue steel helmet circled by a martianlike visor, with miniature antennae on the side.

Along his belt and shoulder harness I counted thirteen pouches, and I could see from the colored markings that some were grenades, smoke bombs and incendiary flares, as well as more Ct-75 riot gas. As a sidearm he had a bulbous automatic pistol, and he was carrying an L-21 fully automatic rifle.

"This is the new breed of London bobby," Norton said. "Don't bother to ask him the time."

The policeman lifted his visor and smiled. I could see he had heard the joke before. He was about twenty-five, with tight curly hair and a boyish grin; he could have been a Viking.

"There are twelve more like him in the van," Norton said. "They're what the salesmen call my 'top of the line.' The plainclothesmen you saw in Leicester Square are what we use when we're trying to be discreet, God help us; these men are what we use when we pull all stops out."

Norton gestured toward the array of armament. "It's taken me three years to get that equipment. The IRA had to kill more than one hundred people before I got it approved. When we started out they had truncheons and were allowed to draw pistols from—" his tone was contemptuous—"a previously agreed-on arms collection point *after* someone shot at them. The joke is that now I've got them, they spend most of their time sitting in those vans waiting for the politicians to have the guts to call them in."

He turned to the sergeant. "Are you ready? Men all briefed?"

"Yes, sir."

"You know the score. If this man Peace escapes, we're in for a bigger disaster than I want to think about. I want him and he's got to be alive. All right. Let's get on with it."

Norton nodded to me and walked over to the smaller interior decorator's van. Inside it was a military-style communications vehicle with two policemen operating double banks of sophisticated radio equipment with computerized scramblers. At the rear of the van there were two narrow benches. We sat down facing each other and Norton pulled a large street plan out between us.

"Peace is there," he said, stabbing his finger onto the plan. "It's a big Regency house right at the foot of Primrose Hill. We nearly lost him when we went after him at the Institute for Social Change this morning. They did a very complicated evasion operation. There were decoy cars decoying from the decoy cars. They were pretty good. We did lose Michelle and Hairy but we managed to stay with Peace." He grunted. "We were lucky."

"Does he know you have him?" I asked.

"Not as far as I can tell. We've had a micro-scanner on the house. That's like putting a magnifying glass right up to the windows, and he's showing no signs of unease. There are at least five Vikings there with him." Norton pointed out four streets forming a rectangle at the bottom of the slopes of Primrose Hill.

"So far it looks good. We have thirteen vehicles in the area, and it's quiet enough for us to watch the surrounding streets in case he should have an escape tunnel or something stupid like that. The only problem is the demonstration."

Norton turned to one of the communications operators. "What's the word on the demo?"

"No change, sir."

Norton turned back to me. "It's a protest march about evictions and high rents; the leaders are Marxists and they're a bloody nuisance. They like to fight with the police. We don't need that this morning."

He nodded to the operator. "Tell Johnson to let me know if there's the slightest change of direction. I don't want those marchers anywhere near the house. Okay, let's move it."

As we pulled away, Norton sat silently for a moment; then he said suddenly, "So you're betting on Globex. And what's your bet on where the Haldoxicon is?"

"I'll put my money on the Battersea Mall," I said. "I can't think of a worse place."

"If it's there, it's going to be a pig to find," Norton said. "Anyway, we'll know soon enough."

The sides of the van were fitted with magnifying peep-holes that gave good wide-angle vision, and I turned to see where we were. It was partly, too, that I didn't want Norton to watch my face as we approached the target. He could not know that if Peace had wanted to intensify the pain of the memory of Julia, there were few better hideouts he could have chosen.

Primrose Hill was the place of some of the happiest memories of our courtship. I had spent a whole summer with her in part of one of these Regency houses bordering the park. Already too costly to remain as individual residences, many of them were divided even then into a warren of rooms. This was share-a-flat territory. One student to a room: share the kitchen, share the lounge, share the girls if they wanted to. Here, in the disorganized and heedless way of youth, Julia and I had tasted for the first time that happiness of trying to create a life together. And it seemed a special kind of desecration that it should be here that Norton was about to loose his police army of the new age of terror.

We drove for about five minutes, then one of the operators said urgently, "It's Sergeant Johnson, sir. The demonstration's changing direction."

"Put him on speaker."

"It's Johnson, sir." The new voice echoed slightly in the metallic frame of the van.

"The marchers have decided to head for Chalcott Terrace. That will bring them into the target zone."

"Turn them back," Norton snapped. "Don't use your men; try some ordinary coppers first."

"We already have, sir, but the leaders are spoiling for a fight."

"Right," Norton snapped. "We'll be there.

"Get me Henson," he barked to the second operator. "On open voice."

The operator threw two more switches and another voice filled the van.

"Henson, sir. Position Radnor Drive and Sussex Walk."

"All right, Henson," Norton said. "If the demonstrators haven't turned back in exactly three minutes, you take over. I don't want anyone within four blocks of the target house. And I don't care what the *Sunday Times* says about you."

"Right, sir." There was just a hint of laughter in his voice.

"The *Sunday Times* doesn't like my men much," Norton said. "They're always doing articles on our 'ultraviolence' and publishing sketches of our weapons." He grinned. "They call them artists' impressions. They've never dared come near enough to get some real photos."

I looked through the peephole and saw that we were already close to the demonstration.

As the van turned the last corner, there was no mistaking what was going on. A line of regular police constables with arms linked had formed a human chain across the road. The marchers had fallen back, but there was no doubt that their organizers were urging them to try to crash through. Our van pulled to a halt about fifty yards from the confrontation. Norton glanced at his watch but gave no orders, and I knew he wouldn't need to; the three minutes were already almost up. Then I saw the dogs. The demonstrators saw them at the same moment, but the animals' arrival was so startling that the marchers didn't immediately grasp what was happening.

All they saw at first was a yellow florist's van speeding down the street and ending in a controlled skid that sent it almost 180 degrees around with a squeal of tires. The doors flew open and the crowd started to break and run even before the animals were on the street.

The dogs were square-jawed mastiffs, bigger than any I had ever seen used for police work. With their fangs bared and their shoulders high as they poised to spring off the back of the van, they might have been some mythical animal bred for hunting forest game.

The handlers were dressed in almost the same space-ranger outfit as Norton's other men except that they had on heavy blue tunics instead of flak jackets. They held the animals on long leashes and ran with them in a curious stiff-legged gait, which kept them low on the ground. There were about a thousand demonstrators, but the crowd was not big enough to fill the whole street and there was room to disperse. That was lucky, but I had no doubt that Norton would have ordered the dogs in even if the marchers had been packed tightly.

The five handlers moved forward into a fan shape, and the point men kept their dogs weaving from side to side. They had obviously practiced the maneuver a hundred times, and not a single demonstrator tried to circle around them.

Ignoring the shrieks of the marchers, Norton said

brusquely, "That'll do fine. Now let's get Peace while the streets are still clear. Tell Denning to go ahead."

"Jesus Christ," I said, "I'm not surprised the *Sunday Times* doesn't like you."

"We're effective," Norton replied. "That's all that matters." He leaned across to the wall behind my seat and adjusted the spy hole. "You can see ahead now," he said. "Now watch carefully and learn."

I could see the removal van ahead of us now, moving very slowly, the driver in cap and overalls, leaning out as if to check a particular address.

Then the van pulled up outside the target house and came quietly to a halt.

What followed was a classic military enter-and-search operation, but on speeded-up film, and the first shock was the way the police came out of the van.

I waited, tensed, for the rear doors to fly open. Instead, the whole side of the van nearest the curb dropped down and the men came out four abreast and charged the door. Three in the first row were carrying automatic weapons. The fourth had a gigantic wrench-cum-clipper of the kind demolitions firms use to deal with stubborn wire and metal when breaking masonry apart.

Once the men were on the street, our van surged forward and Norton leaped out the back.

"Stay here," he yelled. "Don't come out of the van until I call." I saw him pull out a heavy pistol as he ran after his men. Then he was gone.

Through the peephole I had a clear view of the entrance but I couldn't see inside. I heard the fizzing of riot-gas grenades and the sound of shots, but there were no bursts of heavy fire and I guessed that the police were being careful not to hit Peace.

I wanted to dash to the house to see, but I knew that it would be unforgivable for any member of Norton's team to move out of position. I waited, then almost immediately I saw Norton reappear on the front steps, waving at me to come.

"We've got him," he shouted, and I jumped out of the van and raced up the steps, but once inside the house, I couldn't see Peace.

"Where is he?" I asked, fighting hard to control my anger and bitterness. "I want to do the questioning myself."

Norton smiled thinly. "There's no need for that," he said. "Peace is at the back. We'll talk to him in a minute. We're just arranging his transportation."

There was something chilling about the way he said it, and I saw that one of the policemen smiled too, but uneasily, as though it was an in joke everyone shared but didn't like.

He led me through to the back of the house and out of a small door that opened onto some stone steps down into the back yard. From the steps I could see a blue van I hadn't spotted before, and beside it the yellow florist's van.

"We've put Mr. Peace in the blue van, sir," a young officer called out. "We've got three Vikings dead and two more in the cellar."

Norton nodded an acknowledgment. Then he said carefully. "Now I'm afraid there's going to be a little mix-up. It's one of those things that happens sometimes, but it's better if it doesn't happen at headquarters."

I watched in horrified fascination as the doors of the yellow florist's van were opened and Sergeant Henson jumped out with two massive dogs on a double leash.

Silently he guided them to the blue van. A policeman opened the door and the two dogs sprang for the ledge, held on less than a foot of leash. I heard Peace scream; then Henson snapped a command and the dogs started to snarl. Amplified by the metal sides of the van, the sound was unearthly. Then the snarl turned to furious barking and as Henson let the dogs a few inches farther in, they reared up, saliva pouring from their jaws.

232

Norton waited about ten seconds, then he called out, "Sergeant Henson, I think you're in the wrong van."

"Sorry, sir."

Henson took the dogs away and we walked down the steps, through the yard, and a policeman opened the door of the blue van.

Peace was crouched on the floor of the van, lying face down, his head cradled in his arms, trying to bury himself in the gap between the driver's partition and the ridged floor.

"Sit up."

Peace dragged himself half upright, and he was hardly recognizable as the man I had known since Montreal. He was sobbing quietly and tears were leaving uneven streaks down his dirt-covered face. His clothes were ripped to rags and his body seemed to have collapsed inside a pile of loose skin.

Norton moved in closer and sat down on the floor of the van. He didn't face Peace. Instead, he sat at right angles to him, which gave both a curious look of companionship.

"Two questions," Norton said. "One answer for each. First time. Do you understand?"

Peace moved his lips but no sound came out.

"Who is behind the Vikings?"

"Globex." The sound was a whisper. Half a whisper. Little more than one sibilant. "It's the Globex Corporation."

"Where is the Haldoxicon?"

Peace didn't answer. He started to say something, then his lip began to quiver and the words would not come.

Norton's tone was friendly, almost helpful. "Is it in the Battersea Mall?"

Peace's head moved. I could just see that he was shaking it. " 'Nother . . . one."

"What was that?" Norton said. "Did you say 'another one'? What other one? Another shopping mall? Where?"

Peace couldn't form the words. His chest was heaving.

"One last time," Norton said, "or the dogs come back."

". . . it's not in Britain. It's in the States . . . it's a shopping mall in New York State . . . it's called Indian Fields."

"What?" Norton snapped. "Why there, for Christ's sake? Why there?"

"Because it's the biggest"—the words were hardly audible —"it's the biggest thing Intermark has . . . to destroy thousands will be the ultimate terrorist act."

PART

CHAPTER 19 We were halfway over the Atlantic before I spoke to Norton again.

From my seat in the chartered Boeing 707 beside Jack Wescott, I could only see him moving swiftly back and forth between the rear of the flight cabin where the communications post had been established and the partially screened-off first-class section where the "operational planning team" was in permanent session.

"I wonder if Intermark-One, or whatever they call it, has reached New York yet," Wescott said.

"I don't know. They had two hours start on us. I don't know if they'll fly faster as well."

As we had waited at Heathrow for our security team to assemble, we had watched the Pirate's departure. By the time Intermark's company DC-8 was loaded, we had lost count of the executives and private security men who had gone on board, but it had been well over a hundred. We had only glimpsed the Pirate himself. He had come in a closed black limousine and gone up the aircraft steps, almost at a run, surrounded by six security guards with linked arms. They had boarded and taken off while we were sitting through our fourth delay.

On the surface, our operational planning team had been put together with astonishing speed but I knew that it was an illusion. The hardware—the plane, the radio links, the satellite to feed pictures, the computers and the Telexes—

had been linked up efficiently and smoothly. But as Wescott put it dryly, "The machines are interfacing fine. It's the human beings who are having a few problems."

This was how the multinationals scored every time over governments. It didn't matter strategically to Globex whether the target was in Battersea, London, or White Plains, New York. They could deploy the Vikings as well in either.

Intermark had started to move with the same ease across frontiers, but we had not. With eight words—"It's not in Britain, it's in the States"—Peace had taken away all Norton's momentum. It wasn't just the four thousand miles that separated Battersea Mall from Indian Fields; it was the frontier and the onion skin layers of jurisdictions and political empires and spheres of interest.

To pass the time at Heathrow, Wescott and I had made a list of all the agencies who would be affected now that the Viking threat had crossed the Atlantic, starting with the obvious ones like the New York State Police and moving on down to local forces and fire departments and civil defense units. We had reached eighteen. Then we had added in the British security departments who would want a watching brief, then the broader American jurisdictions—federal, state, city and borough. The grand total was thirty-nine and we had counted the CIA twice to round it off at forty.

Norton was the only British official on the plane, designated as coordinator representing British security interests. Pearson had stayed behind in London, heading a special task force to investigate Globex.

On our aircraft, the factions had formed as soon as we had taken off. Jack and I were alone in one corner of the coach. Around us, there were eleven or twelve taciturn Americans, mostly from the U.S. embassy in London, sitting in twos and threes, creating little islands of subdued conversation in the long cabin. There was no contact between the islands. Communications were between each little faction and "their man at the front." Our man was Norton, but he did not come back to talk to us.

"Did you know it was Globex?" Wescott asked as we talked over the situation.

"I was almost sure," I said, "but not completely. Once I knew they weren't genuine radical guerrillas, I asked myself the classic question in any conflict: Who gains? And of course the classic answer is: A rival."

"So we've finally come into the era of corporate wars," Wescott said. "I suppose it's logical. If you let multinational corporations behave like sovereign states, you must expect them to start fighting wars."

Just then I saw Norton coming down the aisle, his face white with anger.

"Judging from the look of our leader," I said, "I'd say he's just been through a less than perfect international planning session."

"We have real troubles," Norton said, before he was even level with our seats. "We've finally got a break on some information from inside Globex, and it's bad. When they heard about Peace's arrest, the Accountant wanted to back off, but there was a split. Three directors wanted to go ahead with the Haldoxicon. They said no one would ever prove it was Globex. No one agreed with them, so they split off and they've persuaded Hairy to go through with it."

"Christ," Wescott said. "Will Globex help us stop them?"

"They won't lift a finger. They won't move a muscle, if it will tie them to the Vikings."

Norton grunted. "And if you think the enemy has problems, you should hear how we're doing. Sabara has landed in New York and he's trying to take over the security arrangements at Indian Fields. And do you know what we've done? We've created another combined task force and we've invited Sabara to be on it. In fact, we've put everyone on it."

When he had gone, Wescott said, "You realize, don't

you, that he likes you. He thinks you're his kind of folks."

"Yes," I said, "that's what scares me. I look at Norton and I see a mirror image. Without Julia and the mountains, I could be a Norton in a couple of years."

Wescott hesitated.

"Do you want to talk about Julia yet?"

"No," I said. "Later, when this is over."

"In the mountains?" Wescott said.

I paused for a moment before I replied. "Yes. I have only the mountains left."

Wescott did not need to be told to leave the conversation at that. We had been friends for too long for him not to know.

He would try to help me in other ways, mostly by behaving normally and trying to keep my sense of humor alive. Like Gellman, his motto when climbing was "Never go solemn in times of stress," and it had served us in many difficult pitches.

"Do you know why I brought you?" Norton said to Wescott as he strode angrily back down the aisle.

"I had wondered," Wescott said. "Why?"

"Well, it wasn't to keep Russell company, that's for damn sure," he said. "It was because you're a journalist and eventually someone is going to have to make sense of all this, to tell it straight.

"They've set up a field HQ at the mall. The last message from it was 'situation stable,' which means nothing is happening so they haven't the faintest idea what to do.

"As far as I can see from the traffic, half of them down there are romantics and the other half are politicians dressed up as cops."

He turned to go back up the aisle. "The mall opened an hour ago so we'll just be there in time for the afternoon rush —unless the situation has become unstable before then."

After that Norton didn't come back for a while and I dozed and tried not to dream about Julia.

When I woke up, Norton was sitting beside me and he had a sheaf of messages on his lap.

"If it's any consolation," he said, "Pearson and his gentlemen in economic and strategic intelligence are having a worse time than we are. Globex has already started to tie them up in knots."

He tapped the sheets. "They can't accuse Globex of anything, so they've started to try to establish links between the Viking people and the corporations."

He ticked the names off on his fingers. "Hairy—whose real name is Harry Everton by the way—has definite contacts with Globex. He also has contacts with ITT, Bell Northern, Unilever, Exxon, NASA and just about everyone in the United States who has a half-decent laboratory.

"His network of contacts covers about thirty states and he's tied in with people who work for just about everyone. But just try to isolate his links with Globex and make it stick.

"With that bloody man Peace it's the other way round. They've managed to establish so far that he was once on the staff of a think tank in Los Angeles that once worked for one of the West Coast affiliates of one of the divisions of Globex-Chemicon, which is a division of Globex Resources Research, Inc.

"But they haven't managed to find out yet whether, at any particular time, Peace actually worked on any of the contracts with Globex."

"What about Michelle?" I asked.

Norton grunted. "Her real name, insofar as anyone in this business has a real name, is Michelle Coulton. She was born in San Francisco. There's a record somewhere that she once worked for the personnel department of Globex. Someone in London approached Globex very discreetly and was told that they think she may have—for a short time—but they're pretty sure she was fired because of her 'far-out ideas.' They are checking."

He gave me a hard look. "She helped you, didn't she?"

"Yes."

"Will she help us again?"

"I don't think so," I said. "She's pretty screwed up. I don't think she'll be much use to them or us."

"As far as I can see, she's been enough use to them already. She seems to have helped train the nastiest bunch of bastards I've come into contact with in a while. She can be really proud of that."

After a pause, Norton continued.

"There are signs of trouble at Indian Fields," he said. "They've done a security check on the maintenance people at the mall. Over twenty of them left their jobs very recently. A lot of them worked in the cleaning and painting department and there are some who worked with the electronic gadgets. It doesn't look good.

"We've had some data on the mall and it sounds bloody enormous. It's pyramid-shaped and it's got dozens of galleries all around and there are about twenty thousand places you could hide the Haldoxicon.

"At least I've been able to sell them on one idea," he went on. "I've told them to get some optical scanners—any kind they can lay their hands on—from an observatory or a space lab or anywhere. If this is going to be a really big blast, the Haldoxicon is going to be somewhere very high and we aren't going to have time to crawl all over the ceilings with a magnifying glass."

When he had gone back once again to the forward cabin, Wescott tapped his foot against a large canvas carryall he had brought with him on the flight.

"Mr. Norton and I have been thinking on the same lines," he said. "If you promise not to tell anyone back at the club, you can have a look in there."

I reached down and unzipped the bag. As I put my hand in, Wescott said, "I'm rather ashamed of what's inside . . . but I think we might need them."

I reached inside and felt something bulky and metallic with lots of separate packages loose around it. I pulled it out and laughed. It was a complete set of the most advanced mechanical climbing aids, including a high-pressure electro-piton hammer—the symbol of everything that was most hateful to what Jack and I called "real climbers."

"It's the very last word," Wescott said. "You don't actually have to climb yourself. You just send your butler up with this. It's supposed to be able to fix pitons into frozen yeti carcasses if the need arises.

"I bought it on the way to the airport. I have a horrible feeling that Norton is right, and if he is, I wouldn't be surprised if you and I didn't end up climbing something that wasn't meant to be climbed . . . by anyone in his right and sober mind."

CHAPTER 20 At JFK we changed to a helicopter. As we took our seats, Norton threw a brightly colored brochure onto my lap.

"Read the title." FACTS ABOUT INDIAN FIELDS.

"The help is just pouring in from all sides," Norton said bitterly. "The Intermark Public Relations Department is at our service."

I opened the brochure.

> THE INDIAN FIELDS MALL IS THE LARGEST EN-CLOSED SHOPPING MALL IN THE WORLD, it said.
>
> 350 acres of land. 120 acres of retail shopping. Occupancy of the center 350 stores. 70 offices on nine levels. 30,000 customer parking spaces.
>
> Center traffic—900,000 people per week.
> 2,200,000 people per week in peak seasons.
> 900 buses per day as part of the regular stop.
>
> *Customer Survey:* Though the Mall is located in White Plains, customer surveys show that over 100,000 tourists from outside New York State visited the Mall to see the Marvo-Wall and its other unique attractions.

"Every fact a little winner," I said to Wescott when I had finished reading. "What do you suppose a Marvo-Wall is?"

"I'd rather not think," he said. "By the way, what do you make of Norton's new playmate?"

When we had transferred from the Boeing to a waiting helicopter at Kennedy Airport, Norton had been met by a man he had introduced as Captain Leo Kinsky, an old friend from the New York City Police Department.

I nodded toward where they were sitting side by side at the front of the helicopter.

"Charles Kinsky—Leo Norton," I said. "They're the same person."

Wescott nodded. "Naked, I bet you couldn't tell them apart," he said.

The helicopter was flying low over an endless succession of gray and black suburban roofs, but in the distance I could see a break in the pattern, and the tightly packed buildings were opening out on the west shore of the river.

I saw Kinsky coming down the aisle. "Charlie asked me to fill you in," he said.

"We're coming up to Indian Fields now. That's it there." He grunted. "They call it the pyramid. They used to call it the biggest wigwam in the world, but an Indian rights movement got an injunction saying it was a slur on their native heritage."

We were moving in close now, skimming over the gray surface of the river, and the mall completely filled the window. It was as Kinsky said, just a pyramid—a huge pyramid rising for no good reason out of the gray New York suburbs.

Around it, someone had arranged several thousand cars as if laying gifts at the feet of some anonymous pharaoh. As I stared out at it, I heard Norton coming fast down the aisle.

"It's started," he said. "A couple of minutes ago. They've managed somehow to close most of the entrances to the mall. There are about seventy thousand people in there. No one knows how the hell they did it."

We landed on a piece of waste ground on the extreme edge of the huge parking lot. Immediately, the helicopter was surrounded by a score of private police with Intermark emblems at the shoulder. They had small sidearms in black leather holsters, attached to a shoulder harness and broad belt.

Norton got out first and before he had stepped off the ladder a large, fat, crew-cutted security guard with sergeant's stripes on his sleeve put his hand to his pistol and pushed him back, saying, "Hold it right there, Mac. No one gets off till you've been cleared."

Kinsky pushed in front of Norton, flapped a leather folder in the guard's face and snapped, "Reach for that and I'll break your fucking arm."

The guards stepped back and I heard Kinsky say quietly to Norton, "Jurisdiction, Charlie, jurisdiction. . . . I don't like rent-a-cops either, but leave the driving to the NYPD."

After that there were no more obstacles and we were driven through the parking lot by a distraught Intermark manager who had watched the arrival and seemed to feel he would rather be briefing us by loudspeaker from a long way off.

From what he said, it was obvious that the Vikings had been studying the mall for months.

Instead of closing all the entrances, they had shut the five biggest sets of doors, by activating the electronically controlled mechanisms, then damaged both the electronic and manual backup systems. The result was that about seventy thousand people were trapped inside without realizing it.

They had left the smaller exits open to avoid immediate panic. The Vikings had spiked a tape into the public address system asking shoppers not to be alarmed as it was a security drill to ensure that all the safety systems were in working order, "for their continuing comfort and protection." "Exit doors are available in all parts of the mall for those who wish to leave but we hope you'll carry on shopping," the tape had said.

Intermark's engineers apparently estimated that it would take about three hours to evacuate everyone through the small exits and nearly that long to repair the bigger ones.

"If we try to evacuate now, all hell will break loose," the mall official said breathlessly. "If they panic and jam the small doors, it'll be absolute chaos. . . . The best we can do is to leave them as they are."

I noticed that Norton didn't try to explain to him what it meant to have that many people exposed to a spray of Haldoxicon. The man was too agitated and the Haldoxicon wasn't real to him anyway. What was happening was some kind of anonymous "emergency"—people were trapped in the mall and what he was afraid of most was panic.

He couldn't even understand how the Vikings had managed to close all of the five vast entrances at once.

"There are three goddam backup systems," the mall man said. "Three of them. All separate. I don't see how they jammed it."

There was no point in trying to explain it to him. That was what made the Viking Process so effective. There were three backup systems, but each system was itself a central control. No one ever seemed to understand that it was almost as easy to damage three computer systems as one. If you've already poured sand into one engine, it isn't that much trouble to throw what's left into two more parked next to it.

We were let into the mall through an emergency fire exit, and our first sight of the interior was a dingy corridor, leading past a series of offices belonging to junior administration staff.

The mall official led us at a run down toward a white-painted door with "Main Square" on it in black lettering.

When he opened it, I guessed we would be right in the center of the mall, but I still wasn't prepared for the impact of the sight the door unfolded.

"Jesus God Almighty," Wescott said. "What in hell is that?"

From the door, all you could see was color. Facing us, across a wide crowded square with fountains and flowers and artificial trees, there was a glass wall, over two hundred feet high, covered over every inch with splotches and streams and rivulets of every color in the rainbow. It looked as though some insane artist, driven mad by the effort of bringing order into his work, had thrown a gigantic fit of despair and hurled every color he had ever mixed onto the wall.

We stopped running. You couldn't help it. Even in a crisis you couldn't ignore the wall.

Wescott stared up into the roof and said softly, "That, without any shadow of a contest, is the ugliest piece of anything I have ever seen anywhere."

"I know what else it is," I said. "It's about three hundred miles of assorted graffiti trails."

"Yes," Norton snapped. "It can't be anywhere else. The Haldoxicon has got to be at the top of that thing somewhere."

It might be too obvious, I thought. A decoy? A red herring?

But staring at it, I knew Norton was right. The Vikings had not planned for anyone to know Haldoxicon was to be put in Indian Fields. The top of the wall was the perfect place; there would be no point in wasting it.

Kinsky looked quickly around the square. "Charlie, can you get a scanner organized?" he said. "Over there. In that group. The tall guy. Name is Dellinger. Tell him you're with me. He'll find one. I'll get someone who knows about the wall."

"They've already brought Marvin," the mall official said.

"Marvin Hurovitch. The brother of the guy who built the place. He's in the office—with Mr. Sabara."

"The original developers were the Hurovitch brothers. They work out of Newark. Intermark bought them out when it was half built. Marvin did the wall."

He pointed up. "They wanted to have a centerpiece. Wherever you go in the plaza you can see the wall."

From inside, the mall no longer looked pyramid-shaped. The wall cut down one side and at its base, on either side of the ornamental square, there were two stores—an Interfoodmart supermarket and a big department store. Neither had any roof and the shoppers in the upper galleries where the smaller stores were located could look down on the people moving among the aisles. As the mall man said, you could see the wall from everywhere inside the pyramid and no place was protected from anything that sprayed outward and downward from the pinnacle above.

"It has to be up there," I said. "There just is no other place. Let's get to Marvin and fast."

When we reached the general manager's office there were already a dozen police and security men there but there was no sign of Sabara. Marvin Hurovitch had just arrived and was shaking hands with everyone as though he was about to sell them rental space. He was short and fat, with dark crinkly hair and a face that must have looked unshaven the day he was born. He wore a loud red and brown broad-checked suit and I counted five rings on his pudgy hands.

It wasn't difficult to see them, because every minute or so he would take someone over to the window which looked out over the main square of the mall to point out some feature of his wall.

He even seemed to have developed a special technique of greeting. A pumping handshake, a Hi, and then his left hand would reach onto the other person's shoulder and start propelling them toward the wall, almost in a single movement.

"Have you seen the Marvo-Wall?" were the first words I

heard him speak. He said them easily, casually, as though it were in some way possible not to have seen it. He needed to mention it so he simply ignored the fact that the Marvo-Wall was a presence, a force even in the manager's office. The whole of the manager's window was blocked out by a rectangular section of it. The sickly rivers of colors eclipsed everything, and I noticed that the manager had turned his desk sideways as far as was possible without being back to the door presumably to escape it.

Wescott made a quick tour of the room and when he came back, he said quietly, "They're all waiting for Sabara and he won't come. He's holding a conference in the next room. Apparently he hasn't made up his mind whether he's going to try to take over the security operation."

Kinsky stood for a few moments watching the scene. I saw him take in the little factional groups that were already forming. Then he strode across the room and spoke to only one person, a gaunt-looking gray-haired man with rimless spectacles who was standing slightly off to the side, also watching the scene.

The conversation took about a minute, then Kinsky moved right into the center of the circle and grabbed Marvin by the arm with a grip that must have raised a bruise as large as the check on his suit.

He did it with a big glad-handing smile on his face, but it was an arrest. He might have been scooping Marvin off the sidewalk after a street fight instead of cutting him out of a group of people talking on a carpeted floor.

"Marvin. I need to talk to you right now," he said. "Tell *me* about the wall."

Marvin started to protest, but before any sound came out he looked into Kinsky's eye and saw the Norton-look there.

"The wall, Marvin," Kinsky said, in a low, almost venomous tone. "Tell us about the wall."

"I built it," Marvin said, his pride fighting with his ruffled feelings. "I did it for my brother Sol."

"Sol?"

"Yeah . . . Sol Hurovitch. He was the main contractor. He wanted a mural. A really big glass mural that people would come and see.

"He wanted to get Felsinger, the guy who did that one in the Museum of Modern Art, but he wanted two hundred thou. I said I'd bring it in for seventy."

Kinsky looked through the office window at the glaring colors.

"You work good, Marvin," he said. "Cheap, but good."

"It's a concept now. We've got the patent. Marvo-Wall. It's registered. We're going to put them in schools, libraries, hospitals . . ." His voice started to tail off as he saw that Kinsky was not going to be a customer. ". . . union halls."

"That's nice," Kinsky said. "What is it made of?"

"Argo-glass. It's a mixture of plastic and glass. You heat it so that it goes kinda bumpy and then you pour the colors on."

"And nature takes care of the rest . . . is that it?" Kinsky's eye was boring through him now. Marvin looked as though he wished he had committed some crime so he would have something to confess.

"Hell, no." He stumbled over the words. "I do a design. It's all planned. Every one is an original work of art."

"Marvin, we may have to go up the artwork," Kinsky said. "How do you suggest we do that?"

"There's no way," Marvin said. He sounded emphatic again suddenly. Sure of his ground. It was something he knew Kinsky could not contradict.

"How do you clean it, Marvin? The sanitation department likes to have these things cleaned now and again."

"There's a firm over in Jersey. Kleesman's. It's the only one. They have a special frame. They just finished a clean and resurface job three weeks ago."

I turned to Wescott. "If the Haldoxicon is up there, there are no longer any prizes for guessing how it got there," I said. "I expect we'll find Kleesman's had some unusually diligent extra help which has since left the firm."

Kinsky put his hand on Marvin's arm. This time the gesture was friendly, reassuring.

"Marvin. We *have* to go up the wall. The outside doors are closed. We can't get the fire department in here with their ladders. We need some help. We need to go up the wall. Why won't you help us, Marvin?"

It was the moment when Marvin would have signed anything Kinsky asked him to, but there was nothing to sign. And there was no way up the wall.

Kinsky made him explain it several times. The gap between the galleries and the wall was too great and there was nothing to hook ropes onto anyway. You couldn't get in from the top because the pinnacle had been reinforced in case anything striking the building would cause the glass to shatter and fall onto the crowds below. There was no metal frame round the mural. The Argo-glass was fixed to the inner wall by metal stanchions, with heads painted over—as Marvin insisted—to blend in with the design.

They were just going around the options again when Peter Sabara entered the room. As always, there were so many people around him that all that was visible of him was the beard and the huge head bobbing about inside his protective circle.

Sabara didn't say anything. He just looked around the room, as if measuring the strength and status of each of the little groups.

He turned sideways again and had just started to say something when Norton burst into the room from the opposite end, propelling by the arm a young straw-haired man in a blue casual suit.

"We've found it," Norton said. "They've done a scan of the dome. And it's up there. It's lying right along the top edge of the wall."

CHAPTER 21   "So we shall have to decide quickly what we're going to do about it." Sabara's voice was a harsh rasp, more brutal and crude than it sounded on television.

He turned to one of his assistants and took a Telex message from a file the man was carrying.

"Half an hour ago, a rumor started circulating on the New York Stock Exchange that a major disaster was about to befall Intermark. Our price is starting to slip. Now that we have located the Haldoxicon, immediate action is essential."

I thought for a moment that Norton was going to fly at him. I could see the words forming and feel his anger even from the opposite side of the room. Even Norton with all his ruthlessness and world-weary detachment was not ready for the idea that the disaster was being defined in terms of a slipping share price instead of maimed and disfigured bodies.

Sabara saw the anger and ignored it. He turned toward the group I had mentally marked down as the politicals and said harshly, "I don't need to remind you gentlemen of how many jobs are at stake in this area. The economy of this region will not stand any further recession. I want to know what moves from you I can count on."

I looked at Norton again and I knew that if we had been in London, he would have stormed over to Sabara and told him the decisions were out of his hands and that he had only to cooperate with the authorities.

Norton stood silently, a look of total disgust on his face.

They took only three or four minutes to decide, then the man with rimless glasses came into the center of the room. He did not introduce himself and I had the feeling that "If you didn't know who he was, you didn't matter," was his style.

"Gentlemen. I think we should listen to Mr. Norton for a few moments. We don't have much time and I don't think we have any choice but to accept his suggestions. If anyone objects, then I suggest we hear his counterproposals."

No one spoke and the circle widened to leave Norton room to come forward.

Instead, he strode to where he had left a black briefcase I had noticed on the plane, picked it up and went over to the longest wall, where there was a large cork bulletin board on which were pinned brochures, advertising leaflets and pictures of the mall.

With surprising deftness, considering the size of his hands, he unpinned them all and threw them onto the floor. As he was doing it, the officials formed a semicircle around him. They were intrigued, fascinated, but I could feel the vibrations of resentment at this outsider who was taking over their show.

They watched as Norton pinned quickly onto the wall six photographs, all of victims from Foodway City. The disfigured, twisted faces stared out from the bulletin board.

"That's what Haldoxicon does," Norton said. "Any questions?"

Everyone looked at Sabara but no one spoke.

"As far as I can tell through the scanner, there is a cylinder about five feet long and nine inches across lying along the back of the top edge of the wall," Norton went on. "We were able to find it so quickly only because we know how the detonation system works. They put trails of phosphorous paint, which looks just like ordinary paint, leading up to the cylinder. The phosphorus burns and when the trail touches the cylinder, the heat explodes it."

He gestured through the window at the wall. "When you know you're looking for paint trails, it's no great trick to know where they might be around this place."

There was some brief subdued laughter and Norton waited for it to die away.

"The way the Vikings usually work is to paint the trails weeks, even months before they need them. I'm sure we'll find out later that the wall has been cleaned or repainted by a crew that had some new members in it. All that doesn't matter. The important thing—the only thing that matters— is to get that cylinder down before someone explodes it.

"Now we come to the difficult part," he said. "If you fire a bullet at any one of those phosphorous trails, it will start the fuse burning. That means that you can set them off from anywhere in the mall practically. There's no point in looking for Vikings. They look just like any kids on the street. From the crowds I've seen out there, one person in four—at least—could be a Viking. Our best bet is to look for weapons. They might just be able to hit the paint trails on the wall with handguns but they're more likely to need rifles.

"They could be concealed in a hundred places or be carried in bags or suitcases. We'll just have to make sure that we spot them when someone tries to draw a bead on the wall."

There were a few murmured comments, but no one said anything to interrupt Norton. He paused for a moment, then he said, "So we have two problems. We have to climb the wall and deal with the cylinder and we have to try to stop anyone from firing shots at the wall while that's being done."

He pointed in our direction and I could see Wescott's face showed just a flicker of a grin.

"We have two people here who can probably climb the wall. They're professionals and they know what they're doing . . . if we can give them enough time. The only question left is whether we try to evacuate the people below. So let's tackle that."

From the briefcase, he pulled out a large drawing, which I recognized as the Foodway supermarket building. It showed the small Haldoxicon cylinder in the roof and lines were drawn downward in a cone shape, obviously indicating the area touched by the falling spray.

"This is what happened in London," Norton said. "They put a very small canister of the stuff—and it was small, less than six inches long—along that beam." He pointed on the picture to the metal stanchion projecting from the roof. "When it went off, the force was so great that the Haldoxicon covered a floor area over three hundred feet across.

"In that store, it was perhaps thirty feet up, no more. This time, it's about two hundred feet, and as far as I can tell, the canister is at least fifteen to twenty times as big. I was never much good at math at school, but I don't think there is any point in the mall that is safe if the spray is blown outward with any kind of force.

"The Vikings haven't gone to all this trouble to have a damp squid go off. I think they'll have rigged it so that it will spray right out onto the galleries and into the stores on the ground floor and into the main square and the areas leading up to the main square."

He stopped short. "I can make my men available for the climb if you want them . . . the other decisions are up to you."

Everyone looked at Sabara.

He looked around, then he said, "My advisers say I should leave it to you. So I shall. The responsibility will be yours. Entirely yours."

It was an exit line. Not everyone realized it immediately, but Sabara's courtiers did. They had watched him for too many years, reading his body language for signs of approval, and they turned to leave as if hearing some inaudible, ultrasonic command.

The flying wedge formed around the Pirate once more and he strode furiously out of the room.

Norton looked pleased. He spoke briefly to Kinsky, then he came over to us. "What do you need for the climb?" he asked.

"Ropes," Wescott said. "And some mystical inspiration to enable us to climb the absolute unfuckingclimbable."

"You've got that gadget that hammers nails in, haven't you?"

"You know about that?"

"Yes. Airport security at Heathrow told me about it, after they'd checked your bags. That was good thinking."

"Look, Norton," I said. "Obviously we are going to try. But, for God's sake, stop pretending that you can just go up a two-hundred-foot glass wall because you've been ordered to. You knew the Haldoxicon would be up high somewhere. . . . Wescott knew it. I knew it. But no one expected something like this. We have no idea whether that thing will even take pitons."

"Well, you'd better find out," Norton said. "Right now if you can. You can't make time on the climb. The Vikings are holding back. We don't know why. They may not even be going to go through with it. But the chances are that if they're going to, they'll do it when they see you start climbing, so you have got to go up that wall fast, fucking fast.

"I don't know what they're going to decide over there"— he pointed to the intent group of officials gathered around Kinsky. "But there really isn't a helluva lot they can do. They can't clear the mall. The doors are still shut tight and there's nowhere to put them. All bloody hell breaks loose. They'll be better off using the cops to patrol every balcony and watch every corner of the crowd on the ground level . . . looking for a gun. If they start crowd clearing, they won't have a hope in hell of spotting anyone. If the crowd stays put . . . there is just a chance. A slim one, but a chance."

"They're going to be looking up," I said. "Just like Food-way. Once we start climbing that mural, assuming we ever get off the ground, everyone will be watching us."

Norton grunted and pointed at the pictures he had tacked onto the wall. "It really doesn't matter a helluva lot. If that spray falls the way I think it's going to fall, it's really not going to matter."

He shrugged. "So let's get on with it. I'll get the rope . . . you find out about the pitons."

He turned suddenly and shouted across the room. "Marvin, come here will you? These men are going to climb your wall. They need your help."

Then he vanished and we were left with Marvin, but only for a moment. As soon as Kinsky saw us talking to him, he came over.

"You're going to help, aren't you, Marvin?" he said.

"Sure . . . sure . . . I'll help. What do you wanna know?" I could see from his look that somewhere in a corner of his mind, something was reassuring him. You couldn't climb his wall. It was smooth, absolutely smooth. You just couldn't climb it, it was going to be all right.

"Marvin," I said gently. "Is there anything else made of Argo-glass in the mall? Any pictures—samples. Little walls anywhere?"

"In the office through there . . . there's a tableau." He pronounced the word as though he had read it in some fancy builder's catalogue and decided it would give tone to his concept. He looked at Kinsky. "This way . . . I'll show you."

We went through into a smaller office which was furnished for four secretaries. On one wall was a square of Argo-glass—a replica of the monstrosity outside—about twenty feet by twenty feet.

"That's beautiful, Marvin, beautiful," Kinsky said. He closed the door behind us with a carefully calculated gesture of finality that must have scared a thousand suspects.

Wescott opened the carryall full of climbing gear he had carried through from the main office and unwrapped the piton-hammer.

"What's that?" Marvin said.

Kinsky grinned nastily. "Don't worry, Marvin. They're just going to put a little nail through your tableau. Not through you. Just through your tableau."

I could see the words were meaningless to Marvin. A nail through his wall was a nail through his body.

"Don't worry," I said, with a reassuring dentist's smile. "It won't hurt a bit."

Wescott quickly slotted a piton into the hammer and held it against the surface of the glass. He touched the trigger and there was a brutal grinding sound and the drill-like gun shuddered in Wescott's hand. I could see the strain on his face as he held it steady; then, as the piton penetrated the glass, he flicked a switch on the side of the body. The noise stopped and the hammer came away, leaving the piton buried in the glass.

It looked secure but before Wescott could reach out and test it, tiny cracks started growing outward from the base of the piton. In seconds, there was a delicate spider's web of lines the size of a small plate around the gleaming steel piton. Wescott grasped the piton and put his weight on it.

It held and the cracks didn't widen. Wescott increased the pressure so that he was almost balancing on it, with only a small part of his weight carried by his toes. The piton still held. Then slowly it started to tilt . . . very slightly at first, and then to an angle ten degrees from the horizontal position into which it had been hammered.

"It's the air . . ." Marvin said hoarsely. "If air gets in down the side of the nail, it starts the cracks widening . . . it's the way the glass and plastic are fused."

"What happens when you get a crack, Marvin?" I said. "How do you fix it?"

"You have to block up the cracks quickly—" He stopped short, as if realizing that he had somehow revealed to his tormentors the last secret protecting his wall.

"What do you block them with, Marvin?" Kinsky said it first, slightly ahead of Wescott.

Marvin swallowed. "It's called Argo-fill. . . . We had it made up specially by the manufacturer."

"Get some. A lot. As much as you can find. Right now." Kinsky's words were so sharp that Marvin backed away. Then he turned and ran out of the door.

When he came back, he was carrying a ten-pound white plastic bag and a device that looked like a cross between an electric drill and an oil can. It had the body of a drill but instead of a bit there was a thin pipe projecting from the nose.

"There's some in already." Marvin was defeated. He handed the gun to Wescott.

I stepped forward and took it from him. "You can't handle both. Let's see if we can coordinate."

Wescott took the piton-hammer and stepped to the other side of the rectangle of glass. As he did so, Marvin made his final protest. "Could you drill next to the other hole?" he said. "Argo costs sixty dollars a square foot . . . plus a share of the original artistic design."

Kinsky tapped him gently on the forearm. "Bill us, Marvin. Send a bill to the government," he said. "We gotta give this a proper trial."

I stood shoulder to shoulder with Wescott. He put the piton on the gun and held it against the glass. I held the filler nozzle ready beside it and Wescott pulled the trigger.

It seemed to go in more quickly this time and the piton bored smoothly into the glass. As Jack released the lever and pulled away the gun, I aimed a jet of Argo-fill round the base of the piton. I knew the filler wouldn't dry quickly enough to offer any support, but if Marvin was right and the problem was the entry of air, it should do the trick.

Wescott grabbed the steel nail and put his full weight on it levering himself up, so that he was pushing vigorously down from above.

It held and I heard Kinsky say, "You work good, Marvin."

Wescott took his hand off the piton. "With a couple of

years' testing, I'd say the method would be safe to a height of about fifteen feet," he said. "At least this drill won't generate enough heat to light the phosphorus. Now all we have to do is work out how the hell you rope on for two people to make an ascent side by side."

As he said it, Norton burst into the room. He hadn't brought ropes; he had brought the manager of a sports store from somewhere in the mall and his two assistants who were carrying boxes containing virtually every piece of climbing equipment they had in stock.

"Choose what you need," he said. "Make it snappy . . . things are starting to move . . ."

He turned to Kinsky. "They've agreed on a plan. . . . It's not much but it will have to do. They're not going to clear the mall. They're going to try to spot Vikings in the crowd. If anything goes wrong and the trails get ignited, they're going to get the crowds to lie flat and cover their heads."

"How the hell are they going to manage that?"

"We're going to fire over their heads. I've never seen anyone yet who didn't duck if you put a few bursts of automatic fire over his head."

Kinsky grinned. "That was your idea, wasn't it, Charlie? That was one of yours."

Norton didn't smile. "Yes . . . and we may be finding out if it works. They've spotted Hairy in the crowd and lost him again. It has to be him from the description. And the woman with him sounds like Michelle."

CHAPTER 22 "We'll do it by triangles." I said Wescott's words to myself as we sprinted across the main square of the mall, trying to visualize the patterns we would have to make on the wall as we raced toward it.

I didn't see the crowds, parting around us, or the police clearing the way ahead of us. I was thinking only of triangles, imagining the moves that Wescott had planned in the few minutes we had spent staring from the manager's window at the great sea of molten color.

It had never occurred to me not to let Wescott plan the ascent. Neither of us was an ego climber. We knew each other's strengths and weaknesses and respected them, and I knew that Wescott's strength was a curious kind of mathematical imagination that enabled him to see a rockface as a pattern of holds.

This time there were no holds. We should have to make every one and I knew that Wescott could do it far more quickly than ever I could.

He had the kind of mind that allowed him to stare at the wall and divide it into body-lengths and imagine the shapes of our outstretched limbs, moving up the face, calculating as he did it how much rope we would need, where the pitons must be placed, where we must rope and where the leader should advance alone.

We both knew the theory of electroclimbing. We had sat and consumed many pints of beer and jeered at films circulated to the mountaineering club, laughing at the spider's web patterns that electroclimbers created to scale faces that would not "go" by ordinary methods. It wasn't really climbing as it had been originally conceived at all. It was much more of a product of the postindustrial age, when impatience with shortcomings and obstacles had overtaken any joy in natural challenges. Just like Rory, we were going to drill a series of holes in Marvin's wall, thread ropes through the pitons and weave a kind of cradle up the face, drawing it up after us, to economize on rope, using the strands only long enough to hold each of us secure as we did the next drillings.

Jack had never made this kind of ascent before, but I never doubted his ability to do it—or mine to follow and give him the support he would need. We had climbed together so often that coordination between us had long ceased to be an issue. We were like an old dancing couple. No matter how tired we were, or how unfamiliar the steps might be, we could not tread on each other's toes.

If he overreached himself, I would know it instantly and be able to move up and take the strain. If he tried a maneuver that I had not seen before, I would be able to grasp my part in it, without his having to spell out the holds.

Wescott was one of the most imaginative individual climbers I had ever seen. He had never wanted to be an expedition leader; he had no patience with organization and logistics, no interest in disciplining a team or a support group. He was a good team man when he had to be, but his greatest love was to let his imagination free and try a new pitch in a way it had never been tried before.

I was stronger physically than he was and I was better on ice and at very high altitudes. His strength was as a rockclimber. He had the build, lightness of touch, enough strength to control his body, and above all, he had the imagination and decision-making speed.

But as we reached the bottom of the wall and the colors seemed to swamp us from above, I wondered if either of us could seriously hope to finish the climb.

At the bottom, Norton was with us. He didn't say "Good luck," only "You won't be able to bring the cylinder down. You know that. Just cut off the trails somehow. And don't be long about it, these crowds are going to be very difficult to handle."

Wescott smiled. "If you start firing over the crowd," he said, "just make bloody sure you fire away from the wall."

Then Norton was gone and we were alone, inside an empty semicircle cleared by a small cordon of policemen, holding back a crush of fascinated onlookers. It was afternoon showtime, I thought. Watch the monkeys climb the Marvo-Wall. Most of the kids probably wouldn't even realize it was difficult. We had a wall-climbing kit. So what was the problem?

In the few minutes of preplanning, we had rejected the idea of climbing with one holding the piton-hammer, the other the filler-spray. Wescott had them both, linked to his waistband on long lengths of cord. They were clumsy and likely to be a nuisance, especially with the method we were going to use, but if either fell, that would be the end of the ascent and we could not afford to take the risk. We needed to pass them from hand to hand and dared not pass them unattached, so we had chosen the lesser problem of having to be deft enough in the transfer not to tangle each other in the cord.

The triangle method Wescott had chosen was going to involve gymnastic as much as climbing skill. I knew I would find it easier than Jack because I was stronger and he was lighter; but if we husbanded his strength carefully and there were no long delays on the way up, we had a fair chance to make it.

The first step, which was easy to do from ground level, was to drill two pitons in at should-level height. Then, using them as footholds and supported by his partner from below, the first man would drill a third hole as high to the right as he could reach.

Spreadeagled between the three, he would then support the weight of the second man, who would reach out and upward to the left, like the spectacular top man on a gymnastic display pyramid, and insert a new piton.

For the next stage upward, the process would be reversed with the lower man overtaking his partner again and making another triangle—formed of two pitons and the support of the other climber.

The delicate part was the roping. Wescott had devised a system for looping the rope through the rings on the end of the pitons which would ensure—in theory—that if either climber fell, he would be attached to a piton below and have his partner's body as a counterweight to stop him from plunging down off the wall.

Given unlimited time and strength—or adequate rest periods instead—the system could work. But if we started making mistakes or got too tired, we could end up in a spectacular tangle, with only what a medical student climber friend of ours called placebo support—the belief that if you rested your weight on an unsupported rope, it would hold your weight.

Our last fear was voiced by Wescott as he started to drill the first piton. "I read Marvin as one of nature's cost cutters," he said. "I hope to god all of this wall is as strong as the bit in the office."

Between the climbing gear Wescott had brought with him on the flight and what we had taken from the store, we had everything we needed for a normal climb, including boots with a composition sole, and we also had what Jack had nicknamed our idiot-hooks—two hooks attached on each side of our chests for holding the mechanical toys. When he had coined the name I did not need to ask why. If I had, I knew him well enough to hear in advance his answer: "Because only a flaming bloody idiot would climb using a method that needed them."

The hammer and the filler-gun were attached to Wescott's belt, but actually hung from the hooks at his chest. The idea was to take the hammer and drill the piton into the glass—then quickly hook it onto your chest and pick up the filler-gun and release the spray before air started getting into the cracks. When I had the instruments, they would be hooked to Wescott's belt still, but I would use the same method, trying—as he had said with mock pleading—very hard not to strangle him in the process.

The last piece of equipment we had added was one small radio receiver; I had attached it to my belt. It was open on the police band so that we could hear a commentary on what was happening below us.

As Wescott drilled the holes for the first triangle, I listened to the exchanges between the police units on the nine levels and thought once again what an impossible task we had been set. For the police to stop anyone from firing a shot from anywhere on what amounted to nine theater balconies, on the opposite side of the mall to the wall, they would have to have the kind of luck that drew all three winners in a big-money sweepstake.

I thought about it just once, then I put the odds and the crowds out of my mind and concentrated on watching Wescott's body, and waiting for my first move.

The first, the second and the third triangles all went easily. The pitons held; both Wescott and I used the ropes and the cords untangled. We had done twenty-five feet and the system worked.

I could see Wescott was pleased, mainly because the roping method hadn't turned out to be too difficult to manipulate. If you thought carefully about what you were doing, you could thread the loops and pass them to your partner in three moves.

I looked up the wall and tried to visualize the Haldoxicon cylinder above us. From this distance, the only sign of it was a very slight projection over the top edge. It could have been a supporting bracket but I knew it must be the cylinder.

Seeing the target helped. It wasn't a container of devastating chemical; it was a ledge: safety, a place that had to be reached.

When it was my turn to move, I smiled grimly at Wescott as he levered me past his shoulder and slipped the hammer into my right hand. "If you drop it on my head, you owe me a beer," he said, grimacing from the strain of supporting much of my 180-pound weight. "If you drop it twice I'll set Norton on you."

I went up smoothly and Wescott passed me again. Two more triangles. . . . We were a third of the way.

From this height the perspective of the mall changed completely. The crowds had receded and even though the outside light was not bright, the rays filtering from the sky-lights above seemed to collect a fine haze of dust which blurred the outlines of the balconies opposite.

I looked down briefly, then once around the tiered layers of stores which were crowded with people. I realized suddenly that most of the crowds thronging the levels were not watching the ascent. It seemed incredible but we already seemed to have been accepted as fixtures on the glass wall. Two window cleaners perhaps with a funny method of holding on. There were a lot of people watching, many of them leaning against the balconies staring out over the square below, but many more were just shopping . . . gazing at the glittering window displays, scurrying around in search of bargains. Maybe it was because we had ropes, I thought. We were a circus act with safety lines. Dull. No action. If they fall, they'll just slide a few feet. Perhaps if we stood on one piton and waved there would be . . . what . . . scattered applause? Or would shopping still win out?

I watched Wescott drive in the next piton, closing my ears against the grinding roar, and held my breath for the tenth time (was it?) as he flicked the drill back onto his hook and slickly replaced it in his hand with the filler-gun.

The piton held. One more triangle complete. We were

halfway. We were also level now with the orblike chandeliers which hung over the square. As soon as we could see above them, Wescott said, "That's our way down. Look."

We were close enough now to the pinnacle to see right into the darkened apex. There were beams up there and a tiny catwalk, directly over the crisscross of metal bars which supported the chandeliers. The gap looked about fifty feet. With a rope secured to the catwalk, you could slide, commando-style, to the beams below and you were in among the narrow metal supports which crossed over most of the square and on over open-roofed department stores. From this angle, the store looked like a maze. It was all one level . . . hundreds and hundreds of yards of shopping aisles, open to the upper tiers of the mall. Some of the crowds were looking up but most were intent on the display counters.

I visualized the descent. A little bit of tricky maneuvering in the pinnacle to get to the catwalk. Fix the rope. Slide down it to the beams and then . . . what? From this viewpoint, you couldn't be sure where the bars ended, but there had to be a way onto the tiers, and any gymnastics on three-inch-thick metal had to be safer than coming down the side of the wall again, with no certainty that the pitons were still secure. But first, there was the rest of the ascent.

On my chest, the noise of the police radio had become a drone of voices checking and cross-checking between units stationed about the mall. It all seemed remote—a crisis in another town. Radio WXR Buffalo reporting trouble in some shopping mall or other.

Were we taking it too easy? Were we going fast enough? It didn't seem worth thinking about. We were both sweating heavily now. Each time we moved, the strain on the tensing muscles was becoming a little greater. On the last push to heave Wescott above, I had felt pains in my shoulder. Any faster, and one of us could easily lose his grip. We must go steadily. There were no Vikings. The Viking didn't exist. There were only shoppers down there. It hadn't been Hairy or Michelle the police had seen. One panic move now and it would all be over and the crowds would get the show they were feeling cheated of. If they were lucky enough to look up from their shopping at the right moment, they would see the two bodies hurtling past the wonder of Marvin's multicolored vision to crash to the floor between the fountains in the square.

We completed two more triangles. We were two thirds of the way up. Then Wescott slipped.

It happened while he was above me and I saw the detail in awesome close-up. His foot slid on the piton, the piton gave way, and as his heel started to flatten, the glass around the hole cracked. It was blue, running into red—a garish halo behind Wescott's boot. As he gripped tightly onto his holds above, the crack shattered and his foot crashed through and was encircled by the jagged edges of the hole.

"Don't move!" I shouted. At that instant, for some reason, the chanting from a childhood game came into my mind. "Paper wraps stone, scissors cut paper . . ." Argo-glass cuts bone. The edges were jagged and thick. A mixture of glass and plastic, Marvin had said. Broken open now, it suddenly looked 95 percent glass. If Wescott moved an inch in the wrong direction, he would slash open his ankle. If a tendon went, he could not climb. I couldn't carry him, and the Haldoxicon would sit, menacingly above, until some kid in the crowd chose his leisurely moment to fire a shot.

"How stable are you?" I called. I heard Wescott laugh, as he always did when the situation was critical.

"Like a bloody elephant on a water-lily. Any suggestions?"

"We've got to get your foot out and I've got to make somewhere else for you to put it," I said. "If I guide it out, can you hold as you are long enough for me to put in another piton?"

"Yes." His voice was deep and throaty. ". . . if you're bloody quick about it."

"All right," I said. "Lean outward from the face. You've got to straighten your leg. The glass is right against your shin, above the top of your boot. Slide your foot out at the angle it's in until I tell you to stop."

Wescott didn't hesitate. There was so much trust between us after the years as partners that he simply leaned back and suddenly all the onus was on me.

"Stop there!" I shouted. "Now bring the foot out . . . slow and easy." I watched it come centimeter by centimeter. I didn't say anything. He had not panicked. He was in control of the leg and it was moving out exactly at the angle I had set.

"Okay, you're free."

Wescott laughed again. "Yeah . . . free to fall off this fucking wall without nicking my foot."

Without being told, he switched his weight onto one handhold and one foothold and quickly handed me the piton-hammer. It took only a few seconds to pierce the glass —far enough away from the hole to hope that it would stick. Then a quick switch with the filler-gun, and the crisis was over.

Wescott put his weight on the new hold. "What's your price? Two beers or three?"

It was an old custom between us.

"Two," I said. "Three next time."

The maneuver had finally sealed our remoteness from the mall below. We were just climbers. Whatever was down in the valley was something we had enjoyed looking at over breakfast . . . and would see again at nightfall. Our world was a few feet of glass.

We struggled on upward and I could feel that the effort had sapped some of Wescott's reserve energy. His push into the next triangle was not as smooth as before. But it didn't matter. We were almost there.

The top edge of the glass was less than fifteen feet away. One more triangle, and we would be there.

Suddenly, as if from another planet, I heard Norton's

voice. "Russell. Wescott. Get a move on. We've got troubles. Someone tried to take a shot at the wall. We got them. But there are more. Get moving."

"Jesus bloody Christ," Wescott said. "That man doesn't give anybody any peace."

I watched him summon his strength. The last triangle was his. To do it quickly, he would have to call on deeper reserves.

He moved and it was easy. Three pitons and he was up. He grabbed the upper edge of the glass and shouted: "It's here!" He sounded surprised, as though the whole thing had been a hoax. He slid the hammer down and I punched in a hold, to the left of his.

"Put the rope across," he said. "We'll make a cradle."

I did as he said and we secured the ends. Wescott carefully slid the last of the nylon rope out through the running rings. We were there . . . seated at the top of the wall—able to reach out and touch the sinister-looking gunmetal cylinder.

Wescott levered himself up to see how it was secured, then Norton's voice crackled out over the radio. "There's a Viking on level two. Watch yourselves."

"Did you hear that, Philip? You have to watch yourself. Make sure you do that now." The joke was a reflex and it did not interrupt Wescott's survey of the ledge.

I was looking around quickly, too.

"The graffiti trails come right up onto the cylinder," I said. "Look . . . there are four of them . . . you can feel the consistency of the paint. It's thicker than the rest."

Wescott scanned the rim. "The red, the blue, the green and the purple. Right?"

"Yes. And we've got to break them."

"Which is about the equivalent of climbing out onto a branch and sawing it off behind you. You realize that we are attached to the top—"

He had not finished speaking when we heard the shot. It rang out like a fresh new sound. Despite the hum of crowd noise below, it was clear and unmistakable.

I looked down. From the top, you could not see the colors of the wall in any perspective. Only in the last twenty feet did the pattern become clear.

I stared down . . . fighting off dizziness, and I searched through the blaze of colors looking for the telltale black trails but there was nothing.

"They missed . . ." It was Norton on the radio. He could have been beside us. Then his voice broke off. ". . . they're chasing them on the level . . . They're going to try again . . . look out!"

I didn't hear the end of the words.

The burst of gunfire blocked them out. The trail had been ignited. I couldn't see it, but I knew it was racing up the wall toward us because of the strange patterns down in the plaza . . . thousands of ants were doing a bizarre religious obeisance . . . they were folding themselves, curling themselves up . . . putting their forefeet around their heads . . . cringing down under the gunfire.

The trail was coming. I had nothing to stop it with. I could swing a foot and break the glass . . . but would it break? And which trail would be the one? Without thinking, I gripped my shoulder and ripped my shirt down to the waist, tugging at the torn piece frantically, freeing it from the idiot-hook, rolling it round my fist. What good would it do? Could you stop a phosphorous trail with a bit of rag and a lump of flesh? It was ridiculous, futile.

In the same instant that I told myself that it was hopeless, I saw the trail. The little cone of sparks at its head was like a delicate firework threading its way through the rivulets of color. It's on the blue, I thought crazily . . . the blue is coming up. I tried to get my boot around onto the end of the blue trail and swing it back against the wall. I managed one kick and felt the jarring pain in my leg, but the glass did not break.

The cone of sparks was there. I made the gesture . . . knowing with an odd clarity that it was a gesture. I thrust my fist into the rivulet of blue color. I wanted to punch the cone of sparks but they weren't there yet. In my frenzy, I hadn't coordinated. My fist was on the glass, then the sparks hit and I felt a searing pain tear through my hand and on up through the arm.

I was no longer on the wall. I was back on the Anstatt Glacier. I had dropped my glove again. My fingers were stuck to the ice. I was going to lose them. I didn't want to lose them. Then the pain diminished and I couldn't understand why. Had I found my glove again? You didn't find gloves once they had fallen . . . and why was my arm so sticky? Was I bleeding?

Then I felt the arm cool and I opened my eyes and I saw Wescott less than a foot from me holding the filler-gun and I felt the streaks of Argo-fill soaking down my wrist and hand.

The relief made me feel lightheaded. I wanted to say something and I didn't know what. Then the words came . . . I would borrow a phrase: "You work good, Jack. You work good."

CHAPTER 23 "Two beers or three?"

"Six," I said, "and a bottle of scotch to wash them down with."

The pain had almost stopped. There must be some damage, I realized that, but I felt as though I had the use of my fingers. It might be an illusion, but if it was, it was a comforting one. I was almost afraid to wipe the slimy layer of filler away in case the pain returned, but I could hear the tense, urgent commands on the radio and see the crowds below, swirling and surging toward the edges of the mall, then breaking into fresh patterns as they recoiled from the black lines of police trying to contain the panic. I needed my hand. There wasn't much time. There were voices booming out over loudspeakers and I thought at first the Vikings had seized the public address system, but though I couldn't make out the words, I could hear the reassuring, then pleading tone, and I knew that we still had control of that at least.

I levered myself up beside Wescott again and together we examined the cylinder. "We'd better start with that," Wescott said, pointing to a thick daub of purple paint which led off the wall and onto the ugly, bulbous nozzle at the end.

It probably didn't matter which of the detonator trails we worked on first. All four could start the holocaust but the purple one looked more threatening than the rest. I nodded.

"Chip some off and see what happens."

Wescott grinned. "What happens if the cylinder starts to fall?"

I grinned back. "Grab it and hold onto it pending further instructions."

He handed me a piton and took one himself and together we worked from the back of the glass, slowly breaking the edge. It came away like pieces of a chocolate egg, leaving jagged outlines sticking up in place of the smooth top of the wall.

When we had chipped away enough to cut the purple trail completely off from the cylinder, I saw that there was a metal ledge hidden behind the wall. Wescott saw it too and stuck his piton gently under the canister. "If we can cut away the rest of this edge without sliding into oblivion, we should be able to rope the canister on and leave it on the ledge. I can't see any other way it could be detonated. Can you?"

I put my hand carefully over the back and felt under the cylinder. "No," I said. "Let's get a move on before the fireworks display starts again."

In all, it took ten minutes to isolate the canister. I looked down only once as we worked and the crowds still seemed to be swirling in the same patterns, going nowhere. The doors were obviously still closed, but the scene looked somehow less frantic than it had before and I could see the panic was subsiding.

But were there any more Vikings? On the shopping galleries, the police seemed undecided what to do. On two of them, they were trying to guide people down toward the escalators and stairs. On another, a cordon of men were trying to persuade shoppers to go inside the stores, but through the crowds I could see the figures of storekeepers barring the way and I guessed they were afraid of having their merchandise wrecked.

Few if any of the thousands of people could have grasped yet what was happening. It was still an undefined "emergency" with some strange happenings on the Marvo-Wall that they would understand only when the scenes were played back to them on late-night television.

I had spotted at least one TV crew in the mall below, but I knew Kinsky would not be allowing live footage. I wondered if we would ever see ourselves perched up on the edge of this ridiculous monstrosity, two black beetles eating away at the edge of a gigantic all-dress pizza, wondering whether the next bite would send them skittering down to an ignominious death, unnoticed in a sea of people preoccupied with their own fears.

When we had broken away the last piece, I thought of Marvin. "I've never done a climb at sixty dollars a square foot," I said. "What do you think it cost?"

"I don't know," Wescott said. "We'll have to wait till they assess our share of the original artistic design." He grunted. "Let's get the hell out of here."

"Up or down?"

"Up and along," Wescott said. "To the catwalk. I've had enough of electroclimbing for one day."

He reached up and pulled himself over the jagged edge of the wall and onto the ledge beside the Haldoxicon. Carefully, he tested the lengths of cord we had attached to both ends of the canister. "It's okay," he said. "Let's go."

It was a short traverse to the catwalk, and when we reached it, Wescott pulled out a pack of cigarettes. "I don't care if the Vikings pick me off right where I stand," he said. "I must have a drag. It's okay to smoke as long as we're very careful." He handed me one and we sat in silence, high in the pinnacle.

I inhaled and sighed. All I cared about was that the descent was going to be easy.

After my years as an army instructor, nothing with ropes and bars could ever daunt me again. The mountain school's assault course had been its special pride: bigger, more awkward, more challenging than any designed for earthbound regiments. I had done it so many times that I had become as bored with it as a fitter with his assembly line. I had done it drunk and hung over; half asleep and with a temperature of 104; with leg injuries and arm injuries and once with a headache so bad that I had kept my eyes closed through half the route.

In the parts of the back used for upward pulls, I had muscles growing on muscles. Physically, I was on the catwalk, smoking and watching. Mentally I was already down on the ground. Then suddenly I heard the radio crackle and a voice came through, agitated, urgent. It sounded like Kinsky's but I couldn't be sure.

"In the department store, southwest corner, two suspects and one hostage. Surround and withhold fire."

Then the commands and responses started back and forth and as I craned over the catwalk, I heard Norton's voice. "That's Hairy and the woman Michelle. If you can cut out the hostage, shoot to kill. They're too dangerous alive."

I didn't hear the response. Was it Kinsky coming in to endorse the death sentence? It sounded like it, but I couldn't listen.

"They're crazy," I yelled. "They can't kill Michelle. They need her. I'm going down."

Without knowing why, I felt consumed with rage. They did need her alive, but I knew that wasn't the reason. As I tied onto the catwalk and swung over the edge, all I knew was that her death would not be right. Gellman was dead; Julia was dead. If Michelle died it would be too much.

I had to get down. I had the feeling that if they killed Michelle, the whole Viking nightmare would evaporate around me and I would be left with no grip on the real world. I didn't care about Hairy; despite his bulk he had no substance for me. He was a brain, an idea, a symbol of one particular kind of midtwentieth-century horror.

But Michelle was real and I was determined that she should not die.

As I gripped the rope, I could hear shouts from below and I wondered which spectacle the crowds had chosen—the circus tricks above or the hostage drama below.

I started the slide down and I felt the pains shooting through my fingers; even my mechanically perfect hand-over-hand was opening up the burns, but I was too angry to care.

I felt the rope swaying, and automatically I adjusted my position to correct it and looked down to check the distance to the bars.

I only had a few feet to go and despite the pain in my hand, I let myself slide faster. I could see the crowd looking up, but away to the left inside the geometric maze of the department store, there were people running and I could hear shouts and screams.

When I reached a metal bar, I grabbed it and swung my feet upward to lock on in support. I was still seventy feet up but there were lower bars I could transfer to on the other side of the first orb chandelier. After that there were more bars, crisscrossing over the department store, carrying signs and decorations. I still couldn't see a way down, but I guessed that there would be links to the galleries on the other side of the chandeliers.

I set off at a monkey run, back hanging down, parallel to the bar, feet locked over it, keeping to an "instructor-setting-a-good-example" position, despite the years that had passed.

Above me, I could see Wescott beginning to shin down the rope, and beyond him, the awful mess of color, spiked now with the nails, full of holes and cracks leading up like animal tracks to the spiky broken edge up above.

I swung my head around and looked down into the maze. I was still too high to see clearly, but the chasing had stopped; whoever it was, the police had lost them and they were circling in between the counters, searching and pushing aside the crowds who were torn between fear and curiosity, wanting to watch a real live police drama unfiltered by a TV screen, yet afraid that suddenly the reality would become too strong and the game would be spoiled.

Looking out over the silly sawed-off top of the department store, I tried to guess where a fugitive would hide.

There were a dozen places, but I was sure that it would be somewhere with a top. The department store was a classic paranoia box, like the open-plan offices that were the new fashion. I felt suddenly certain that if Hairy was in control, he would want to feel covered. It wasn't the reality that mattered. You couldn't really be seen clearly from the galleries. They were too far away for you to be more than a dot circulating in the maze. It was the feeling of security that a roof or a ceiling gave when you were in a panic and on the run.

Ahead of me, I saw a place where I could rest and hide and look around and give the watchers below time to forget my presence.

I was near an intersection in the rods and close to a section that supported a monster lettered sign saying INDIAN FIELDS. The letters were big enough to hide behind and I swung upward and grabbed hold of one "I" and flattened myself against it.

Standing upright, I could see the whole store. The police were moving slowly, and seemed to be trying to pen some invisible figures into the corner to my left. I looked over it and saw there were no covered areas. From the ground, it would look like a good place to hide with boxes and packing cases and a jumble of racks and counters.

But there were no roofs. I thought quickly, where, in this kind of store design, would there be roofs. On the toilets? Yes. But that would make too conspicuous a hiding place for a man and a woman and a third hostage. But fitting rooms would be perfect. I scanned the floors below, looking for the clothing departments. Craning over the letters, I spotted them to my right—men's and women's—not far apart—and beyond them, a series of little covered cubicles. It was not far. I could make my way along behind the letters, and if there was someone in there, I would be hidden from them by another of the orb chandeliers.

I edged carefully along, still hidden behind the letters. It was a guess and yet I felt it as a certainty. As I moved I wondered who was watching me from below. No one seemed to be looking up. I had ceased to be an aerial show when I slipped among the signs and decorations. Surely they would be too preoccupied . . . police, fugitives and onlookers. There was action down there and I could hear the excited buzz of voices and the tramp of feet.

Then I saw Hairy. He was standing by one of the fitting room cubicles, peering down a tiny corridor. He had a gun in his hand and he was pointing it sideways into the cubicle. He was wearing a leather university student jacket and from the way it was pulled tight around the neck and sleeves, I guessed that he had chosen it to hide the telltale hair. It was all stuffed inside and his freak hair was tied tightly in a sailor's pony tail and tucked down the back of the jacket.

The hair knot reminded me of Michelle, and just as the image came I saw her, standing beside him. There must have been a third person there, too, because Hairy still had the gun pointed inside the cubicle. He was arguing with Michelle but they must have been almost whispering because I could make out no sound at the height I was.

I decided to move quickly. They were too preoccupied to look up. It was the right time to take a chance.

There was still enough double-barring left for me to swing along upright, with feet on one bar and hands above on the other.

Watching the tableau from above, I could only guess what they were arguing about; but if I was to do anything, I had to get lower, down onto the lowest level of bars running across the store. The police were still at the other end of the store, systematically searching the sections closest to the main square.

I decided to take a chance. Using a vertical bar that was still obscured by one of the hanging signs, I slid down to the lower level. No one looked up. But when I moved next, I would be seen, if not by Hairy, then by someone outside the fitting room area, and there would be shouts and pointing and I would have lost my chance.

I balanced myself, for one last time, with my hand on the support above, then made three quick steps along the bar and jumped.

I remembered the impact and the jarring sensation and the shriek that I knew must have come from Michelle. I felt some pain, then there was the sideways motion and I saw the side of the cubicle coming up to crash against my head.

Then there was nothing and when I came to, Wescott was standing over me.

"You flaming bloody idiot," he said as he helped me to my feet. "In all the years I've known you, that's the daftest thing I've ever seen you do."

"Don't worry," I said. "I'm all right and it felt good. I've been in a cage too long. I'm finally out of it now. Just tell me. Did I get him?"

"Yes," Wescott said. "You smashed his skull with your feet and snapped his neck. Are you satisfied?"

"And Michelle . . ."

"She broke your fall and you broke her shoulder blade. She'll be okay."

As he spoke, I saw Norton looming at his back.

"But you're going to have to wait a damn long time for your reward," Norton said. "There's no screwing where we're putting her."

He looked me up and down. "Can you walk?"

"Yes."

"Then you'd better come to the office with Wescott. They want statements."

He turned and strode back down the corridor.

Wescott grinned. "That sound of muffled drums you hear

in the distance is you being drummed out of the antiterrorist lancers. You've been officially reclassified as a romantic and transferred to the 'all for love and the world well lost brigade.' "

He stopped short and, just for a moment, looked serious. "That's not how it was, is it?"

"No," I said. "There's nothing between Michelle and me. But I'm glad she's not dead. There's still part of me that resists the idea of annihilating everyone in one gigantic burst of law and order rage. But I am on Norton's side."

"He knows that," Wescott said. "That's why he's so pissed off at you. I think he was going to offer you a job and he doesn't hire romantics."

"Don't worry," I said. "I'll square Norton."

As we walked down the corridor, neither of us looked up at the wall. The crowds in the ornamental square were thinning down now, and in one corner a space had been cleared for the television crew. They were interviewing Kinsky and their lights formed a pool of artificial brightness, even in the light of the dome.

"They want you more than Kinsky," Wescott said. "They want to interview the avenging angel who swings from chandeliers and leaps into space."

"Later," I said. "I want to talk to Norton first."

"And there's someone else." Wescott pointed to a young man in a synthetic-age version of a gray flannel suit and grinned. "I think this may be your day for job offers."

I walked over to the man and stopped, facing him, without offering to shake hands.

He seemed nervous and had the unmistakable look of a man who has something important to say and doesn't know how to say it.

"My name is Michaelson. . . . I work for Mr. Sabara."

"And he wants me to work for him, too," I said. "Is that what you came to tell me?"

My bluntness obviously shocked him as much as if I had spat on his highly polished briefcase.

"Well, yes . . . no . . . yes. . . ." This was not how he had rehearsed the conversation; he had been sent on a delicate mission—to feel me out and report.

"Tell Sabara he can stuff his job offer," I said. "In my book, the only difference between Intermark and Globex is that Globex thought of the Vikings first. I'm not interested in helping the Pirate play catch-up games. Goodbye, Mr. Michaelson."

I turned and walked back to Wescott.

"Still unemployed?" He smiled.

"Yes," I said, "they wouldn't go over a hundred thousand dollars. Let's go and see Norton."

We climbed the stairs to the first level of the mall and I found that most of my limbs seemed to be working properly.

There was some soreness at the base of the spine and the back of one leg was stiff, but I was sure nothing serious was wrong.

When we got to the manager's suite, we found Norton in the small room Sabara had used.

"Sabara's gone," he said. "He left when you were halfway up the wall. I could get to dislike that man very much."

He still sounded angry but I was out of my cube now, and in no mood to be respectful.

"You want to know why I saved Michelle," I said.

"So you have an explanation."

"Yes," I said. "I did it to save you from making a fool of yourself . . . again."

Norton looked up, surprised. "What do you mean?"

"If you're going to start fighting corporate power seriously," I said, "you're going to have to get more sophisticated about fighting corporations. Michelle can give you evidence . . . real evidence, about motivations. She can tell you how Globex got her to do all the things she did. You need to know what levers the multinationals have to pull to put together an operation like that. There's no one in the world who can tell you more about that than Michelle, and you were going to have her killed."

Norton stood up. "I'm waiting to hear from Pearson on the Globex investigation. And there'll be a watch placed on Sabara."

I laughed. I couldn't help it. It was such a lame remark from such a powerful man.

"You'll be able to do all the Sabara watching you need on television for the next few days," I said. "He's going to be one of the most visible men in the world, restoring confidence in Intermark, rebuilding the shambles of his car-rental operations and the hotel chain. You'll be sick of the sight of him.

"And when you put your watch on him, will you know what you're looking for? Even if you see what he does, you won't understand it."

Norton grunted. "If I offered you a job, would you take it? Corporations are not my kind of enemy. I know that. I need help."

"Am I to take that as a real-live offer?"

"Yes."

"Well, I'll take it," I said, "but not right away. I need some time first."

"To seek solace in your bloody mountains, I suppose."

"I need some time to think," I said, "about Julia . . . about a lot of things."

"Don't take too long. Sabara may try to take his revenge."

"Yes, and there'll be others," I said. "Corporations copy each other very fast."

Norton pointed to the papers on the desk. "So all that's left for now is the statements."

"I'll be back in a minute," I said. "The television people want me."

Norton let me get as far as the door, then he snapped out suddenly in his interrogator voice, "When you tell them you saved Michelle for her evidence, what will you say when they ask why you didn't save Hairy?"

"I'll say Hairy was the one with the gun," I said and started down the stairs toward the television lights.